Country SINGER

HE HELPED HER BECOME A COUNTRY SINGER AND SHE GAVE HIM COURAGE TO FACE HIS FATE.

outskirts
press

Outskirts Press, Inc.
http://www.outskirtspress.com

ISBN: 978-1-9772-6259-2

Library of Congress Control Number: 2023906233

Cover Photo © 2023 www.gettyimages.com. All rights reserved - used with
permission.

Outskirts Press and the "OP" logo are trademarks belonging to Outskirts
Press, Inc.

PRINTED IN THE UNITED STATES OF AMERICA

CHAPTER 1

Ed Goff was barely three hundred miles into the trip, heading west on Interstate 80, when freezing rain began to pelt the car. He immediately flipped on the windshield wipers and the headlights and slowed the Toyota SUV. Gripping the steering wheel even more tightly, he was glad there were few cars on the road; in bad weather he always worried about being smashed by a careless driver. He hoped the road would not get more hazardous before he reached Ohio, where he intended to stop for the night. Even though it was only approaching five, darkness had already overtaken the dreary day, adding to his uneasiness because driving at night was becoming an issue—another woe of getting old.

Wondering how extensive the storm was, he turned on the radio and scanned the stations till he found one just as they were giving the weather report. The forecast called for a cold front to move swiftly through, with the sleet changing to snow. He wished he had checked the national weather forecast before setting out and waited a day before starting the nine-hundred-mile trip to his hometown in Illinois. One thing he was glad about, that he'd allowed three days to make the journey, which normally took a day and a half. He intended to be in time to attend the Christmas Eve Midnight Mass in the church in which he was baptized and had been an altar boy. The last time he was there was for his dad's requiem Mass nearly thirty years ago. During the intervening years, he had thought of making the trip to visit his parents' graves and for his high school class reunions, but he always found a convenient excuse not to do it. This time, he finally had a most compelling reason.

The sudden swerve of the SUV on the rapidly icing road startled Ed into instant alertness and he promptly slowed the vehicle to the posted minimum speed of forty miles per hour. Feeling somewhat unnerved and needing to relieve himself, he warily eased the SUV onto the iced-over shoulder and waited for the two cars a short distance behind him to pass. He got out and hurried to the front of the SUV, then relieved himself, feeling uneasy and somewhat uncouth. Once back in the SUV, he felt less stressed but quite chilled and promptly reached for the large thermos of black coffee resting on the passenger seat next to a road atlas and a carrying case of Frank Sinatra CDs. He hurriedly unscrewed the top and took two hearty swigs. When done, he flipped on the overhead light, then reached for the atlas and opened it to the Pennsylvania map. Having just passed a highway mileage marker, he was able to determine that the next exit was about twenty miles; he figured it would most likely take him about forty minutes to reach it, driving at minimum speed on the treacherous road. Just before starting up again, he cranked his head to the back seat to make sure he had not forgotten the quilted bedspread and several other survival items for winter travel, the most prominent being a fifth of Wild Turkey.

Once again on the road, Ed thought how quickly time moves and catches a person unaware of the passing years. It seemed to him like yesterday that he was young and strong, just married and embarking on a new life with Ann. But in many ways, it was more like an eternity ago, and he wondered where all the years had flown. He had no doubt he had lived them all, but they were like a dream he could barely recall. He had vague glimpses of how life was then and his ambitions, though very few came to be, and here he was, all alone and quite surprised by old age and a fast-approaching demise. He vividly remembered seeing elderly people when he was young and thinking they were a lifetime away from him, and in no way could he imagine being that old, but here he was, just like them. Old age had crept up like a thief in the darkness and stolen his youth without warning. Just getting out of bed was a major chore every morning, always hoping there were no new pains. Even naps were not taken by choice now but rather happened on their own.

But perhaps the greatest regret of it all, he thought, was for all those things he'd intended to do and never did. He shook his head in disgust for wasting his life, especially the last eight years. There wasn't a single worthwhile accomplishment to embrace and cherish, and he uttered loudly, "What a goddamn shameful waste of life." Even this trip to visit his hometown was only prompted by a foreboding circumstance. Deeply engrossed in his thoughts, Ed was startled by the intense blue lights of a state trooper cruiser pulling up alongside the SUV. He immediately slowed it to a crawl and lowered the window, which the trooper did as well, then motioned for Ed to halt.

"Shall I pull off on the shoulder?" Ed said in a shaky voice.

"No, there's no traffic behind, so stay where you are. The shoulder is a sheet of ice."

"Did I do something wrong?" Ed queried nervously.

"Not at all, just wanted to make sure you're not running out of gas or unable to cope with the road conditions," the trooper answered kindly. Ed was surprised by the trooper's friendly demeanor. He was always skeptical about cops, thinking them to be bullies who took advantage of their authority and pushed people around just to get their jollies.

"So far, I'm handling it."

"You're about fifteen miles from the next exit, and I would highly recommend you exit there for the night," the trooper urged. "I'd be happy to escort you."

"That would be great. I was going to stop there anyway."

"I'll pull up in front and get you to the exit."

"Just one more thing, if you don't mind. Is there a motel there?"

"Yes, and a gas station right off the exit; the motel's a quarter of a mile or so down the road."

"Thanks so much," Ed said with an appreciative smile.

The trooper nodded and raised the window, then pulled the cruiser in front of Ed's SUV and slowly started to accelerate. Twenty minutes later, Ed was greatly relieved when he saw the exit sign for Mercer, Pennsylvania. Just before the actual exit, the trooper turned on his right-turn signal and flipped his high beams a couple of times, then continued down the highway. Ed acknowledged him by doing the same and cautiously eased the car down the slick decline onto Pennsylvania State Highway 19, which was even more treacherous than the interstate. Fortunately, as the state trooper said, the gas station was no more than a hundred yards away. Much to his relief, as he pulled in, Ed also noticed a brightly lit Motel 12 sign a short distance down the road. Before getting out, he reached for the parka draped over the passenger seat and, once out of the SUV, quickly put it on, along with his gloves. When he got to the pump, there was a notice taped just below the grade selection, requesting cash customers to prepay before dispensing the gas. He shook his head and headed inside the convenience mart. Standing at the counter was an attractive, very young, honey-blonde-haired woman talking to the beefy, middle-aged clerk behind the counter, who immediately stopped the conversation and looked toward Ed.

"Nasty out there, ain't it?" he said vociferously.

"Getting there," Ed answered as he approached the counter with a polite nod to the woman who at close range, appeared to have a slight bruise on her left cheekbone. She acknowledged the nod with a friendly smile.

"So, what can I do you for?" the clerk said in a less intense tone.

"Need about thirty dollars' worth of gas," Ed said with a nod to the pumps and pulled out his wallet from the inside chest pocket of the parka, retrieving two twenties and handing them to the clerk.

"That's all you need?"

"Yes."

"You going back on the interstate?" the clerk guessed as he rang up the sale on the cash register and handed Ed a ten-dollar bill.

"Not tonight. It's too treacherous, and I doubt there'll be too many cars on the road after me," Ed said, stuffing the bill in his wallet.

The clerk rubbed his chin thoughtfully. "Hmm. If

5

that's the case, maybe I'll close up. You headed to the motel?"

"Yes."

The clerk glanced at the young woman. "Maybe this gentleman can give you a ride there."

Ed looked directly at her, saw the disappointment on her face, and kindly said, "I'd be happy to—not a problem."

"Guess I'm out of luck hitching a ride tonight, so I'll take you up on the offer. Thank you," the young woman said, shaking her head disconsolately.

"Tell Fred I sent you," the clerk said with a nitwit grin.

Ed motioned for the young woman to proceed to the door, and he looked over to where she stood for some kind of travel satchel because it seemed the only thing she had with her was an oversize leather shoulder bag.

"No luggage?"

"It's on me," she said, glancing down at the shoulder bag and continuing to the door.

Once outside, Ed looked directly at the young woman and offered his hand in greeting. "I'm Ed."

"I'm Kristen, and I appreciate the ride. Thanks so much," she said, shaking Ed's hand and following him to the SUV.

"I'll pump the gas, and if you don't mind, would you please move the stuff from the passenger seat to the back?"

"Sure," she said agreeably as she pulled open the door.

Minutes later, with both tasks completed, Ed started the car and glanced at Kristen, who looked apprehensive.

"Please feel safe," Ed said reassuringly with a kindly smile.

"I'm sorry. It's been a rough day," Kristen said with relief.

"You must be freezing in that light car coat."

"I have a warm hoodie under it."

"So, where you hitching to?" Ed asked as he slowly proceeded to the motel.

"Las Vegas."

"Any special reason, if you don't mind me asking?"

"A girlfriend of mine lives there, and from what she's told me, it sounds like a cool place to be, and there are lots of jobs."

"That it is," Ed agreed and gripped the steering wheel even more firmly as the SUV fishtailed suddenly. He straightened it and slowed the SUV to a crawl to avoid sliding into a shallow ditch running along the road.

"It's really bad, huh?" Kristen said, pulling her hand back from the dashboard.

"You OK?"

"I'm fine," she said with a reassuring smile. "So, when were you in Las Vegas?"

"Years ago, when my wife was alive," Ed said uneasily.

"You're a widower?" Kristen said without thinking.

"Eight years."

"Sorry."

"That's life, as Sinatra once sang," Ed said dismissively, not wanting to sound pitiful. He detested people who dwelled on their misfortunes and forced others to listen to stories about them.

"Guessing you're a big Sinatra fan, from all the CDs you had on the seat."

"Love his music," Ed said sprightly.

"I read he was really cool and a great ladies' man."

"There'll never be another like him," Ed said with

fondness. He then added lightheartedly, "So where are you escaping from?"

"New York, the city."

"We're practically from the same place; I'm from Staten Island," Ed said, glancing at Kristen with a warm smile.

"You're headed someplace special for Christmas?" Kristen guessed.

"Moline, Illinois."

Kristen knew only one city in the state. "Is it close to Chicago?"

"About one hundred seventy miles northwest, right off I-80, across from Iowa."

"Going to visit family?"

"None left."

"Friends?"

"Not that, either. Just the town, my parents' graves, and attend the Christmas Eve Midnight Mass at the church we used to go to," Ed said. "Guess that must sound kind of weird."

Kristen was affable. "Long way to go to a Midnight Mass."

With that said, Ed turned into the Motel 12 parking lot and drove up to the registration office door.

"Hmm. From the looks of all the cars parked in front of the units, they may not have any vacancies."

"The red neon sign under the motel name said they had vacancies." Suddenly, Kristen looked queasy.

"Something wrong?"

"Yeah," Kristen confessed. "I'm traveling a little light on bucks."

"I'll treat you to a room," Ed said without hesitation.

"Thanks, but that wouldn't be right. I'll just sleep in

the SUV, if you don't mind. You've got that big old quilt back there that should keep me warm."

"No way I'll let you do that. Let's not argue about it. We'll go inside and register," Ed said firmly.

"That's very kind of you—I'll have to repay you some way," Kristen said uneasily.

"There are no strings attached," Ed said, letting her know he was no satyr.

Kristen nodded. "OK, but it's not fair."

"Just one thing more: to avoid unnecessary idle chatter, let's pretend you're my granddaughter."

"OK, Grandpa," Kristen kidded.

"Now let's go in and get us the rooms," Ed said, then pushed open the SUV door and started for the registration office, with Kristen a step behind.

A slender, sallow-faced man in his fifties behind the counter lifted his eyes from a magazine, then hopped down from a high stool and said in a raspy voice, "Good evening. I'm Fred. Welcome to Motel 12, the best in Mercer."

"Good evening. We need two rooms," Ed said as he approached the counter, Kristen at his side.

Fred shook his head. "Sorry, just one room left, but it has two beds."

"Is there another motel nearby?" Ed asked with an exasperated sigh.

"No, sir, we're the only one."

"But you said the best in Mercer, which indicates there's at least another."

"No, sir, this is the only one," Fred said feebly.

Ed was uncertain and looked at Kristen. "Think you'll be all right with us sharing a room?"

"Don't know why not, Grandpa," Kristen said, tongue in cheek.

"All right, we'll take it," Ed said as he handed the man a crisp fifty-dollar bill, then began filling out the registration card.

Fred retrieved a key attached to an old-fashioned oval plastic tag with a room number on it from a drawer and handed it to Ed. "You're in room twelve, all the way at the end."

Ed nodded as he took the key and grinned. "Guess that's where you got the name for the motel—twelve rooms, I mean."

Fred failed to see the humor in the remark and said dryly, "Don't know about that. Oh, there is no TV since the satellite dish iced over, so you'll have to find some other form of entertainment. I got a couple of old magazines you can have."

"Thanks, we'll be fine," Ed said and with Kristen proceeded to the door.

When they got outside, she burst out laughing. "If he only knew—Grandpa."

"Yeah, we'd be sleeping in the SUV, most likely," Ed said with a chuckle.

The sleet had turned to swirling snow, which had already blanketed the car, but Ed didn't mind; it was the last remaining thing in the world he got excited about.

"It's magical."

"Yes, I love it, too," Kristen said, sticking out her tongue to catch the flakes as she climbed into the SUV.

"I hope this won't be awkward for you," Ed said with some concern.

"I'm OK with it if you are," she said without hesitation.

Once in the room, Ed set his suitcase and the cooler on the oversize dresser opposite the two beds, and Kristen did the same with the thermos and road atlas. He immediately went to the heating unit under the window and raised the temperature all the way up.

"So, which bed do you prefer?" Kristen said, looking at the two.

"If you don't mind, the one nearest the bathroom. I get up at least a couple of times during the night, and I wouldn't want to stumble over your bed in the dark," Ed said.

"You have some kind of medical issue?"

Ed didn't want to go into a long explanation about older men and their prostrate problems. "Just old age."

"You don't look more than sixty, which I read is now considered middle age," Kristen said knowledgeably and slung her shoulder bag onto her bed.

"Guess you haven't dealt with too many old people," he said as he removed his parka and tossed it on his bed.

"So how old are you?"

"Seventy."

"That's just slightly past the new middle age," Kristen said kindly.

"And you're what?"

"Twenty-two, going on fifty," she kidded.

"Why fifty?"

"There's mileage on this bod."

"I don't get it."

"Guess I better explain..."

"You don't have to."

"I'll tell you the whole story if you care to hear it, so you don't have to wonder."

"It's up to you, but really, you don't have to," Ed said, grabbing a chair near the dresser and sitting down as Kristen plopped down on the edge of her bed.

"For last four years I was living with a musician who got hooked on drugs."

"Was he doing it when you met him?"

"No, he was straight. I'd just turned eighteen when we met at the Port Authority Bus Terminal in New York after I split from home in Albany. I had no place to go, so I was hanging out at the terminal for a couple of days when I met Chuck. He was coming back from visiting his folks in New Jersey and spotted me in the waiting area, dozing on a bench, and came over and introduced himself. We talked awhile and connected. I went with him to his place, thinking he was really cool, being a musician, and especially because he had a place of his own, whereas all I had was a bench in the bus terminal. It was either that or becoming a cheap street hooker." Kristen paused and pulled her legs underneath her and took a deep breath. "I can't tell you how many times in those two days pimps tried to recruit me. That's where they get a lot of young runaways and turn them into sidewalk whores. I was determined not to become one, so I went with Chuck. Things were really great for the first two years; he had steady gigs playing bass guitar, and I got a job as a waitress at a homey Italian restaurant. Then I got pregnant; Chuck went wild and insisted I get an abortion, which I reluctantly did to save our relationship because I truly loved him and didn't want to lose him." She shook her head. "After the abortion, things started to change for some reason I couldn't figure out, other than perhaps deep down, I resented Chuck for making me abort the baby."

"How old was Chuck at this point?"

"He was twenty-six, and I was twenty," Kristen said, removing her car coat. "Wasn't long after that he started staying out till all hours of the night and lying that he was playing late-night gigs, which I doubted because he was constantly broke and borrowing money from me. It continued that way for some time, and then it really started getting bad. He began coming home all drugged up. When I bitched about it, he would lose his temper and smack me around, and not long after that, he started doing the drugs at home." Kristen paused, tearing up. "Funny, through it all, I still loved him, and on his good days, when he was sober, he would tell me that he truly loved me and we would get married soon. But with his habit steadily growing worse, he needed a lot more money to buy the junk, so he talked me into pole dancing at a skin bar where he once played. I stupidly agreed, hating myself for lowering myself like that. Whatever I made, which, on weekends, would be several hundred bucks, he would spend most of it on drugs and just leave me enough to buy some food. To cope with him and what I was doing, I started to smoke grass and occasionally even do coke for the courage to get up on the stage. At that point, the coke and the other junk weren't enough for him, so he had the pushers come to the house while I was at the skin joint, and they would all get high, shooting the big H up their veins till they zoned. Then one night, it finally happened: two pushers shot up Chuck so badly that he passed out, and when I got home, they raped me. Next morning when he sobered up and I told him, he just shrugged and said, 'So what?' and told me I might as well get used to it because that was how he was going to start paying the pushers. Two days ago while halfway sober, he attacked me sexually and violently. When I tried to stop him, he gave me the souvenir you see on my face and other parts of my body, which you can just imagine. When he went to take a crap, I grabbed my bag, threw a couple of things in it, and split, with the intention of buying a bus ticket to Las Vegas, only to discover the lousy bastard stole my credit card from my wallet, and of the nearly four hundred dollars I had in cash, he left me only ninety-five bucks."

Ed shook his head. "Hard to believe someone so young has been through so much."

Kristen smiled. "Well, it led me to meet a very nice, kind man."

Ed wanted to hold Kristen and tell her how sorry he was and that it would be OK, but he thought better of it. He did not want her to feel uncomfortable or misconstrue his motives. It was the last thing she needed to concern herself with after what she had already experienced. He thought about her remark about going on fifty. Now he understood.

"Maybe you should reserve that lofty praise until you know me better. I could be a nasty old man," Ed joshed to lighten the mood.

"I don't think so," Kristen said, looking directly into Ed's eyes.

He smiled and glanced at his watch. It was nearing eight. "Listen, you probably haven't eaten in quite a while and must be starving."

"That I am," Kristen readily admitted.

Ed got up and walked over to the window to partially pull open the thick drape. "It's still snowing and doesn't look good for going out—think we're stuck here for the night."

Kristen reached into her bag and, after an intense search, pulled out two granola bars and held them up. "I have these munchies."

Ed shook his head, walked over to the phone on the nightstand between the two beds, and dialed the front desk. "Fred, this is Ed Goff in unit twelve. Is there a pizza delivery place nearby?"

"There's one in Mercer about half a mile from here, but they don't deliver, and they're probably closed with the icy roads and now the snow."

"Thanks," Ed said sourly and hung up the phone, then turned back to Kristen. "Well, that's out; looks like you're going to have to feast on the granola bars."

"We'll share them," she insisted and held out her hand for him to take one.

"You have them both. I'm OK. I had a late lunch," Ed fibbed, certain Kristen hadn't eaten in some time.

"That's not fair," she protested.

He smiled and walked over to gently squeeze Kristen's outstretched hand. "We're not going to argue, are we?"

"No," she said sweetly.

"Oh, there should be a couple of Cokes in the cooler to wash them down," he remembered.

"I feel so badly for you," she said with genuine concern.

"I have a bottle of Wild Turkey in the suitcase, which is better than a steak any day."

"We could have a party," Kristen quipped as she jumped to her feet and headed for the cooler to retrieve a Coke.

"I don't think so."

"You don't like to party?"

"I do when there's more than two."

"Sometimes two can be more fun," Kristen said suggestively as she popped open the can, then returned to the edge of her bed.

"I think you need to eat," he hinted and proceeded to get his drink.

Minutes later, Ed watched with amusement as Kristen gobbled up the granola bars while he sat in a chair across from her, sipping the Wild Turkey, thinking how much he enjoyed her company. The liquor sedated the pain in his gut substantially and mitigated his awkwardness with her. He had never known any female like her, even in his youth. In some ways, there was still the residue of a little girl, but in other ways, she was worldly and definitely a free spirit. Even her physicality was telling—shoulder-length straight blond hair, soft blue eyes with defined eyebrows, and full lips. He guessed she was about five seven and slightly slender, with small bones and fine skin. There was an inner beauty and goodness about her that also added to her attractiveness, and Ed wondered what made her run away from home but didn't want to ask because she had already amply shared her soul. Touched deeply by her predicament, he decided to help her out however he could.

"Wow, it's getting hot in here," Kristen said, fanning herself, and rose to her feet to remove her light jacket and hoodie, leaving her in a tight white T-shirt that showed the outline of her braless, pouting breasts.

"Turn down the thermostat," Ed suggested as he momentarily gaped. Then quickly turned his eyes away, feeling bad about his reaction.

Kristen noticed and wanted to put Ed at ease, so she said matter-of-factly, with a grin,

"They're real, in case you're wondering, but I don't know how they got so big since I'm thin."

"I apologize," Ed said fervently, focusing on Kristen's face.

"You're a man, no matter the age, so don't feel guilty doing what comes naturally,"

Kristen said dismissively and started for the heater. "What should I lower the temp to?"

"Whatever you like," Ed said with relief.

Kristen promptly adjusted the temperature setting and bounded back, stopping a couple of steps from Ed. "You suppose I could have a nip of the Wild Turkey for a nightcap?"

"Help yourself," Ed said, motioning to the bottle and plastic cups next to the open suitcase.

After Kristen got her drink, she returned to the end of her bed and lifted the cup in a toast. "Here's to our friendship and a great day tomorrow."

"I'll second that," Ed said, lifting his cup as well.

After taking her sip, Kristen took a tenuous breath and looked at Ed. "Hope I'm not being presumptuous, but you are going to give me a ride tomorrow, aren't you?"

"Count on it," Ed said without hesitation.

Kristen finished her drink before Ed, rose to her feet, and stretched. "I know it's early, but if you don't mind, I'm going to wash up and hit the sack. I'm really beat."

"I will as well. It's been one hell of an eventful day," Ed said with a laugh.

Kristen ruminated momentarily, as if trying to work up the courage to finally look directly at Ed. "I hate to ask, but do you have a shirt I could borrow? Otherwise, I'll have to sleep in this one and wear it again tomorrow."

"I have something even better, an extra pair of flannel pajamas that will keep you nice and warm, but you'll have to grow into them a bit," Ed joshed and promptly retrieved a pair from his suitcase.

"Not a problem," Kristen said as she took them from him and headed for the bathroom.

As soon as Kristen closed the bathroom door, Ed

poured another half cup of the Wild Turkey, hoping it would sufficiently suppress the ever-present pain for the night and enable him to get at least a couple of hours of uninterrupted sleep.

He couldn't believe what a joy she was to have for company after eight years of monastic life, but even more, he appreciated having someone to care about and having that emotion be reciprocated. With cup in hand, he sauntered to the window and pulled the drapes apart slightly to look out. The parking lot was fully blanketed with several inches of snow, but it was beginning to taper off, and he wasn't sure whether to be glad or not. Somewhere deep within, he wanted the trip to be extended so that he could enjoy Kristen's spirited company.

"Still snowing?" Kristen said as she stepped out of the bathroom.

Ed turned and grinned, seeing Kristen lost in his pajamas. "It's letting up."

Kristen smiled broadly, threw her arms up, and spun around. "What'd you think—too sexy?"

"You'd be a smash, modeling that on a Victoria's Secret runway," Ed teased.

"More likely in my undies would be more appreciated," Kristen said provocatively.

"I think you'd better get to bed, and no more nightcaps for you."

"OK, Grandpa," Kristen kidded and started for her bed.

Ed headed for the bathroom, then suddenly stopped. "I just thought of something. Did you cancel your credit card?

"No," Kristen said, instantly in a panic. "I didn't even think of it."

"You had better do it right away." Kristen hurried to the nightstand.

"What's your limit?" Ed asked.

"I think it's three thousand," Kristen guessed.

"When you get customer service, be sure to tell them the credit card was stolen, not lost."

"I'll do that, thanks."

"While you're doing that, I'll get ready for bed as well."

Kristen nodded. "Oh, I left my T-shirt on the shower rod—I washed it."

"I promise not to wear it," Ed cracked.

A few minutes later, Ed emerged from the bathroom in mismatched pajamas that sent Kristen into mild hysterics.

"Yes, I know they don't match," Ed said, having already noticed he'd absentmindedly packed the mismatch.

"I'm sorry, it just tickles me," Kristen blurted out through her laughter.

"Yeah, I must look like a clown," Ed said with a chuckle.

"We make quite a pair." Kristen shook her head.

"So, how'd you make out with the call?" Ed said when they stopped laughing.

"Great; nothing has been charged, and thanks again for telling me," Kristen said and slid under the covers, looking very much like a little girl.

"Glad it worked out, and if there is anything at all I can help you with, please feel free to ask." He pulled the cover back and got in bed.

"You have great-looking silver hair. Makes you look very distinguished, like Cary Grant."

"Maybe next time around," Ed said lightheartedly.

"Oh, there will be something I'll need, if you don't mind a couple of shirts and a charging cable for the cell phone. I left the one I had at home."

"We'll get whatever you need in Mercer," Ed said thoughtfully.

"I already checked it out on the cell; we'll have to go to Hermitage, which is the next exit off the interstate, about fifteen miles from here. They have a Target, a Walmart, and a bunch of food places, like Bob Evans."

"Bob Evans is great for breakfast," Ed said enthusiastically. "Used to stop at them when Ann and I made the trips to visit my folks in Illinois."

"I guess that's where we'll part company," Kristen said with regret.

"I'll buy the biggest breakfast you can eat, and after that, you can get whatever you need." Ed felt bad, thinking about it.

"I'll treat you to breakfast," she offered.

"Are you going to give me a hard time again?"

"No. I just feel like a big sponge."

"You're not, and just so you know, I enjoy your company very much."

"I love being with you as well," Kristen said with a fond smile.

"Before nodding off, can you check the weather for tomorrow on your cell?"

"Oh, sure," Kristen said. "Looks like it'll be cold and cloudy, with possible flurries through most of Ohio, then heavy snow."

"Well, at least no freezing rain."

"Won't the snow slow the drive?"

"Somewhat. Are you in a hurry?"

"Not at all, quite the opposite." Kristen's tone was jaunty.

"Good. We'll just take our time. Now, are you ready to close those baby blues?"

"You want me to set the alarm clock?"

"No, you can sleep as long as you want. I'll be up early without the alarm, so if you're ready, do the light."

"Good night, and thanks for everything," Kristen said sweetly, then clicked off the bright nightstand lamp.

"Good night, and have beautiful dreams."

"Just one more thing before I close my eyes."

"What?" Ed said, wanting to laugh at her childlike ways.

"You have a lady friend?"

"No."

"It must be awfully lonely for you."

"I'd be lying if I said no," Ed admitted.

"How very sad," Kristen murmured, then turned on her side.

CHAPTER 2

I t was pitch-black when Ed awoke and panicked momentarily, not remembering where he was. He felt there was something different about the bed and the layout of the room, even though he couldn't quite see. He rubbed his eyes, hoping to improve his vision, but that only made them tear, and he wiped them with his sleeves. A minute later, with his sight improved, he finally got the sense of the room and realized where he was and the circumstances that had prompted the most pleasant dream he'd had just before waking. He'd dreamed of Kristen rather than Ann, and in the dream, he was young and with her in a sailboat somewhere on a dark-blue ocean beneath a cloudless sky, sailing to an undetermined destination. He glanced over to the other bed, where Kristen was sleeping peacefully, and wondered if it was chance that brought her to him or fate, with a reason not yet known. One thing was certain: she had brought him more joy in just a few hours than he'd known since Ann's demise.

Glancing at the red-numbered clock, he saw it was nearly seven; this was the longest he had slept in years. Sometimes on bad nights, when he couldn't fall asleep, this would be about the time he'd just be nodding off. Feeling the urge to relieve himself, he kicked the covers off and planted his feet on the carpeted floor, then waited a moment to make sure he was in full control of his balance, which of late was becoming an issue, another curse of growing old. Once sure of his stability, he navigated his way to the bathroom and, after closing the door, flipped on the lights and peered into the mirror. He was surprised: for a change, he didn't look half-bad, other than needing a shave. With teeth brushed and face shaved, he was ready for a shower. Without looking, he reached up to pull the shower curtain back and instead had a handful of Kristen's damp T-shirt. He shook his head and chuckled, then suddenly remembered Kristen did not have another top to wear and have to settle for just her hoodie and the light car coat. He decided that after they ate, he would take her shopping for some clothes, but in the meantime, he'd lend her one of his shirts.

All showered, he shut off the light and gently pushed open the door. Much to his surprise, he found Kristen sitting up in bed with the nightstand lamp aglow.

"Good morning. Hope I didn't wake you."

"No, I've been up for a few minutes, and good morning to you, too," Kristen said cheerfully.

"You sleep well?"

"I did, and you?" Kristen stretched.

"The best in years, and I owe it all to you."

"Me?"

"Yes, and I even dreamed about you."

"You dreamed about me?" Kristen was curious.

"Yes."

"Care to share?"

"I don't know," Ed said hesitantly, not quite sure if she might misconstrue his dream.

"Please."

Ed walked over and sat down on the end of his bed. "It was a vivacious dream—the first I've had in many years."

Kristen's eyes widened, and she said bluntly, "Was it sexy?"

"Nothing like that, but it could have been because in the dream, I was young like you, and we were on a sailboat alone on the way to islands unknown."

"That's awesome! Then what?"

"I woke up."

"That's a bummer—why'd you do that?" Kristen blurted out, disappointed.

"So I wouldn't be embarrassed, telling you the rest of the dream," Ed joshed.

"You can talk freely to me. I'm a big girl."

Ed nodded. "Yes, in most ways."

"Not all?" Kristen said with a surprised look.

Ed shook his head. "You still have some beautiful little-girl ways about you that add to your charm."

"Thank you," she said pertly. "Shall I get ready?"

"Yes," Ed said as he rose to his feet, then walked over to the draped window for a look outside.

"Is it still snowing, I hope?" Kristen said as she hopped out of bed and started for the bathroom.

"You hope?" Ed said with a puzzled look.

"Yes. It would give us more time together if we're snowbound."

"It must have stopped after my last peek last night; it all looks about the same."

"See you in a bit," Kristen said, disappointed, and closed the bathroom door.

"Take your time," Ed hollered.

With a sudden pain in his gut, Ed walked over to the dresser and took a gulp of the Wild Turkey straight from the bottle, then rubbed his stomach in a circular motion, hoping to ease the pain as the whiskey made its way down. He didn't like the idea of taking a drink this early in the morning and then driving, especially with someone in the car besides himself. He felt angry but unsure of whom to blame for his problem. The temptation, of course, was to blame God, but deep down in his heart, he knew otherwise. Totally absorbed in his thoughts, he was startled by Kristen's voice when she called out through the partially open bathroom door.

"Ed, could you please get my hoodie? It's on the end of my bed. The T-shirt is still too damp to wear."

"Would you like one of my flannel shirts?"

"Thanks. That would be great, and I promise not to stretch it," she kidded.

After handing her a flannel shirt through the door, Ed returned to the chair and took another slug of the booze. A moment later, he felt the pain slowly ebb, much to his surprise. He stuck the bottle back in his suitcase and was about to close it when he suddenly remembered his toiletry kit and underwear in the bathroom and waited for Kristen to come out. Moments later she emerged with a huge grin on her face, wearing the way-too-big flannel shirt.

"Looks like you've lost serious weight," Ed cracked.

"Don't know how, after the huge meal last night," Kristen shot back. "Oh, don't forget your stuff in there, or I can get it for you."

"If you don't mind, and you can put your wet T-shirt and whatever else in the plastic bag on the floor with my underwear."

"You think they'll get along?" Kristen kidded.

"Like ice and snow."

"Kristen and Ed—it rhymes."

Before leaving, Ed scanned the room and noticed the cell phone on the nightstand and motioned to it. "Think you're forgetting something."

Kristen looked and shook her head. "I don't know what's wrong with me."

"Not a thing that I can see."

"Thanks, that really made my day."

After starting the SUV and turning on the heater, Ed got back out with a large ice scraper he retrieved from under the driver's seat and began the task of removing the snow and ice from the windshield. Kristen offered to help, but Ed insisted she stay in the car since she had no gloves and was dressed in light layers. It took him several minutes to clear the front and rear windows, and then he finally got back into the SUV, to be welcomed by the warmth and Kristen's smile.

"You must be frozen; you should have let me help."

"I don't want you getting sick," Ed said.

"That goes for you as well," Kristen said with true concern.

"All right, what'd you say we turn in the key and get you that huge breakfast at Bob Evans?"

Once out of the snow-covered parking lot, Ed was happy to see that the state road out of the motel had been plowed and sanded, including the ramp to the interstate, which appeared to be in fairly good shape. Less than half an hour, they were seated in a booth at Bob Evans restaurant.

"Very homey," Kristen said, looking around as she removed her car coat and placed it on the bench seat next to her.

"Reminds me a lot of a place in Moline," Ed said as he removed his parka.

"How long since you've been there?"

"Thirty years."

"Oh, wow; probably changed a lot," Kristen guessed.

"No doubt, grown old like me."

He could see Kristen did not particularly like him referring to himself as old, maybe because it conjured up infirmity and death. "You know," she said, "they say age is a state of mind, and you are very youthful in your ways and looks."

"You're very kind, even if that's an exaggeration, and I'll try my best not to be old," Ed said with a grin.

Kristen smiled. "Glad to hear it."

"Now, let's take a look at the menu and get you fed," Ed said as a plump waitress with a happy face approached with two mugs and a coffeepot.

"Good morning. My name's Emma. Welcome to Bob Evans."

"Good morning," Ed and Kristen said simultaneously.

"Coffee for both?" she asked as she placed the mugs on the table.

"Yes, please," Ed replied.

"You folks on a long Christmas road trip?" Emma queried.

"Yes, on the way to Illinois," Ed said with a wink at Kristen.

"Saw this morning on the Weather Channel some serious snow coming that way," Emma said as she filled the mugs and then peered directly at Kristen's bruise.

"I didn't pay attention and ran into a door the other night," Kristen fibbed to stem any questions.

"That's a shame. You have such a pretty face."

"Thank you."

"They say how soon the snow is coming?" Ed asked.

"Late afternoon or early evening," Emma said fretfully.

"Well, that'll put a cramp in our drive," Ed mused.

"The cream's on the table, and I'll be back to take your order," Emma said and turned to go.

"Don't leave; we'll give you the order now. My grand-daughter is starving," Ed said with a wink at Kristen. "You still serve the 'Big' breakfast?"

"Sure do," Emma said and reached for her order pad.

Ed looked at Kristen with prompting eyes. "What do you say?"

"You want me to?"

"That's what I promised."

"OK."

"Good, and I'll have a bowl of oatmeal and whole-wheat toast."

Emma glanced at Kristen. "How do you want your eggs, dearie?"

"Scrambled, please."

Emma jotted down the order and left promptly.

"From what she said, it looks like we may have a longer trip after all," Ed said, lifting the coffee mug to his lips.

"Do you mind?" Kristen said with a probing look.

"Not one bit."

"I'm so glad," she said happily.

"I'm puzzled. Why?"

"Like I said, it'll give us more time together."

"You may regret it."

"Why in the world would I?"

"Lack of commonality. I'm an old man."

"Meaning what?"

"You'll get bored. We probably have very little in common to talk about."

Kristen shook her head as she reached for the creamer. "You just might be pleasantly surprised at how much we may have to talk about—would you like some cream?"

Ed shook his head. "I don't use it; see, that's a minus one already."

"That has nothing to do with what we're talking about," Kristen protested.

"OK, I'll concede that one, but I think I'll get a note-pad and make a list."

"I already have a pad, and I will note, instead, all the things we do have in common."

Ed smiled and lifted his mug in a toast. "Here's to commonality."

"And you losing." Kristen clicked Ed's mug.

"Early Christmas toast?" Emma said cheerily as she approached the table with a large tray and set it down.

"That was quick," Ed said with surprise.

"It's still early and we're not that busy, for some reason," Emma said as she served the plates.

"Kristen, sweetie, you lucked out."

"Well, enjoy, and I'll be back for refills."

"Thank you, Emma," Ed said with a nod and looked over at Kristen, who was staring at the food in disbelief.

"You weren't kidding when you said big breakfast. This is more than two could eat."

"We'll get a doggie bag," Ed joshed.

"I'll share some of this with you," she said, glancing at Ed's oatmeal and toast.

"Do the best you can."

"Are you on a diet?"

"Sort of, and I don't want to overeat since it tends to make me tired when I drive."

"Wish I could drive and give you a break," Kristen said sympathetically.

Ed was surprised. "You don't know how to drive?"

"I took driving lessons in high school, but I haven't driven since."

"Well, then, I'll give you a chance to get behind the wheel again."

"You trust me?"

"Like you told me, you're a big girl."

"I can't wait," Kristen gushed.

Ed finished his oatmeal and a piece of toast and sipped his coffee, watching with amusement as Kristen struggled with her big breakfast. Sensing his eyes on her, she looked up, shook her head, and pushed the plate away.

"No more. I'm stuffed."

"You did good."

"I could have used some help," Kristen said and dabbed her lips with a napkin.

"Here comes Emma; maybe she'll have the rest," Ed cracked.

"Well, looks like someone has a way to go," Emma said when she reached the table with a coffeepot in hand.

"Not on your life," Kristen said, shaking her head.

"I'll tell you the truth, sweetie, only the brawniest of men finish that meal."

"I'm relieved," Kristen said and pretended to wipe her brow.

"Refill on the coffee?" Emma stood ready to pour.

"No, thanks, just the check, please; we've got to hit the road," Ed said, glancing at his watch.

It was a short drive to Target, which wasn't Ed's preferred choice, but it was conveniently located, and he didn't want to waste time looking for something more upscale if, in fact, there was anything like that. In the store, he grabbed a shopping cart, much to Kristen's surprise.

"I really don't think we need a shopping cart for what I'm getting."

"Let's do it, just in case," Ed casually suggested.

"Well, OK," Kristen said.

With the cell-phone cable in hand, Kristen pointed in the direction of the women's department. "I just need to get a couple of things."

"Lead the way," Ed said, wheeling the cart.

Kristen knew exactly what she wanted and wasted little time choosing undies and a top. "I'm done. See, you didn't need the cart."

"That's just a start," Ed said, looking around. "I want you to get all the things you really need—more undies, warm wearables, and whatever else comes to your mind; then we'll top it off with a parka and a travel bag."

Kristen was flabbergasted. "I can't let you spend that kind of money on me."

"Are we going to argue about it?" Ed chided with a grin, using the now-established phrase.

"It's just not right."

"Please do it for me—there are no strings attached, if that's what you're thinking."

"I feel like a sponge, taking advantage of your goodness," Kristen protested.

Tell you what, let's call them Christmas gifts, which you can't refuse. I have no one to do that for, so please don't take that pleasure from me."

"OK," Kristen murmured, and Ed could see she didn't dare to look directly at him as tears filled her eyes.

"After you finish here, let's stop at the grocery department and get some snacks and drinks for the trip."

An hour later, on the interstate, Kristen was beside herself, going through the shopping bags and looking at the items excitedly. It was the first time since she was a little girl and her dad was still alive that she'd received so many things at once.

"You spent nearly five hundred bucks on all this stuff," Kristen said emotionally. "How do I thank you?"

"You're doing it."

"I am?" Kristen said with a puzzled look.

"My thanks is seeing you so happy."

"But that's nothing," Kristen said and leaned over and kissed Ed on the cheek. "Thank you again."

"It's my pleasure."

Kristen looked intently at Ed. "You have any family?"

"No, just a few friends."

"No one at all?" Kristen said in disbelief.

"My wife came here from Italy when she was ten to live with her aunt and uncle on Staten Island. Her parents were killed in an auto crash. So that was her only family here in the States.

"She did have extended family in Italy, though," Ed said distantly. "My parents emigrated here from Belgium right after World War I and had no one here, either."

"We're both orphans, then."

"Surely you must have some family?"

"Yes, on Mom's side, but for whatever reason, we weren't close and hardly ever saw them," Kristen murmured.

"Can I ask you a personal question?"

"Anything you like," Kristen said without hesitation, stuffing all but one of the items back in the shopping bags and tossing them on the back seat.

"What made you run away from home?"

"My dad died of a heart attack when I was thirteen, and Mom just couldn't handle it, so she started drinking heavily. It wasn't long before she became a lush, but at least she drank at home. Then, for some reason, she started hanging out at the bars, and that's where she met Jack, the scum," Kristen said bitterly. "A few months later they were married, and that's when it all started. I was fairly developed for my age, and of course, the pervert noticed. At first he made me believe he was an affectionate stepdad and playfully tickled me all over, including my breasts. I didn't know any better, and since Mom didn't say anything, I thought it must be OK. From there it started to progress. He would come up to my room after I got in bed and pretend to tuck me in and, of course, touch me everywhere. I told Mom, but she said he was just trying to be nice and that I shouldn't reject him. He would booze her up out of her mind so that he could get at me without her knowing what was happening. Then one night, he got her so damn drunk that she passed out, and that's when he came into my room, took off his clothes, and got in bed with me. He said he would just cuddle me. After that, he started having sex with me while she was zonked out. I told her, but she wouldn't believe me. I guess her brain was turning to mush, and besides, I think she was afraid he would leave her—then she couldn't afford to buy booze."

"You didn't tell anyone else?"

"I was too ashamed."

Ed shook his head angrily. "The goddamn, lowlife mongrel."

"You're the first one I've ever told this to," Kristen said softly.

"Did he ever stop?"

"Yes, when I got in high school," Kristen said, avoiding Ed's eyes. "I think he was afraid I might finally tell on him."

"I'm so very sorry," Ed said with feeling and squeezed her hand.

"That kind of thing happens more often than you can imagine," she said knowingly.

"Have you had any contact with your mom since you left?"

"No, and I don't think I ever will." Her words were bitter.

"Maybe one day you'll be able to forgive her."

"Would you?"

"I honestly don't know," Ed said with a deep sigh. "Forgiveness is one of the hardest things to do in life."

Kristen, feeling uneasy, was eager to change the subject and looked out the window. "Looks like we've lucked out—no flurries yet."

"Can you check it out on your cell?"

"Will do." Kristen busied her dexterous fingers. "Appears to be good through most of Ohio."

"And then what?"

"You really wanna know?" she teased.

"Reluctantly, yes."

"Flurries, turning to serious snow."

"I'll tell you what, we had better make reservations somewhere near the end of Indiana."

"You have any specific place in mind?"

"A town with more than one motel," he said with a grin.

"Hang on a sec." Kristen busied her fingers again. "Ah, Chesterton has a few—Days Inn, Quality Court, and a few others."

"Great. Pick the best one and make a reservation for two rooms."

Kristen was disappointed. "You want us to have separate rooms?"

"I thought maybe you'd prefer it, and don't worry, I'll pay for it."

"Can't we share a room like last night?"

"I don't have a problem with it if you don't," Ed said agreeably.

"I'm so glad," Kristen said jubilantly.

Ed reached into his pocket for his wallet and handed it to Kristen. "If you open it, you'll see a Visa card; you'll need it to make the reservation."

Kristen did as Ed suggested and, a minute later, finalized the reservation. She replaced the card in his wallet, then peered at the worn photo of Ed and his wife in a plastic holder, taken when they were young. "She was beautiful."

"That she was," Ed said tenderly. "It was taken at the Copa on our first date."

"How long were you married?"

"Thirty-eight years."

"Sounds like you had a successful marriage," Kristen mused. "Did you have kids?"

"We had a son. He was killed in Iraq," Ed said with finality to preclude further questions.

"I'm very sorry," Kristen said with utmost sincerity.

"What religion are you, if you don't mind me asking?"

"Born a Catholic but lost the faith," Ed said indifferently.

"May I ask why?" Kristen said with a perplexed look.

"During Ann's battle with leukemia, I just couldn't understand how a supposedly caring God could turn His back and ignore all the prayers and watch that kind of suffering."

"But didn't you tell me one of the reasons for this trip to your hometown is to attend a Christmas Midnight Mass? Doesn't that mean you still have faith?"

Ed was tempted to tell Kristen the full story but decided he didn't want to divulge his terminal illness and have her feel sorry for him. "I'm doing it mainly for my parents as a sort of final Christmas present. They, like Ann, were fervent believers."

"When's the last time you went to church?"

"Ann's funeral, eight years ago."

"That's a long time," Kristen murmured.

"Losing faith is like getting a divorce; you're left with a whole lot of bitterness and enmity," Ed said poignantly. Then he added, "I'm sorry. I don't want to let my thoughtless comment sway you in your faith."

"You're not; I haven't been to church since my dad died. We used to go every Sunday, and I was in the choir, but after he died, Mom stopped going, like you—she was too drunk to go anyway."

"I shouldn't be spouting off. Please forgive me," Ed said contritely.

"Right now I don't know if I believe in anything. You lost your faith in God late in life, and I was too young to develop one."

"Sounds like we're both pretty much in the same place," Ed said thoughtfully.

"And guess what?"

"I give up."

"That's another thing we have in common, which reminds me—I said I was going to make a list of all the similarities we do have," Kristen said. She reached for her shoulder bag and pulled out a slightly worn notepad and a pen and began to write. "That's three."

"Wait a minute, what are the other two?"

"We both love the snow and each other's company."

"That's unfair. I don't have a pad," Ed protested.

"Don't worry, I'll keep track of yours on a separate page---which will be a waste of paper because there won't be much to write about our not having anything in common," Kristen teased.

"Can you get me a drink from the cooler, please?"

"Sure. What would you like, Coke or water?"

"Water will be fine."

Kristen pulled out a small bottle from the cooler beside her feet, unscrewed the top, and handed it to Ed.

"Before I join you in a drink and if you don't mind, I'll change out of your shirt and into something that fits."

Ed seemed totally ill at ease. "You might want to hop in the back."

"That would be kind of hard to do, and it's all right, I don't mind," Kristen said and started to unbutton the shirt.

"Well, at least push your seat all the way back," Ed said firmly, focusing his eyes on the passing lane.

"I've been looked at hundreds of times in the raw by lots of men," Kristen said.

"Well, just the same, I'll keep my eyes on the road. Let me know when you're done."

Kristen smiled and shook her head, finding his nobility hard to believe as she changed into a turtleneck sweater. "You are truly a gentleman, the first I've ever met."

"Don't give up; there are others out there."

"Unfortunately, not that many—you can look now."

"Hopefully, you'll find some of them."

"Yeah, right," Kristen said sardonically.

"Just one more personal question, and you don't have to answer."

"You can ask all you want."

"I've always been curious: How do girls find the nerve to get up on a stage and strip in front of a bunch of lecherous men?"

"It's brutal, and very few girls do it sober; they resort to booze, drugs, or both before they hit the stage. When I first started, Chuck would have me smoke a joint, and sometimes when I just couldn't do it, he had me snort a little coke."

Ed shook his head. "A real caring jerk. You're lucky you didn't get hooked on the junk."

"I probably would have had I stayed."

"Somebody up there is looking after you," he said kindly.

"For sure my dad," Kristen murmured, then retrieved a Coke from the cooler. "Would you like one, too, and something to munch?"

"No, thanks, I'm good, but you go ahead."

"You think we'll make it to Chesterton before the snow?"

"Well, let's see, we've got about two hours left in Ohio and another two in Indiana, so depending on how fast the snow is moving, we should be able to make it."

"Well, if we don't, we'll survive. We've got lots of snacks, drinks and booze, and that big old quilt back there to keep us toasty," Kristen said playfully.

"Damn!"

"What?"

"I should have gotten hot coffee for the thermos."

"You want to try to get some at the next exit?"

"Definitely, yes," Ed said. He needed a bathroom break and a shot of booze to kill the developing pain in his gut. Twenty minutes later, he pulled up at a minimart gas station off the exit.

"Guess I'd better use the ladies' room as long as we're here," Kristen said girlishly.

"Good idea, and here's fifty bucks: thirty for the gas, the rest for coffee and whatever else you want to get."

"You want anything?"

"No, I'm good, but if you do, by all means, get it."

As soon as Kristen was inside the mart, Ed rushed over to the rear of the SUV and opened the tailgate and the suitcase. After a quick look around, he took a long swallow of the booze, then hurried back to pump the gas. Once done, he headed for the minimart just as Kristen approached the door with the thermos in hand. He reached into his pocket and handed her the SUV key.

"Start the engine and blast the heat. It's really getting cold."

"I just might drive off and leave you here," Kristen kidded.

"Well, then, I better give you more money for gas," Ed shot back.

Kristen scrunched her face and said sweetly, "I'd be lost without you, don't you know?"

Ed smiled affably. "That makes us a pair."

"You finally admit it, so I won't have to make those lists."

"I guess not."

"I'm so glad," Kristen said joyfully.

"Did you get yourself some cream for the coffee?"

"Yes, a whole bunch of those little ones. I have them in my parka pocket."

"See you in a bit, then," Ed said and headed for the men's room.

When Ed got back, Kristen was sitting in the driver's seat, listening to a country music radio station and singing along with the woman. She looked up, somewhat startled, and pushed open the door.

"Sorry."

"No, stay."

"You want me to drive?"

"The safest place to learn is on an interstate, especially when there's very little traffic and the road is flat and straight."

"What if we get stopped?"

"We'll just tell them you forgot your wallet in Albany."

"We might get arrested."

"Then let's hope we're in the same cell with two beds," Ed cracked.

Kristen shook her head. "Well, all right. It's your car, and I hope you have money for bail."

Once in the SUV, Ed motioned for Kristen to drive. "Keep your eyes on the road, and be ready to brake."

"This is fun," Kristen said excitedly as she pulled out of the gas station and headed for the interstate.

"You could have left the radio on and listened to country music."

"I wanted to hear the weather report, and the cell is running low on juice. I just came across this country station."

"Damn, I should've gotten you a charging cable for the car as well."

"We'll be OK if we don't use it unnecessarily, and as far as the music, I'm not into hip-hop and the other junk," Kristen rationalized. "Believe it or not, I love country music, and my daddy did as well."

"A New York girl and country music—hmm."

"Most of the country songs tell tender stories that touch the heart and the soul," Kristen said emotionally.

"You sing along with all the songs?" Ed guessed.

"That and also karaoke on my cell, but only when I'm alone."

"Can you make an exception and let me hear you sing?"

"I don't know," Kristen said timidly.

"Please, just one," Ed begged.

"You might laugh."

"That I would never do, and besides, I have a feeling you have a beautiful singing voice from the way you string your words together when you speak."

"You can tell from that?" Kristen said disbelievingly.

"Yes," Ed said honestly, having heard countless actors doing commercials at the ad agency.

"You really gonna make me sing?"

"No, I'm not going to make you, but I would love to hear you."

"OK. This was my dad's favorite, sung by Sammi Smith. He played it all the time, and the name is 'Help Me Make It through the Night.'"

"I've heard it, and I like it very much," Ed said and eagerly waited for Kristen to find the karaoke app on her cell phone.

When she finished, he was astonished by the superb richness of her voice and the way she added her own style to the words.

"Like it?" Kristen asked.

"Incredible."

"Are you teasing?"

"Absolutely not. Why haven't you pursued a singing career?"

"I didn't think I was any good since I'd only sung a few years in a church choir before my dad died."

"You have extraordinary talent. You shouldn't waste it," Ed said.

"I have no idea how to get started."

"Maybe I can help in the time I've got left," Ed blurted out without thinking and then bit his tongue.

"What do you mean? Do you have a life-threatening medical issue?" Kristen said with concern.

Ed felt cornered and wanted to tell Kristen the truth, but he knew it would upset her and she'd perhaps dismiss his suggestion.

"It's an old combat wound from Vietnam that has acted up, and no, the wound is not life threatening," Ed said honestly, refraining from mentioning the real reason.

"You know the music business?"

"No, but I have extensive experience in advertising and promotion—over forty years on Madison Avenue with a top-notch ad firm."

"So how and when do we get started?" Kristen said eagerly, buoyed by Ed's reaction and recalling her dad's as well.

"You're on the clock as of now," Ed said with an encouraging smile, "which means endless hours warbling country songs."

"You're gonna get sick of hearing me."

"I'll enjoy every minute."

"OK, but don't say I didn't warn you," Kristen said blithely.

"So, how's it feel to be driving?"

"I love it, but I can't believe I'm doing it; thanks so much for trusting me."

"And I thank you for giving me a break," Ed said with a grin. "Let me know when you want me to take over."

"I can do it as long as the weather holds up."

"Well, that being the case, I'll close my eyes and snooze, if that's OK with you."

"Go ahead. I'll wake you if there's a problem, and I'll practice singing while you're resting."

Ed adjusted the seat to the reclined position and re-laxed. He hope it would give Kristen more confidence, knowing he trusted her driving. Not long after he dozed off, a strange and disturbing nightmare filled his head. He was in a dark and frightful place, with walls all around, desperately trying to find a way out, but the more he tried, the darker it got, and a smell of death filled his nostrils. He suddenly felt a tug on his shoulder and shot straight up in the seat and mercifully saw Kristen's lovely face, slightly discomposed.

"You were having a bad dream. Are you OK?" Kristen said breathlessly.

"Thanks to you, now I am," Ed said with great relief. "I was having a nightmare straight from hell."

"You did scare me momentarily," Kristen confessed.

"So sorry. How's the driving, and where are we?"

"I'm doing OK, and we're way more than halfway through Ohio, believe it or not," Kristen said proudly.

"Great driving; you must be starving," Ed said, glancing at the dash clock.

"I could stand a Coke and a snack."

"Want me to drive so you can eat?"

"No, I'm fine unless you have doubts."

"I have full confidence you can multitask," Ed said with a smile and reached into the cooler for the Coke and a sandwich. He popped open the can and placed it in the drink holder between the two seats, then partially unwrapped the sandwich and placed it in her hand.

"Are you having one?"

"I'll just have a Coke for now," Ed said, feeling the pain in his gut coming back and wishing he could have a slug of Wild Turkey instead of the soda.

"Just remembered, I have your change in my parka on the back seat," Kristen said as she was about to bite into the sandwich.

"Keep it for the next time you want to get something."

"You're so good to me. How am I ever going to repay you?"

"I've already given you that answer: with the joy you bring me."

Kristen shook her head. "That's hardly enough. I could pole dance for you," she teased.

"That's not ever going to happen," Ed said reprovingly. "Now eat your sandwich, and no more talk like that."

"Sorry. I just want to do something to repay you."

"Not that way," Ed said firmly. "I just had a thought for when we get to Chesterton."

"What?"

"Maybe they have a karaoke bar for your public singing debut."

"I don't think I'm ready for that yet. I'd probably make a fool of myself."

"I would never let you do that," Ed said staunchly.

"You really think I can do it?"

"From the way I heard you sing, you're more than ready, and time is of the essence."

"I wish I'd met you a long time ago."

"We can't do anything about that, so let's concentrate on now and give it all you've got. Have you done anything other than country?"

"No."

"You want to try something different just to see?"

"If you want me to," Kristen said agreeably.

How about a duet with Frank Sinatra? There's a song I have in mind." Ed reached back for the CD case and then searched out the album. "Ah, got it."

Kristen glanced over. "What is it?"

"Name of the song is 'Something Stupid.' Have you ever heard it?"

"I don't think so."

"Frank sings a duet with his daughter Nancy. You can do her part."

"Can I listen to it first?"

"By all means," Ed said as he slid the CD into the dash and raised the volume.

It took Kristen but a moment to pick up the rhythm and the beat. When the song ended, she looked at Ed confidently. "Play it again."

Ed couldn't believe his ears as he listened to Kristen harmonizing with Sinatra and totally wiping out Nancy's pitiful voice.

"Awesome," Ed said with a huge grin when Kristen finished. "You made it sound like you recorded it with him."

Kristen glanced over at Ed with a satisfied smile. "You're not just saying that to make me feel good?"

"I am, but also because you're that good."

"I think you're slightly prejudiced."

"If you weren't driving, I'd give you a hug."

"You can do it while I'm driving," Kristen teased.

"I think not."

"OK, then when we stop."

"We'll see."

"You want me to do the song again?"

"It's up to you."

"You're not tired of listening to me?"

"I'll never tire of hearing you sing, like I've already said. You can do it twenty-four-seven. Sometimes I listen to Sinatra nonstop for hours, but now I've got you."

"You might be sorry."

"Nothing you do makes me sorry."

"You'll tell me if something does?"

"And you do the same. Are you ready to do it again?"

"Yes," Kristen said and tore into the song with even greater intent; when she finished, she punched off the CD player and looked over to Ed, who was leaning back in the seat with his eyes closed. "Are you napping again?"

"No, I'm having a beautiful vision."

"What of?"

"You performing at Carnegie Hall."

"I think you're way overvisualizing."

"Are you open to advice from someone who has been around the block once or twice?"

"From you, yes, I am."

"Dream big and never settle for less—that's the difference between those who succeed in the world and all the rest."

"Uh-oh."

"What?"

"There's a state trooper with lights flashing coming behind us like a bat out of hell," Kristen said nervously.

Ed glanced back. "Relax. He's not after us."

A moment later, the state trooper passed, doing at least ninety miles per hour, and Kristen let out a long sigh.

"I'll share something with you that you may not believe, but it's absolutely true. I've dreamed of performing on a big stage. Not Carnegie Hall, of course."

"I'm glad you have, and tonight, if we find a karaoke bar, it'll be the start of your dream."

"I love you, Ed," Kristen said tenderly.

"I love you, too, little thrush."

"Thrush? What's that?"

"It's a small songbird Thoreau once extolled."

"And you think I'm worthy of that comparison?"

"Absolutely."

They drove in silence for the next few minutes, each musing about their spontaneous declaration of love. Kristen was not sure exactly how she meant it because that feeling was new to her—somewhere between how she loved her dad and she'd once loved her boyfriend. Ed, on the other hand, had no such conflict; he loved Kristen for her free spirit and the joy she brought him. Memories he had long forgotten and feelings that were all but dead. For the first time since Ann, he felt that someone really needed him, and he, in turn, needed her. It was a part of life he once took for granted and only now realized how much he'd missed when it vanished. He found himself becoming deeply entwined in Kristen's life and felt it was beyond his control, as if some invisible force had taken over, and he was merely a pawn.

"This girlfriend in Las Vegas you mentioned—how long have you known her, if you don't mind me asking?"

"I met her at the skin bar a couple of years ago. She was a pole dancer like me and came from similar circumstances, except it wasn't a stepdad who was doing it to her; it was her perverted father. Her mom was a tramp who had a boyfriend in every bar in Jersey City. Morgan ran away when she was sixteen and hooked up with a pimp as soon as she got to New York. She wised up after getting brutalized and diseased and broke it off with the Black pimp. A year ago she decided to head for Las Vegas and start a new life.

"What is she doing for a living there?"

"She's a cocktail waitress at a casino, so she tells me."

"Doesn't sound like you believe her."

"I'm not sure," Kristen said honestly.

Ed shook his head, thinking how ignorant he was of what was happening in the world around him.

"So, what are you in the mood for eats when we stop?"

"Can I have anything?"

"Whatever your little heart desires."

"Steak smothered in onions, fries on the side."

"It's a deal, and after, hopefully we'll find a karaoke bar."

"I'm ready for it if you think so."

"That's what I want to hear from now on."

"I wish I had your optimism."

"You will by the time I'm through with you."

"You know something?"

"What?"

"You bring me up when I'm floundering."

"And you do much more for me."

"Why do you say that?"

"You've brought sunshine where there was only gray."

"Don't know about that, but as far as I'm concerned, it's you doing everything for me."

"It just seems that way."

Kristen smiled tenderly. "You are the most caring and generous man I've ever known."

Ed rubbed his chin, then smiled. "Been a while since I've had someone to be that with."

"Your wife and son were very lucky."

"I got much in return from them."

"It seems like you've had more than your share of bad."

Ed shrugged and glanced at a road sign. "We're in Indiana."

"And it looks like snow ahead."

"You've made great time; let's stop at the next exit and gas up, and I'll drive. You must be totally exhausted by now, and the snow is about to overtake us."

"I'm getting there," Kristen confessed.

"You want some coffee?"

"Yes, please."

Ed fixed Kristen's coffee and handed her the cup.

She took a sip. "Yum. You having some?"

"How can I resist that Colombian aroma?" Ed said with a grin and poured himself a cup.

"When were you in Vietnam?"

"In 1966, just as the war was cranking up."

"How long were you there?"

"Five months when a bullet ripped through my gut. Then they had me in intensive care for a month in Saigon before they shipped me to Walter Reed."

"You got shot in the gut?"

"Yes."

"Have you been in pain since then, or did it just flare up?"

"It's been on and off for many years, but lately it's gotten worse."

"Why have you been trying to hide it from me?"

"You're very observant," Ed said, "and simply put, I don't want it to become a disruptive issue and me sounding like a whiner."

"I think I understand," Kristen said kindly, "and you're one hell of a man."

"Well, I'm glad that's out. Now I won't have to try to fool you anymore and can feel free to partake of the Wild Turkey."

"You don't have pain medication?"

"I have an unfilled prescription. It's very potent, and if I use it, I can't drive."

"If that's the case, I'll do all the driving."

"That's very sweet, but let's share for now."

"Besides the pain medication, there is nothing they can do for you?"

"Unfortunately, no," Ed said with a shrug.

"Wish I had the power to make it go away." Kristen's words were tender.

"Believe it or not, you're helping a lot."

"Does the pain stop you from eating?"

Ed nodded. "Yes. I don't have much of an appetite."

"Should you be drinking booze?"

"It helps dull the pain."

"I feel so bad for you, having no one to look after you."

"I have you right now."

"I'm glad you think that," Kristen said emotionally.

"Ah, we're coming to an exit just as the flakes start to fly. Like before, you pay the man and I'll pump the gas, and by all means, do get whatever you like," Ed said, reaching for his wallet.

The snow was light all the way to Chesterton, and Kristen more than once volunteered to drive, but Ed wanted her to rest in case there was a karaoke bar and she got to sing. The room at the Quality Inn was a significant improvement from the one at Motel 12, which was a step above a homeless shelter.

"Firm mattress." Kristen beamed happily as she bounced on the bed.

"Glad you like it," Ed said with a grin, enjoying Kristen's youthful antics.

"Wonder if the TV works," Kristen said once she stopped.

"Give it a try. The remote is on the nightstand. Maybe we can get an update on the weather."

Kristen sprang to her feet, grabbed the remote, and turned on the TV. "Perfect timing; they're doing the weather."

"No significant accumulation, that's great," Ed said happily when the weather report concluded. "Why don't you get the phone book from the drawer and see about steak joints?"

A moment later, Kristen looked up from the phone book and smiled. "Kelsey's Steak House has great reviews.

"Make a reservation if we need one, and as long as you're looking things up, see about a karaoke bar," Ed said as he pulled out the fifth of Wild Turkey from the suitcase and poured himself half a glassful, then settled in an armchair.

Kristen finished her search and made a sour face. "There's a karaoke bar in Portage called Dan's 21, but it's about twenty miles from here."

Ed glanced at his watch. "Not a problem. We've got plenty of time to have dinner and then head out there."

"You're not too tired?" Kristen said with genuine concern.

"Even if I was, it wouldn't matter. Tonight is going to be the start of your country fame and a new life."

"I'm a little scared," Kristen confessed and ambled over to Ed. "Can I have a sip to calm my nerves?"

"Pour yourself a mouthful or two and no more."

"You embolden me when I'm doubtful," Kristen said earnestly.

"And you, my thrush, light up my life," Ed said jovially, clicking Kristen's glass in a toast.

Dan's 21 was packed and lively, which Ed was glad about for Kristen's sake. He wanted her to have a spirited audience for her debut. Looking around, he spotted a just-vacated table near the small stage and guided Kristen to it.

"I don't know about this," Kristen said apprehensively when they were seated.

"After what you've been doing, this should be a piece of cake."

"There were never this many people, and I had some help to boost my courage the first time I took the stage."

"I'll get you a drink."

"Wish you could get up on the stage with me and we could do a duet like Frank and Nancy."

"I would gladly if I could carry a tune past the first syllable," Ed kidded and squeezed Kristen's hand.

"Good evening," a young, attractive waitress in skintight blue jeans and a pink sweater said as she stepped up to the table. "My name is Tammy. What can I get you guys?"

Ed glanced over at Kristen and motioned for her to order first. "I'll have a vodka and Coke."

"And you, sir?"

"A double Wild Turkey, no ice."

Tammy noted the orders on her pad and turned to go.

"Wait, before you go: They do karaoke here?"

"Yes, every night except weekends, when we have a live band. It's break time right now, but it'll be starting back up in a few minutes. Are you going to sing?" Tammy said with a curious look at Ed.

"No, my granddaughter is. How does she go about it?"

"I'll tell Lynn, the MC, and she'll put your grand-daughter on the list. What's the name?"

"Kristen Cole."

"Please have Lynn put me toward the end of the list since we just got here and I need to get more comfort-able," Kristen said nervously.

"Will do. What song you gonna do?"

"'Help Me Make It through the Night.'"

"Ah, a Sammi Smith song," Tammy said knowingly.

"Yes."

"I love her voice," Tammy said and left.

"I hope it's a long list so I have time for two drinks," Kristen said half seriously.

"One is all you're going to get," Ed said firmly. "Do what public speakers and many professional entertainers do."

"What?" Kristen said eagerly.

"Focus on one person in the audience and pretend it's just the two of you."

"I'll try."

"That's my girl," Ed said encouragingly and squeezed her hand.

"I just thought of something: Why don't you be my manager since this whole thing is your idea?"

Ed smiled and shook his head. "You will need a real pro who knows country music and can guide you through the showbiz maze. I'm just here to get you started."

"But I will need you to give me courage and believe in me, and there is no one in the whole world who can do it like you," Kristen said with pleading eyes.

"Why don't we talk about it later? Right now, you need to concentrate on your performance and nothing else, OK?"

"Yeah, I guess," Kristen said downheartedly.

"Oh no, we can't have any of that." Ed reached over and lifted Kristen's chin. "Let me see that confident, beautiful smile."

"I'll try."

"Got your drinks," Tammy said as she approached the table.

"Your timing is perfect," Ed said.

"You're all set," Tammy said to Kristen as she set the drinks down. "You are fifth in line, and to ease your mind, it's a very supportive crowd tonight; good luck."

"Thanks," Kristen said with a nod.

"I'll be cheering for you," Tammy said with a grin and left.

Ed picked up his drink in a toast and motioned for Kristen to do the same. "Here's to the launch of your music career."

"I hope you're right," Kristen said demurely.

The audience was just as the waitress had described, very friendly and supportive of every singer, even though each failed to even stay in tune. Nonetheless, they received hoots and hollers when they finished from the very vocal crowd. Kristen tensed when the singer before her left the stage, and then she gulped the last drop of her drink.

The full-figured MC with a roundish face and too much makeup looked out at the audience with a playful grin. "Ladies and gentlemen, and I use those words loosely, our next singer is Miss Kristen Cole, a first-timer here, so let's put our hands together and make her welcome."

Kristen rose deliberately and made her way to the stage to cheers and whistles from the men, who appreciated her good looks and figure after the previous local chippies. When she got to the stage, the MC hugged her and looked out at the crowd.

"All right, you all, here's Miss Kristen Cole doing her version of one of the best country songs ever recorded by so many: 'Help Me Make It Through The Night.'"

Kristen clutched the stand-up mic and looked out at the crowd, then glanced at the MC standing by the karaoke machine and nodded. "I'm ready."

"Watch the monitor for the words," the MC urged.

"I just need the music," Kristen said.

"Ladies and gentlemen, Kristen is doing the song on her own," then hollered to Kristen, "hit the Play button."

Once again, there were whistles and hollers in support of Kristen's choice, including Ed, who gave her a thumbs-up.

Kristen smiled nervously, and within a few lyrics, she lost herself in the song and the moment and, just as Ed suggested, focused on a couple at a nearby table. Throughout her performance, there were cheers and applause, and when she finished, those who were seated rose and gave her a standing ovation and began to holler for an encore. Ed could hardly contain his emotion, thrilled by the response of those in the audience, who yelled at the top of their lungs.

"Do another!"

Kristen looked over to Ed, also on his feet, who nodded, and she held up her hand.

"It's a little livelier—hope you like it, 'Son of a Preacher Man,'" Kristen said and waited for the MC to cue it on the machine. Once the music started, Kristen removed the mic from its stand, took a step forward, and began jauntily. The crowd went wild as Kristen exploded with voice and body, prompting many of those seated to their feet in a like response. Ed felt that the crowd knew they were seeing someone very special who was headed for stardom. When finished, a breathless Kristen bowed several times to thundering applause and whistles, then hurried off the stage into Ed's open arms.

"I am out-of-my-mind proud of you," Ed declared as he hugged her with all his might.

"You're the one they need to thank," Kristen said joyfully and kissed Ed on the cheek repeatedly.

No sooner were they seated than a young man approached the table, wearing an oversize grin.

"My name's Wayne. I own the bar, and I just want to tell you, Kristen, you are one hell of a singer. You must be a pro."

Ed promptly and proudly interceded. "Believe it or not, this is Kristen's debut. She's never sung anywhere but church."

"You're right, I don't believe it," Wayne said and looked at Kristen. "You put most of the professional country singers to shame. I'd be honored if you let me join you and get a round of drinks."

Kristen smiled. "Thank you so much for the offer, and

please don't take it personally, but this is a very special moment I only want to share with this man."

"Well, I can't say I'm happy about it, but I understand, and have as many drinks as you like. I'll have Tammy bring you whatever you're having."

"You handled that like a pro," Ed said happily.

"I've had a lot of practice at it," Kristen said, tongue in cheek, "and I really do only want to share this special moment just with you."

"You have no idea how much I appreciate you saying that, and in return, I will put your mind at ease, if you haven't already guessed. I'll gladly accompany you to Las Vegas and get a manager to help you become a country star."

"It's a far reach," Kristen said dubiously.

"Believe," Ed said forcefully.

"Shouldn't we go to Nashville instead?"

"No, Las Vegas is the heart of the entertainment world and has an abundance of entertainment gurus. With some luck, we can find a top manager who knows the country business so you can skip the paying-your-dues thing and go straight for stardom."

CHAPTER 3

They crossed the Illinois state line Saturday midmorning, with snow gently swirling. According to the latest weather report, the prediction was for six or more inches and definitely more for the northwestern part of the state, where they were headed. They were both a little tired from the night before, having stayed on at the karaoke bar longer than Ed had planned, but he wanted Kristen to bask in the glory of her incredible singing debut. He knew she would face some hard times getting started and needed all the self-confidence she could garner. She had the natural-born talent and a unique voice he hoped would get her the much-needed attention in the initial weeks and months of competing with established country singers, which would not be easy. With his grave medical condition, time was of the essence in getting Kristen started quickly.

"I still can't believe last night," Kristen mused happily.

"No doubt about it, you certainly made a hell of a statement."

"And it's all because of you. You gave me the courage to do it."

"I think eventually you would have got there on your own. I just gave you a slight nudge."

"A little more than that," Kristen said with a grin.

"Hopefully I didn't bruise you badly."

"You want to see where?" Kristen kidded.

"I'll pass." Ed shook his head.

"Why won't you let me do something nice for you?"

"There's a million and one reasons why not." Ed was adamant.

"One day you'll want me to, and I'll say no," Kristen teased.

Ed let out a languishing sigh. "What am I going to do with you?"

"Want me to tell you?"

"How long are you going to keep this up?"

"I'm done for now," Kristen chirped with a grin.

"At last," Ed said, relieved.

"Will we see Chicago from the interstate?" Kristen asked eagerly, suddenly noticing all the road signs for the city.

"It's too far away."

"I wish I could see it," Kristen said, disappointed.

"One day you might, when you're doing a concert at Soldier Field."

"That's too far away for me to imagine."

"Believe and always think big," Ed said, reaffirming the ongoing thought.

"You really believe in what you're telling me?"

"Absolutely, as long as you don't get distracted."

"Distracted?" Kristen said with a curious look.

"Ignoble guys, like the one you were living with, will come at you from all directions."

"You don't have to worry about that. I've learned my lesson and will never make that mistake again," Kristen said resolutely.

"So happy to hear it—sometimes experiences like that can be positive life changers," Ed said thoughtfully.

"Like meeting you."

"It might have been somebody else just as caring."

"I doubt it very much. You're one of a kind, with a heart of gold." Kristen squeezed Ed's shoulder.

"Even if I push you?"

"I know you're doing it for me."

"Not only are you beautiful and talented, but you're also very smart."

"Are you fooling me?"

"Absolutely not."

"Well, then, I thank you," Kristen said, her ego soaring. "So how far are we from your hometown?"

"About a hundred seventy miles, but with the snow to deal with, it might take us a lot longer to get there than the four hours it normally would."

"You think we might get stuck?"

"At the rate it's coming down, it's a possibility."

"Should we think about making a motel reservation before that happens?"

"A very good thought; I'm just not sure where because we don't want to stop too soon if we can go farther."

"Are there many towns along the way with motels?"

"I'm not sure; it's been thirty years since I've made this trip. Why don't you get the road atlas from the back seat and see the towns along the way."

Kristen reached over the seat and retrieved the atlas, then searched out the appropriate page and scrutinized the map. "OK, here we go: LaSalle is a little more than halfway there, then Princeton and Geneseo, which are not that far from all those adjoining cities."

"The whole area is called Quad Cities. Moline is one, and the ones across the river are in Iowa," Ed said readily. "I guess Princeton probably makes sense."

"You want me to look up motels there?" Kristen said and reached for her cell phone, which rested on the dashboard.

"Yes."

In less than a minute, Kristen had the answer: "There's just one: Days Inn. Should I make the reservation?"

"Yes, we can always cancel it," Ed said and handed Kristen his wallet with the credit card.

It took only a minute for Kristen to make the reservation, and as she clicked off the cell, she said, "Can I ask a silly question?"

"Shoot."

"How come you don't have a cell phone?"

"I don't go out much, so why have one? And I do have a landline. Those little things are too damn complicated for this old brain to deal with."

"I'll have to teach you how to use mine so you can get one. Then if by chance we're apart, I can reach you, and vice versa."

"Guess you've never heard the proverb 'you can't teach an old dog new tricks,'" Ed said with a grin.

"That only applies to dogs," Kristen fired back.

"Huh . . . never heard that one."

"See, you just learned something new, even from me," Kristen said lightheartedly.

"You're not only a great copilot, but you know quite a bit," Ed said with a grin.

"What about reservations in Moline?"

"This time of year, we don't have to worry; there's a whole bunch of motels in the Quad Cities area," Ed said. "Now, what do you say we have some coffee? Snow always makes me want to have a hot cup."

"I'll join you," Kristen said as she reached for the thermos on the floor.

"Be careful—don't burn yourself," Ed warned. "It was steaming hot when they filled it."

Once finished with the task, Kristen began to hum classic country songs, much to Ed's delight, and prompted him to give serious thought to the finances required to accomplish the dream. He immediately thought of his will, which would have to be rewritten, with new provisions made.

"You're deep in thought," Kristen finally said after several minutes.

"I've got some serious decisions to make."

"Concerning me?" Kristen said pensively.

"Yes."

"Can I help?"

"Not at this time—I just want to be one hundred percent sure of your commitment."

"Haven't I shown it?"

"You have, but I detect a smidgen of doubt."

"I need you to assure me a little longer so I get over it."

"You have my word."

"Can we please not talk about it anymore? I can't stand to think that you have a doubt," Kristen said emotionally.

"I'm sorry. Please forgive me; this goddamn pain in my gut is affecting my thinking," Ed confessed.

"Is it that bad?" Kristen said with concern.

"Yeah. I could really use a slug of Wild Turkey."

"Why don't you pull over and I'll get it from the suitcase?"

"Thanks," Ed said and eased the SUV onto the shoulder.

When Kristen came back with the brown-bagged Wild Turkey, she said, "Let me drive."

Ed was somewhat reluctant. "Are you sure you can deal with the snow?"

"Yes. I'll drive slow," Kristen said reassuringly.

They switched places, and before Kristen started up, Ed took a slug of the booze, then mused, "Hell of a way to deal with pain."

"I hope I'm not partially to blame," Kristen said quietly as she steered the SUV back onto the road.

"In no way. It just comes and goes, without rhyme or reason," Ed said, not wanting her to feel she was to blame.

"Why don't you see a doctor when we get to Moline?" Kristen pleaded.

"I saw one before I left New York, and this is something I'm just going to have to cope with."

"I just can't stand to see you suffer like this."

"I'll be OK in a few minutes. You know what would help me?"

"What?" Kristen said eagerly.

"You doing some country songs."

"What would you like to hear?"

"Whatever you want to sing."

"Hand me the cell phone, please," Kristen motioned to her phone on the dashboard in front of Ed.

After finding the app, Kristen began to sing, pausing only to find songs she was happy with. Ed leaned back in the seat and marveled at her soothing voice as she sang the tender songs. Even though he was not knowledgeable in the intricacies of music, he did have a fairly good ear for the tunes and words, having listened to thousands of hours of Frank Sinatra and other great singers over more than fifty years.

Deep in thought, he began to formulate a plan to ensure Kristen's success, ready to commit whatever he had to financially make it happen. He knew his attorney and good friend, Ted, no doubt would question his sanity, having just days before drawn up the will that donated all his worth to charities.

After nearly an hour of continuous singing, Kristen stopped and looked over at Ed, who was beaming. "Mind if I take a break?"

"Not at all. You helped me forget the pain, my precious thrush."

"I'm so happy. I will gladly sing for you anytime, for as long as you want, if it helps."

"I'm ready to drive and give you a much-deserved break, especially with the snow starting to accumulate."

"You sure?"

"I'm OK now, thanks to you."

Once out of the SUV, they both stretched before making the switch, with Kristen, as was her ritual, catching snowflakes on her tongue, much to Ed's delight.

"They're tiny and feel almost dry," Kristen said when they got back inside the vehicle.

"Good—that means we're less likely to slide."

"So how come you left Moline?"

"I didn't want to end up working on an assembly line building tractors for John Deere for the rest of my life."

"What about college?"

"I wanted to go, but there was no money. My dad made just enough for us to get by."

"What'd he do for a living?"

"Worked for Rock Island Railroad in the repair and maintenance yard, and on weekends he did some carpentry work, which actually was his trade, but he had to give it up when the housing market dried up. He did some work on weekends whenever he could, and sometimes

I would help him when he needed additional hands. The summer after graduation, while my white buddies were all getting ready to go off to distant colleges, I decided to head for New York."

"I'm puzzled—white buddies?"

"We lived in the poor section of town, which was mostly Mexican. All through grade school, most of the kids I played with were Mexican, and they were my close friends. In the summer when I was old enough, about ten or so, I would go with them to the nearby truck farms and pick strawberries. At the end of the day, I'd wind up with about four bucks and dark enough tan to pass for one of them. When I got older and could push a lawnmower, I would go out in our neighborhood and do lawns. In the winter I would shovel snow. That was my self-generated weekly allowance."

"Sounds like you had it pretty rough."

Ed shrugged. "Nothing compared to you, and I apologize for sounding like a kvetch."

"A what?" Kristen asked with a puzzled look.

"A crybaby."

"I don't think that at all; you just stated realities."

"Think I'm becoming a wuss in my old age," Ed said self-critically.

"So what happened when you got to New York?" Kristen asked eagerly.

"Got a cheap hotel room near Times Square and tried to get an office job, but unfortunately, I didn't have much luck, so I ended up working all kinds of other jobs, including at the fish market. As if things weren't bad enough, some lowlife broke into my crummy room and stole my good suit and shoes, temporarily halting my search for an office job. I almost called it quits, but my pride wouldn't let me, so I stuck it out, and I finally got a job with an ad agency as an all-purpose errand boy. After a couple of months, my boss suggested I go to Pace College and learn artwork and business advertising. He also suggested I move to Staten Island, where the living costs were lower and accommodations a lot better and safer than in Manhattan. From that point things started to look up, but unfortunately, my plans were temporarily interrupted by the draft board and a stint in Vietnam. Once I recovered from the wound and was discharged, I went back to the ad agency and also resumed my education. I met Ann a year later. She was a secretary. We were married six months later. I continued at Pace College and got my degree, and eventually the firm made me a partner. I stayed with the agency till I retired, when Ann got sick."

"Wow, that's quite a story," Kristen said.

"I got lucky on both counts."

"Ann lived on Staten Island, too?"

"Yes, not far from where I had an apartment."

"Sounds like you had someone up there looking out for you, too."

"Yeah, a part-time angel," Ed cracked.

"Was Ann the only girl you dated?"

"There were others before I met her."

"You settled on Staten Island after you got married?"

"We lived in an apartment for a couple of years, then inherited her aunt's house when she died."

"You know something?"

"What?"

"You are one persevering man with serious smarts."

"Wisdom comes as you age if you've got half a brain to start with," Ed said temperately.

"You also have great insightfulness, the way you figured me out."

"That's because you shared your soul."

"I trust you just like I did my dad," Kristen confessed.

"I take that as a great honor and promise never to hurt you or allow anyone else to."

"And you know what else?"

"What?" Ed said, holding back a chuckle.

"I love you," Kristen murmured.

"I do you, too," Ed said, just as the car fishtailed.

"Oh, God!" Kristen shrieked and grabbed the dashboard.

"It's OK," Ed said calmly and brought the car under control, stopping halfway on the shoulder. "It's starting to get a little chancy."

"Think we can go on?" Kristen asked in a shaky voice.

"We just hit a patch of ice, but the snow is still not that bad, and we're safe in this big SUV," Ed assured to calm Kristen down.

"Glad I wasn't driving," she gasped as a state trooper pulled up alongside and motioned for Ed to halt.

"You folks OK?" he hollered through the open window on the passenger side.

"Yes, thanks. Think I hit some ice."

"The plows and sanders are on the road not far behind. I would suggest you let them get ahead, but it's strictly up to you."

"Thanks, Officer," Ed said with a nod.

The state trooper touched the brim of his hat in acknowledgment and slowly drove off.

"I'm becoming fast friends with the state troopers in every state," Ed kidded as he started to drive.

"If they clear the road, you think we'll make it to Moline?" Kristen said anxiously.

"At the rate they clear the road, it will take us forever,"

Ed said, glancing at the car clock. "What do you say we have a cup of joe?"

"Coming right up," Kristen said and reached for the thermos.

"I was thinking, depending on the weather, maybe we can spend an extra day in Moline and I'll show you the sights."

"I'd love to see your old stomping grounds and the John Deere tractors," Kristen said with a grin.

"Just don't expect too much," Ed kidded back.

"What kind of a kid were you?" Kristen said as she handed Ed the coffee.

"A lousy student and a rowdy."

"I find that hard to believe, you being such a gentleman now."

"I told you, I grew up in the poorest section of town and hung out mostly with Mexicans who were looked down on, and being with them, I was, too, so we formed a little gang to retaliate—no one messed with us after that. The few who tried ended up black and blue."

"But you said you were an altar boy!"

"Only till seventh grade," he said with a grin. "One Sunday at an early morning mass, my Mexican buddy and I got a hold of the wine before the priest showed and got blitzed. We were banned for life from ever serving as altar boys."

"Your parents find out?"

"The parish priest contacted them after the nine o'clock mass they always attended and let them know."

"You get punished?"

"Oh yeah, couldn't leave the house for a month, except to go to school and help the church janitor three times a week."

Kristen shook her head in disbelief. "Just can't picture you a ruffian, belonging to a gang and doing bad things."

"You wouldn't believe the things we did."

"Were they really bad?"

"Some were."

"Like what?" Kristen eagerly asked.

"If I tell you, it'll ruin my squeaky-clean image," Ed kidded.

"I promise it won't; just tell me one or two," Kristen pleaded.

"I'll tell you a funny one. It was when we snuck into the girls' gym changing room and hid in the stand-up lockers that had slits at the top of the doors you could see out.

"But didn't the girls try to open the lockers you were in?"

"Oh yeah, but we secured the doors from the inside so they couldn't open them. We certainly got an eyeful, and by lunchtime, most of the school knew what we did."

"So you got caught?"

"No one dared to squeal on us, although I think some of the teachers had a pretty good idea."

"You did this with your Mexican gang buddies?"

"There were only three of us on this caper," Ed said with a grin and took another sip of coffee.

"What grade were you in at that time?"

"Tenth."

"Please tell me another."

"This was during summer vacation. One night we stuck one of the guys in the trunk of a car we 'borrowed' and partially closed the trunk. We had him stick out his bare leg, which we smeared with a bottle of catsup, and then we sped down the main street in Moline and Rock

Island and across the bridge into Davenport, Iowa. Other drivers saw it and, of course, called the cops. There must have been about a half dozen cop cars from the three cities chasing us, but they never caught us. We ditched the car in a dark alley and got the hell out as fast as our legs would carry us to a waiting getaway car. It was on all the TV stations that night and in the papers the next morning as well. It was awesome," Ed said fondly.

"And you never got caught, of course," Kristen said and shook her head. "You really were rowdy."

"It was the most fun time in my life. Nothing ever came close to it."

"Did you have a steady girlfriend?"

"No, didn't want one for reasons I'll skip," Ed said slyly, "but enough about me. Tell me about your high school life."

"It wasn't much. Didn't have many friends because of my drunkard mom—was too ashamed have them come over the house, and I really struggled to get passing grades," Kristen said reticently, her eyes downcast.

Ed sensed Kristen was uncomfortable talking about it and decided not to press her. "Sorry for bringing up a bad memory."

"Not your fault. I'm just trying to forget that part of my life and not have it encroach on the now. So you think we'll find a karaoke bar in Moline?"

I would think there's at least a couple in the Quad Cities. Why don't you check it out? Ed suggested with a nod to Kristen's cell.

Kristen got right to it, and a couple of minutes later, she happily announced, "There's four: one in Moline, one in Rock Island, and two in Davenport."

"Then we'll definitely have to stay an extra day," Ed said, looking over to see Kristen's reaction.

"No complaints from me," she said enthusiastically.

"Sounds like you're really into it," Ed said happily.

"Hope they like country."

"Take my word for it, they do, and they'll eat you up."

It was after four when they were settled in their room at the Fairfield Inn in Moline. The drive had been much more taxing than Ed had anticipated, with the plowing of the interstate spotty at best, but fortunately, the snow was not as intense as the weather reports had originally indicated. Kristen offered to drive several times, but Ed did not want to put her in a calamitous situation and instead asked her to sing, which she readily agreed to do, much to his joy.

"These are some digs," Kristen extolled, looking around the spacious room with two queen-size beds, a desk, comfortable chairs, a mini fridge, and a microwave.

Ed was amused by Kristen's naivete and teased, "How about that—even a coffeemaker and Colombian coffee."

Kristen promptly glanced over. "You want me to make some?"

"Not right now," Ed said and rubbed his gut. "I think I need a drink"

"I'll get it. Why don't you sit down and relax?" Kristen hurried to Ed's suitcase, which he'd set down on the stand by the dresser.

"Thanks."

"All that driving in bad weather probably aggravated it," she said as she handed him the drink.

"I'm sure it did," Ed said to pacify Kristen's concern.

"After you finish, maybe you should take a nap," Kristen suggested thoughtfully.

"Think I'll do that, and if you're up to it and want to do something while I nap, you can check out this place.

The sign in the lobby indicated they have a workout gym, a game room, and a pool."

"Hmm, maybe later I'll take a dip," Kristen said playfully and smacked her lips.

"You want a taste?"

"You mind?"

"No, I just hope I'm not teaching you a bad habit."

"Your're not," Kristen said and took a swallow, then looked out the window, "I think the snow is stopping."

"Great. We can for sure get out to a restaurant."

"And after, to a karaoke bar," Kristen added.

"We've got to do it tonight. Tomorrow is Christmas Eve, and I doubt there'll be much going on."

"Are you too tired for it?"

"Not a problem," Ed said, thrilled with Kristen's eagerness to perform.

"I'll look up the karaoke bar in Moline," Kristen said, taking out her phone.

"Good thinking."

It took her a minute to find Kelly's Bar on Fifty-Second Avenue.

"That's right around the corner from here."

"Good. We can make it for sure, even if we have to walk."

"These may be the last karaoke joints till Omaha."

"Is that the way we're going?"

"Yes," Ed said and slowly rose from the chair. "And now, if you don't mind, I'll take that nap. You don't have to go out; you can watch TV if you like. It won't bother me."

"I think I'll check out the place, just like you said, and stretch my legs. Then maybe I'll work on my song."

When Ed awoke, Kristen was on the love seat by the window with a notepad and a pen, looking quite intense, as if searching her mind for the next word or sentence. Feeling Ed's eyes on her, she looked up and smiled.

"Well, it's about time."

"Looks like you're deep in thought," Ed said as he sat up.

"Trying desperately to rhyme a sentence," Kristen said with a frustrated sigh.

"Writing a letter?"

"No, a song, silly."

"Is it your first?"

"I've written others, but they stunk, so I trashed them. It's always such a struggle."

"Don't lose heart. The worthwhile things in life sometimes are."

"Once again, I'm floundering, and you're there to pick me up," Kristen said with a sneaky smile.

"What?" Ed said suspiciously.

"Words from the song," Kristen mused.

"So, what discoveries did you make downstairs?"

"It's all really nice, and I can't wait to take a dip in that beautiful blue pool."

"What about the bathing suit?"

"I'll figure something out."

Ed ignored the comment and looked out the window at the darkness, illuminated by a yellowish hue from the parking lot lights. "What time is it anyway?"

"Almost six," Kristen said, glancing at the clock radio on the nightstand.

"Think I'll call the desk and see about a good restaurant nearby. Any preference?" Ed asked as he reached for the desk phone.

"No, you choose."

"Chinese?"

"Sounds good."

It was a little after ten when Ed and Kristen got to Kelly's Bar, which was packed and quite loud.

Surveying the place, Ed spotted a vacant table by the far wall and hurried to it with Kristen in tow. Several minutes later, a youngish waitress with a pretty, oval-shaped face and dark hair wearing blue jeans and a colorful Christmas sweater approached the table.

"I'm Cindy. What can I get you?"

"A double Wild Turkey straight up and a vodka and Coke," Ed said. "Oh, and when does the karaoke start?"

"It's just about to," Cindy said as she took down the order.

"Where do I sign up?" Kristen said hastily.

"Normally at the bar with Sue, but she's on the way to the stage," Cindy said, glancing over in the direction of the small rectangular stage. "You going to sing?"

"Yes."

"I'll be glad to tell her," Cindy said amiably, still holding her order pad. "What's your name, and what're you gonna sing?"

Kristen gave the pertinent information, and Cindy, true to her word, made a beeline for the stage, handed Sue the scribbled paper, and pointed to the table. Sue glanced in the general direction where Ed and Kristen were seated and nodded.

The wannabe singers, all female, were barely passable, but the crowd was kind and applauded generously, no doubt feeling the effect of their drinks and the Christmas spirit. Ed shook his head as he polished off the remnant of his drink and looked around for Cindy to order another before Kristen's turn on stage

"Damn, she must be lost or on a break," Ed said impatiently just as Cindy came into view, heading for their table.

"Sorry for not showing up sooner, but I had to take a makeup break."

"I forgive you," Ed said with a grin. "I'll have a repeat, and plain Coke for Kristen."

No sooner had Ed spoken than the full-figured girl on the stage finished her song and received her due applause. Sue looked over and called Kristen's name.

"Knock 'em dead," Ed said and squeezed Kristen's hand.

Sue welcomed Kristen with a smile and introduced her and her song. When Kristen finished "Am I That Easy to Forget," she received resounding applause and cheers lasting nearly a minute, much to her surprise.

"That was awesome," Sue hollered over the boisterous din. "You a pro?"

"No," Kristen hollered back, not believing Sue's comment.

"Honey, you're missing one hell of a calling if you're not."

"I hope to change that very soon," she said confidentially.

"They absolutely love you. Can you do another?"

Kristen looked over to Ed, who was up on his feet like everyone else in the place, beaming like a father seeing his newborn for the first time.

"I think not," Kristen said and took several more bows before stepping off the stage while the audience pleaded for just one more.

"You were absolutely magic," Ed said as he hugged

Kristen and planted a kiss on her forehead. "I thought you'd do an encore."

"I looked over to you and was on the verge of tears thinking about what you've done for me and how much I love you," Kristen said emotionally.

Ed was deeply touched. "That goes both ways, and they also loved you."

"I felt it."

"Don't mean to interrupt a tender moment, but I had to come over and meet the next great country star," a very fit, middle-aged man said to Kristen. "I'm Russ Kelly, the owner."

"Thank you, that's very kind," Kristen said politely and shook his outstretched hand.

"And I assume you're Kristen's granddad or manager?" Russ said to Ed and offered him his hand as well.

"More or less on both counts," Ed said with a grin and shook Russ's hand.

"May I join you for a couple of minutes?"

"Certainly," Ed said, motioning to the chair without the parkas.

Once they were seated, Russ got right down to business. "Are you from this area?"

"We're from New York, just passing through."

"That's too bad."

"Why?"

"I was ready to offer Kristen a very generous performance contract to sing on weekends for as long as she wants, and I do realize it would have been for a limited time since she's definitely headed for stardom," Russ said with an admiring look at Kristen.

"I appreciate the offer and your observation, but obviously, we'll have to pass."

"Well, it was a shot in the dark," Russ said sportingly. He then added to Kristen, "Someday soon, when you're a huge country star, maybe you'll remember this place and stop by."

"You're very kind," Kristen said with a warm smile.

"Well, it was a pleasure to meet you both, and I wish you the very best, Kristen. I'll send Cindy over with whatever you're drinking, which, of course, will be on the house for however long you're here," Russ said and reluctantly walked away.

"That does it," Ed said with a huge grin. "You're on your way, my little thrush."

Moments later, Cindy came with the drinks. "I had no idea when I first served you that I was in the presence of an up-and-coming country star. Would you mind signing an autograph?"

"Not at all," Kristen gushed.

"This no doubt will be the only chance I have to get it, and when you're a huge country star, I'll be able to say I once served you a drink and be able to prove it," Cindy said and handed Kristen a pen and her order pad.

Kristen scribbled a brief note and signed it. "Thanks for asking, and I included a note."

"Thanks so much," Cindy said happily and promptly left.

"Get used to signing autographs; there'll be thousands," Ed teased.

"I just can't believe it," Kristen said dreamily.

Ed picked up his drink and raised it in a toast. "To your fabulous future, my little thrush."

"And you in it," Kristen said with a smile.

Throughout the evening, they were interrupted by well-wishers asking Kristen to sing again, sign autographs, and pose for selfies. At a little past midnight, Ed had reached his limit physically and suggested they leave, especially because Kristen was starting to feel her drinks and getting giddy. Driving back to the motel, Kristen could not stop her giggles and silliness, but Ed didn't have the heart to ask her to stop after she'd dedicated the night to him. She given it all and deserved to cut loose.

In the motel parking lot and out of the SUV, Kristen wasn't finished being playful quite yet and began to frolic in the snow, challenging Ed to a snowball fight. He likewise was mildly under the influence and felt sporting, so he pursued Kristen around the parked cars, then in the open area, where Kristen suddenly flopped down on her back and made the imprint of a snow angel.

When she was done, she got back to her feet and made a couple of snowballs to fling at

Ed with a joyous laugh.

"OK, you win. Now let's go inside. It's too cold out here," Ed pleaded.

"You give up?"

"Yes."

"Guess what I'm gonna do next?" Kristen said playfully as they started for the motel door.

"I'm afraid to ask."

"I'm going for a swim."

"You have no bathing suit," Ed said with some concern and hoped it was just playful talk.

"Not a problem," Kristen said forthrightly as they entered the motel lobby, which, at that late hour, was deserted, except for the lone youngish male clerk behind the check-in counter, absorbed in some game on his smartphone.

Once in the room, Kristen got right to her intended

deed and, after retrieving a couple of things from her bag, made a beeline for the bathroom. Ed, slightly exhausted but invigorated by the games in the parking lot, happily plopped down on his bed and savored the momentary youthful feeling that Kristen had awoken in him from very long ago—sadly smothered by the passage of time. His reflection was suddenly jarred by Kristen's voice echoing from the bathroom.

"Ed, can I borrow your robe?"

"It's on the bathroom door," he said without hesitation.

Moments later, Kristen emerged in the robe and grinned. "Your things fit me perfectly."

"You do justice to my clothes," Ed kidded back, "and pray tell me, what is your intent?"

"Going down to take a swim, like I said."

"You magically found a bathing suit in your bag?"

"No, but something passable; you want to see?" Kristen asked, reaching for the tie at the waist of the robe.

"No, it's OK, but promise me it's passable."

"You'll see when we get to the pool. Just make sure I don't drown or get attacked by male sharks," Kristen teased.

Ed shook his head and reluctantly rose, although he earnestly hoped the pool was closed. "Lead the way, you little pain."

The desk clerk was somewhat baffled but affirmed the pool was open and no one was there. At the poolside, Kristen removed the robe and, to Ed's relief, was wearing a black bra and matching panties.

"I don't believe it," Ed muttered as he averted his eyes.

"It's OK. I have two pairs of black panties on," Kristen assured Ed, then dove into the water.

He promptly turned his head to the entrance door and took a deep breath, hoping no one would show.

"You should come in; the water's perfect," Kristen hollered, a short distance from Ed.

"You enjoy it," Ed called back, feeling like he was standing on burning coals.

When Kristen had her fill, she swam up to Ed, who held the robe high in front of him and promptly wrapped her in it.

"Next time, you have to join me," Kristen insisted.

"Yes, when we both have bathing suits and I'm thirty."

"I didn't reveal anything, did I?" Kristen said defensively, fastening the robe.

"I didn't look."

"It's your loss," she teased.

"What am I going to do with you?" Ed said good-naturedly as they started for the door.

"Be there for me always," Kristen said fervently.

"I'll do my best," he murmured, heavyhearted.

CHAPTER 4

C hristmas Eve morning was dark and dreary, and even though he'd been awake for some time, Ed didn't feel like getting out of bed. Instead, he turned to his side and listened to Kristen make her usual sleeping sounds. Her face, barely showing from under the covers, looked happy and content. Ed thought about the previous night's happenings and smiled broadly, still not believing what had transpired. It was the most fun night he'd had since he was young. Kristen's joy and un-restrained spirit made him feel alive and endeared her to him more each day. She untied the knots of lifelong restraints and set his spirit soaring. The more he thought about her influence on his dreary life, the more he real-ized he was totally enraptured with her. She was filling the empty space in his heart he'd endured for so many years. In no way was she replacing Ann, but most defi-nitely, she was creating her own spot. With that thought, he decided to thank her with a very special Christmas gift, one he hoped she would cherish long after he was gone. Invigorated by that idea, he decided to get up and get on with the day, which included a visit to his parents' graves.

Showered and shaved, he emerged from the bath-room to find Kristen still sound asleep. It appeared she had not budged from where he last saw her. He was glad because once again, he was dealing with the pain in his gut and did not want Kristen to see. He swiftly took a long swig from the bottle and settled in the chair, waiting for the alcohol to ease the pain. He began to feel the welcome relief just as Kristen stirred and opened her eyes.

"Good morning, my little thrush," Ed said gladly.

"Good morning," she said wearily, "and what's the thrush again?"

"A thrush is one of the most poignant songbirds in the world, inspiring poets and songwriters, and a most appropriate name for you."

"You really know how to start a girl's morning," Kristen said happily and sat up.

"You had quite a time last night," Ed said with a grin.

"Did I do something bad?" she said with slight concern.

"You went swimming in the raw," Ed joked.

"No, I didn't," Kristen insisted and immediately peeked under the covers. "I have sleepwear on."

"Yes, I put them on," Ed said on the verge of laughter.

"Did you really?" Kristen said, mouth aghast.

Ed burst out laughing. "Really got you."

"Payback is gonna be hell for you," Kristen said with a devilish look.

"I'm only reciprocating your suggestive teasing," Ed said coolly.

Kristen relaxed and chuckled. "OK, we'll see who wins."

"Is that the thanks I get?"

"Yes, and no more free drinks for you because of me," Kristen teased.

"And that goes for you as well, none at all from now on," Ed said seriously.

Kristen shrugged, not really taking Ed at his word. "So what's on the schedule for today?"

"After breakfast I'm going to the cemetery, and you can practice singing. When I get back, which shouldn't be more than a couple of hours, we'll go shopping at the mall; and you can buy a robe and a dress."

"You want me to get a dress?" Kristen said with a puzzled look.

"Yes, something for church tonight."

"You want me to go to Midnight Mass with you?"

"It would be nice to have you with me, but it's strictly up to you."

"I'm not Catholic."

"They'll let you in anyway," Ed teased.

"I haven't been to church or dressed up for Christmas since my daddy died."

"Then maybe it's time," Ed said casually.

"OK, I'll go."

"I'm really glad."

Kristen smiled affectionately. "It's the least I can do after all you've done for me."

"Get yourself ready and let's have breakfast, and then I'll head for the cemetery."

"This will be the first time we'll be apart."

"You probably need a break from me."

"I'll never tire of being with you," Kristen said firmly.

"One day you'll find someone your age and move on."

Kristen shook her head and said forcefully, "No way; you're stuck with me for the rest of your life, don't you know?"

"I'm a very lucky man," Ed said happily.

Once Ed was out of the motel parking lot, the main streets were fairly well plowed and somewhat slick only in spots. Ed stopped at a flower shop and picked up two Christmas wreaths, then asked the young woman to refresh his memory on the best way to get to the cemetery. He felt somewhat disoriented, even though there didn't seem to be changes in the streets or the structures. For some reason, it all seemed somewhat strange. Once he got to the cemetery, he decided to park the car just outside the gate, not wanting to get stuck inside, where narrow roads might be piled up with snow. Even though he had a general idea where the graves were, it still took him nearly twenty minutes to find them, and only by viewing countless names on the headstones, some of which he had to brush the snow off in order to read. After placing the wreaths up against his parents' headstones, he backed up a couple of steps, bowed his head, and spoke out loud.

"Been a long time since I've been here, so please forgive me for your unattended graves all these years. This will be my one and only visit, though it looks like I'll be joining you very soon. No doubt Ann and Brandon are with you, and the extended family. Merry Christmas, and I love you all."

Ed stood silent for several minutes more, recalling significant times as a family. He wiped away the tears and hurried to the SUV, the ice-cold wind swirling the snow across the cemetery like a giant invisible hand. Driving back to the motel, he reminisced about Christmases past when he was young and wished he could experience just a sliver of one. Driving absent-mindedly, he was surprised when he suddenly saw the motel a block away, with no idea how he got back. Seeing a liquor store, he decided to stop and buy a couple of bottles of Wild Turkey for the continuing trip.

His spirits lifted when he opened the door and Kristen rushed over from the love seat with pad and pen in her hand and hugged him mightily. "I missed you so very much."

"So nice to have someone who does," Ed said happily and removed his parka. "You've been writing the whole time?"

"Mostly singing and just started writing a short while ago, but the words are still not meshing," Kristen said, sounding disappointed.

"Can I help?"

"I'd love that, but you really can't since it's about you, and I want it to be a stunner when you hear it."

"Maybe you're having a hard time because I'm not worth singing about," Ed kidded.

"It'll come to me, even if it kills me. No way I'm gonna give up," Kristen said passionately.

"That's my girl," Ed said steadfastly and glanced at his watch. "It's getting close to lunch, which I thought we might have at the mall."

"Can I have just a few more minutes with this thing?"

"By all means. It'll come to you," Ed said in a calming voice.

Kristen looked at Ed and smiled broadly. "You're always doing that when I'm vexed, and I love you for it."

With lunch out of the way, Ed and Kristen agreed to meet back at the entrance of the restaurant because it was fairly central in the mall, then proceeded to their individual shopping destinations. Kristen went to purchase her things, for which Ed gave her more cash than necessary and suggested she buy whatever else she needed. He in turn headed straight for a jewelry store, still uncertain what to get her. There were several shoppers in the store, meandering between the long glass display cases, each one with a specific type of jewelry in it. Like the other shoppers, Ed eased his way between them until he came to the necklaces and decided one of them would be the ideal gift for Kristen. He scanned several and finally saw what he thought would be perfect: a solid-gold heart on an eighteen-inch chain. Several minutes later, a middle-aged, slender, neatly dressed woman finally came over.

"Sorry for the delay, but as you can see, we're really busy.

"Not a problem. I'd like to see that solid-gold heart," Ed said, pointing to the item.

"Dainty and beautiful and one of a kind," the saleslady said as she opened the case, retrieved the heart, and handed it to Ed.

"What's special about it?" Ed said as he viewed it.

"All the others are somewhat flimsy; this one is solid gold and inscribed on the back."

Ed flipped it over and squinted, but he could not make out the minute words. "I'm afraid the inscription is beyond my eyes."

"Yes, of course, that goes for me as well," she said with a pleasant smile. "The inscription reads: 'Follow Your Heart.' I looked at it with a jeweler's eyepiece when we got it in the store, which is how I know."

Ed was elated. "Perfect, I'll take it."

"It's pricey."

"Whatever the cost, it will be worth every penny," Ed said easily and handed her his credit card, totally unperturbed when she told him the price.

When they got back to the motel room, which was neatly made up, Kristen was eager to show off her robe. As soon as Ed settled in the chair, she pulled it out from the shopping bag and modeled it. She then retrieved a long-sleeved burgundy dress and held it up against her body.

"Hope you like it—a bit expensive," Kristen said reluctantly.

"It looks great, and you'll look gorgeous in it," Ed said with a happy smile.

"Thanks so much," Kristen said joyfully and rushed over and planted a kiss on Ed's cheek.

"Did you have enough money?"

"Yes. I've got some left over." She glanced at her parka.

"Keep it," Ed said dismissively.

"Did you put up a tree after Ann passed?"

"No, just didn't care anymore."

"Oh, how sad."

"A Christmas tree is a celebration of joy and love; when you're alone, there's not much of either one."

"I guess not," Kristen murmured and laid the dress on her bed.

"Sorry, I didn't mean to sound pathetic."

"I think you have every reason, but this Christmas you're not alone, and for sure I won't let you be sad."

"You're a gem," Ed said glowingly.

"And a sponge; all I'm doing is taking from you and giving nothing in return," Kristen said self-critically.

"Not so, you've given me more than you'll ever know."

"It's just not right that you're spending all this money on me," Kristen said sincerely.

"I have no one else to spend it on, and I sure as hell can't take it with me," Ed kidded.

"But I'm not even a distant relation."

Ed shook his head and grinned. "Are you going to give me a hard time?"

"No," Kristen said demurely and scrunched her nose like a bunny. "Would you like me to fix you a drink?"

"That's a timely idea, and you can join me with a small one," Ed said, hesitantly recanting what he had said earlier.

"No, thanks. I'll just have a sip of yours."

"I'm proud—you remembered."

"You're gonna have to get some more," Kristen said as she poured the drink.

"I got some coming back from the cemetery; it's in the SUV."

Moments later, Kristen handed Ed the drink.

"You want your sip?"

"No, you go first."

"I'm liable to give you germs and cooties," Ed joked and took a swig.

"You can give me all the germs you want and whatever else," Kristen said with a shrug.

Ed handed Kristen the drink. "Now, about tonight . . . if you don't feel like going to Midnight Mass, it's OK."

"But what about the dress you had me buy?"

"You may need it for another time."

"I want to go."

"It'll be nice to have you at my side," Ed said happily.

"How far is the church from here?"

"About twenty minutes."

"You think they'll let us in?" Kristen kidded.

"We'll sneak in the back door, stop at the priest's dressing room, and have a swig of the cheap wine," Ed joshed.

The church looked more tired and worn since the last time Ed had seen it, including most of the Mexican parishioners, who were much like the church. There were very few young people and even fewer whites since he was a kid, which did not surprise him after so many years. The one thing he found most hard to believe was the low turnout and lack of Christmas joy. He felt a letdown, having thought he would see a glorious celebration like the ones when he was young. The Mass, conducted all in Spanish, added to his disappointment, and he felt the only thing worthwhile was hearing "Silent Night," even though it was sung in Spanish. Forcing himself to disregard it all, he tried hard to reconnect with the Almighty, but to his dismay, he felt nothing. The bond was gone, and his belief as well. Had it not been for Kristen, he would have walked out, just like he had of late on many things, always feeling more empty than before. He cut the prayer short, thinking it was totally a waste of time, and glanced at Kristen, who, to his surprise, seemed quite taken by the proceedings, especially when the priest melodized some of the prayers and even more so when the choir sang. He was glad at least one of them found something worthwhile in attending. After the priest gave the final blessing and wished all a joyous Christmas, Ed let out a grateful sigh, took Kristen's hand, and hurried out.

"Guess you weren't into it," Kristen said as they headed to the SUV.

"Sorry to say I wasn't; guess my expectations were

unrealistic. Like everything else in the world, even the church has changed."

"Did you by chance recognize anyone—your buddies, I mean?"

"At this stage, one of them could have been sitting on my lap and I wouldn't have known him," Ed joshed.

"Did you date Mexican girls?"

"Yes, and whites."

"And which were more fun?" Kristen said lightheartedly, hanging on to Ed's arm as they briskly walked.

"The whites, of course," Ed cracked.

"Why?" Kristen blurted.

"Are you getting into my sexual life?"

"No, I'd just like to know why the white girls were more fun."

"In one word, they were much more 'willing.'"

"And you no doubt took advantage of it," Kristen teased.

"You think I would have done such a thing?" Ed teased back.

"In one word: a great big yes!" Kristen said emphatically.

"What made you come to that conclusion?" Ed said as he opened the SUV door for her.

"I think under that conservative exterior was a big ladies' man," Kristen said once Ed got in as well.

"Young lady, you are treading where angels shouldn't," Ed said lightheartedly.

"You know I'm right. You just won't admit it."

"I don't know about you, but I'm chilled to the bone. Reach in the back and pull one of the bottles of Wild Turkey from the bag," Ed said as he gunned the engine to get the heater going.

Kristen retrieved a bottle and handed it to Ed. "Feels ice cold."

"Only the bottle, not the booze once it hits your inners," Ed kidded as he unscrewed the top and took a swig, then looked over to Kristen. "You want some?"

"Yes, please. I'm freezing wearing a dress, which is why I seldom do." Kristen took a small swallow. "You want any more?"

"No, thanks, and Merry Christmas."

"And you, too, with all my love," Kristen said affectionately and kissed Ed on the lips.

CHAPTER 5

The room was flooded by bright sunshine when Ed opened his eyes at a little after seven. He still slightly felt the effects of the Wild Turkey, which he'd consumed freely when they returned from the Midnight Mass; it was more than he intended to have. Once in the motel room, he just wanted to shut the world out, especially memories of past Christmases, which now, in the morning, seemed rather fatuous. He also decided, now that the sun was shining brightly and the roads were clear of snow, it might be wise to get on with the trip. There really was no good reason to delay it because most places of interest would be closed, and the weather was unpredictable this time of year. Above all, time was of the essence, and he couldn't afford to waste it. With his mind made up, he got out of bed and headed for the bathroom to get ready. When he emerged a little later, Kristen was scurrying from the wardrobe closet back to her bed with a shopping bag in hand. She stopped when she saw Ed and smiled happily.

"Good morning and Merry Christmas."

"Merry Christmas," Ed said warmly, "hope you had beautiful fairy-tale dreams."

"I did, and they put me in a very Christmassy mood, and I've got something for you," Kristen said happily.

"By any chance a Christmas present?" Ed said playfully.

"How could you have ever guessed?" Kristen teased back with a beaming face and handed Ed a yuletide gift bag.

"You really shouldn't have; thank you so much," Ed said appreciatively and removed a Sony battery-powered compact CD player and Anne Murray country album.

"I do hope you like her, and the reason I chose this CD is for a very special song she sings, and most appropriate for what you mean to me," Kristen said emotionally.

"I can't wait to hear it, but first let me get your gift," Ed said, then set the bag down on the bed and walked over to the closet, where he retrieved a small dark-blue felt box from his parka and handed it to Kristen.

"You've already given me a ton of Christmas presents," Kristen protested sincerely.

Ed smiled and said tenderly, "The others will wear out, but this one will last forever—open it."

"It's beautiful!" Kristen cried. She jumped up at Ed, wrapped her arms around his neck, and kissed his face repeatedly, including the lips.

Ed gently lowered her. "There's an inscription on the back. Hope you can read it."

Kristen instantly removed the necklace from the box, focused her eyes on the minute inscription, and read it aloud: "'Follow Your Heart'—how very perfect," she said lovingly, looking into Ed's gentle eyes with tears in her own. "I will cherish it eternally and over any gifts I may ever receive. Will you please put it on me?"

"Be happy to."

Once the gift was secure on her neck, Kristen fingered the heart and excitedly said, "I want to see it in the mirror," and rushed to the dresser.

"It's perfect on you," Ed said happily.

After admiring her reflection, Kristen rushed back, wrapped her arms around Ed's neck, and looked deeply into his eyes. "I will never remove it as long as I live."

"You may tire of it."

"Not ever," Kristen vowed, fingering the gold heart again. "This must have cost a fortune."

Ed shrugged. "OK, here's the deal for today; I think we should get on the road after breakfast and take advantage of the good weather."

"You don't want to see the old haunts?"

"After the church fiasco last night, not really in the mood," Ed said dismissively.

"I feel bad that you traveled all this way, only to be so disappointed."

Ed shook his head. "Don't be. If it wasn't for the foolish idea, we would never have met. Now why don't you get ready, my little thrush. We've got miles to cover by nightfall."

"You want to hear our song first?"

"Please."

It took Kristen no time to pop the CD into the portable player and motion for Ed to sit next to her on the bed.

"The name is 'You Needed Me,' and I hope you love it just as much as I do because it must have been written just for us. I'll key the song and omit the others."

Ed blocked out all thoughts and listened intently to each and every word that Anne Murray so splendidly vocalized. When the song was over, tears filled his eyes, and he was barely able to speak. "Is that really how you feel about me?"

Kristen nodded and murmured, with tears swelling in

her eyes as well. "This will always be our song, even after I write mine."

It was nearly ten when they got on the interstate and crossed the bridge into Iowa. The sun was bright, and the road was in splendid condition to make good time, which Ed hoped to do. Kristen sensed Ed needed cheering and decided to sing a snappy song. She punched it up on the cell phone and tore into "Blue Bayou."

"Thanks. That really helped," Ed said with a loving smile when she finished.

"I'm so glad, and I'll sing more if you want," Kristen said cheerfully as they sped through Davenport on the elevated interstate.

"I'm fine now," Ed said emphatically.

"This is all part of the Quad Cities?"

"Actually, there are more than that, but the guy who dubbed it couldn't count past four," Ed wisecracked.

"So good to hear you laugh."

"You're an angel in disguise."

"I'm far from it after what I've done," Kristen said forthrightly.

"Not as far as I'm concerned," Ed insisted.

"So how far do you think we'll get today?"

"I'm shooting for Omaha."

"You know what's there?" Kristen said excitedly.

"Great steaks," Ed kidded.

"No, silly, that's where they have the national karaoke championships every year and all kinds of weekly contests."

"That's great. I worried we wouldn't see another karaoke joint till we got to Vegas," Ed said with relief.

"They probably have more places than any other city in the country," Kristen said knowingly.

"Well, that being the case, we're in big-time luck, and if you want, we can spend a couple of days there and take advantage of them. That way, by the time we get to Las Vegas, you'll be a pro already," Ed teased.

"So glad we came this way instead of the southern route."

"You know about the I-40 route?"

"Yes, the truck driver who gave me the lift to Mercer told me about it, and if you hadn't decided to go with me to Vegas, I would have parted company with you where we saw all the signs for Chicago and hitched a ride going south, then I-40. But you know what I think? Fate interceded, and you came into my life, and here we are, you and me forever," Kristen said happily.

"I wonder if it was fate or predestined," Ed mused.

"What do you mean?"

"I've always believed that our lives are preplanned through our genes, and we just follow the predetermined route---good or bad."

"Wow, that's heavy," Kristen said, pondering Ed's words.

"Just something you might want to keep in mind when things don't go the way you planned."

"You know, in the five days I've been with you, I have learned so much, and I see things so differently now."

"I'm happy that you've absorbed some of my hard-learned truths. Maybe they'll help when you contemplate your new life."

"There's so much I need to learn yet, so don't you dare check out on me anytime soon,"

Kristen said seriously.

Ed was perplexed once again: he wanted to be honest with Kristen and tell her about his terminal condition, but he knew that doing so would devastate her and, more than likely, destroy the incredible musical career waiting for her.

"I'm not a kid," Ed cautioned.

Kristen shook her head and insisted, "You're not that old. Please, let's not talk about it anymore; it makes me upset."

"OK. Would you like to drive since the weather is nearly perfect and the road is so straight?"

"Thought you'd never ask," Kristen said eagerly.

It was nearly ten when Ed and Kristen checked in at the downtown Hilton Garden in Omaha. Having made their reservations earlier by phone, they first stopped off at an Italian restaurant and had dinner since it was getting late; they didn't want to have to go out again once they were settled in the room. Ed was ever so grateful for Kristen's smartphone, which guided them to their intended destinations without a single misstep, with no need to ask for directions.

The streets aglow with Christmas lights and decorations somewhat rekindled Ed's fading holiday spirit. He was glad he had chosen the Hilton since it was first class—from the lobby and amenities to the spacious room, far superior to the others they'd stayed in. Kristen drove nearly all the way since Ed had to resort to several slugs of Wild Turkey to ease his pain.

She crashed on the bed, parka and all, once the bellhop left.

"Think I'll just stay like this for the night," Kristen kidded in an exhausted voice.

"I'm sorry for not helping you drive that much."

"It's OK. I'll get with it in a few minutes; not as bad as

I'm making it out to be," Kristen said sportingly, not wanting Ed to feel even more badly.

"You're a real trooper—and one hell of a driver," Ed said gladly and removed his parka.

Kristen sat up and removed hers as well. "You know what I'm gonna do?"

"I'm too tired to ask," Ed cracked.

"Soak in a tub till I'm like a prune."

"Just don't fall asleep because I'm not coming to the rescue," Ed kidded with his parka in hand, then took Kristen's as well and hung them in the closet.

"You can look all you want," Kristen teased as she got her things from her travel bag.

"I thought you promised not to talk like that," Ed said with an exasperated sigh.

"That wasn't lewd," Kristen said playfully. "But OK. I think while I'm soaking, I'll give Morgan in Vegas a call and wish her a Merry Christmas."

"Good idea. And while you're at it, ask her about first-rate condos."

"For you and me?" Kristen said eagerly.

"Yes, of course, unless you have different thoughts."

"No, I was hoping you'd say that," Kristen said happily and started for the bathroom.

"Oh, look up karaoke bars as well."

"Then we'll be here for a couple of days?"

"Yes, since you said they have quite a few. You need to perform in front of audiences as much as possible."

"Great," Kristen said exuberantly.

"I'm impressed," Ed said with an approving nod.

"Now if you'll excuse me for a while, I'll go soak."

Ed stretched out in the oversize stuffed chair and removed his boots, then gazed out the window at the city skyline, which looked very much in season with the dominant red and green hues highlighting the streets. With a population of less than half a million, the city stretched out in all directions, giving the appearance of being a much bigger city. He suddenly felt a sharp pain and rushed to the suitcase, retrieving a bottle of Wild Turkey and taking a quick swig before pouring some into a glass. With drink in hand, he sat down again and tried to formulate a plan of what he needed to do in the next few days. He was certain that he would need to make a trip back to Staten Island and meet with Ted, his attorney, then put the house up for sale and dispose of a lifetime of possessions. The things he once so highly prized now seemed totally inconsequential. Still in deep thought, Ed was surprised and unaware of the time when Kristen emerged from the bathroom in a nightshirt, looking quite refreshed and perky. Seeing the drink in Ed's hand, she walked directly to him.

"Your gut again?"

"That and my life," Ed said heavyheartedly.

"I can't leave you alone for a single minute," Kristen joshed, hoping to snap Ed out of the down mood.

"It's getting that way," Ed easily conceded.

"Can I have a sip?"

"Sure," Ed said agreeably.

After taking a swallow, Kristen sat down on the edge of the bed directly across from Ed and reluctantly said, "Well, I spoke to Morgan."

"And she floored you?" Ed guessed.

Kristen nodded. "Chuck got busted for dealing drugs a couple of days after I left."

"How'd she find out about that?"

"She keeps in touch with one of the girls at the skin bar who knows Chuck."

"Sounds like Chuck got his just reward."

"Now and then it happens, I guess," Kristen said indifferently.

"So what's happening with Morgan?"

"She's a cocktail waitress at Golden Nugget."

"You tell her what's going on with you?"

"Yes, I told her I met an extraordinary gentleman who is beyond generous and has led me to a whole new life, including singing. Of course, she doesn't believe it, thinks something funny is going on."

"You told her how old I am."

"Yes."

"And she thinks what?"

"That you're having sex with me."

"Well, I really can't blame her," Ed said thoughtfully. "You are a beautiful, desirous young woman most men would give their right arm to be with."

"See what you're missing?" Kristen kidded.

Ed shook his head and sighed. "Did you ask her about the condos?"

"Yes, but she was disappointed because she thought I was going to move in with her. She did say there is no shortage of condos, so once we get there, I'm sure we can find one very easily."

"I assume she's big-time pissed at me for being the reason you're not moving in with her?"

"She's not. In fact, she's looking forward to meeting you."

"Maybe we can make it up to her," Ed said benevolently.

"How?"

"From what you've told me, she's had a tough life and, like you, needs a break."

"You are amazing," Kristen said, shaking her head.

"After helping one sorry waif, you want to take on another?"

"Call me a fool," Ed said dismissively.

"Totally wrong. What you are is the most kind and decent man," Kristen said from the heart.

"Appreciate you saying that. So did you check out the karaoke joints?"

"There are more than a dozen; the biggest appears to be Music Hall, which hosted the National Karaoke Championships last year."

"That's the one we'll do," Ed said enthusiastically.

CHAPTER 6

B ack in the room after a leisurely breakfast, Ed reviewed the brochure of what to do and see in Omaha while Kristen gathered up the clothes to be laundered, of which there were quite a few. The one place Ed thought might be fun and give them both a chance to stretch their legs after the long drive was the Old Market, only a short distance from the hotel. The brochure described it as jammed with charming buildings hosting art galleries, an array of unique shops, and many restaurants. It further stated that it all could be seen in a few hours, depending, of course, on the time spent at each point of interest. With the plastic laundry bag overflowing, Kristen sat down on the bed across from Ed and let out a sigh.

"I can't believe we have all this laundry."

"It's been several days."

"Anything look interesting?" Kristen said, glancing at the brochure in Ed's hand.

"Yes, thought we might visit the Old Market. It's full of quaint places, knickknack shops, and art galleries, which I'd really like to visit."

"Are you into art?"

"I was at one time. I used to buy artwork at outdoor fairs from starving artists, as the saying goes—a lot cheaper than the galleries and, in most cases, quite good."

"That confirms it," Kristen said with a grin.

"What?" Ed said with a puzzled look.

"You've been a philanthropist from way back—first starving artists and now young women who've lost their way," Kristen kidded with a grin.

"Hmm . . . that's something I never considered being."

"You truly have a very good heart. By any chance, do you also collect stray animals, too?"

"I only stick to people. Animals are not my forte."

"You really going to try to help Morgan?"

"Yes, if I can," Ed said firmly.

"It's not going to be easy," Kristen warned. "She's pretty much set in her way of life, and you can imagine what that is."

"I'm willing to give it a try with your help."

"I'll do all I can."

"If it doesn't work out, then we'll just chalk it up to a case of 'you can't win them all.'"

"So how's this laundry thing work?"

"Just call room service and they'll send somebody to pick it up."

"Are we gonna head out now?" Kristen said eagerly.

"Get your coat and gloves after you make the call."

With the sun out and a cloudless sky, the temperature was not too bad, and with all the shops to choose from, it was easy to stop in and warm up. It was still early, so the number of shoppers and strollers was limited, which made it easy to visit a greater number of the quaint shops, all still very much in the seasonal spirit, with goods in ample supply. After they'd browsed through a handful, Ed suggested they visit an art gallery, to which Kristen

Fred Preiss

readily agreed, sensing this was what Ed really wanted to do, and she was ready to spend some time in one place. A few minutes later, they stepped inside a unique art gallery named Master's Artworks. Ed was delighted and taken aback by what he viewed displayed on the walls. The paintings were copies of the greatest oil works of the old masters, and from a scrutinizing look, Ed thought most of them were quite good. With only a handful of viewers around, Ed took his time to appreciate each painting and to explain to Kristen the history of the original painting and the artist. He was pleasantly surprised by Kristen's eagerness to learn.

"How in the world do you know all this stuff?" Kristen said in awe.

"It's a hobby I started not long after I married Ann. Actually, she's really the one who ignited the art-appreciation spark in me. An uncle of hers in Italy was an artist, and over the years, he sent us several of his paintings, some of which I sold to our friends for him."

"You have many paintings?"

"Yes, not a single room without at least a couple of paintings."

"Of the old masters' paintings, which are your favorite—I mean scenic or people?"

"Both, but leaning more toward scenic, like Claude Monet's *Water Lilies* and *Tulip Fields*; Winslow Homer's *Breezing Up*; and of course, Van Gogh's *The Harvest*, *Yellow Wheat*, and *Fields of Poppies*. And for portraits, Rembrandt's *Woman Cutting Her Nails*; Goya's *Doña Isabel*; Holbein's *Henry VIII*; and of course, the most famous painting in the world, da Vinci's *Mona Lisa*."

"Pardon me. I don't mean to be forward, but my sister and I couldn't help overhearing you educating your granddaughter about the old-world artists. Are you an art critic or an aficionado?" a very attractive, blondish-gray-haired woman with sparkling hazel eyes and a lithe figure said as she approached with what appeared to be her younger, look-alike sister.

"Actually, I'm neither—just an amateur who loves the old masters' great paintings."

"You certainly sound like your knowledge of fine art is much more than amateurish."

"That's very kind of you to say."

"Forgive me for being presumptuous, but by any chance, are you from the New York area?"

"Yes, Staten Island, to be exact; I guess the New York accent gives me away."

"I'm from Yonkers, and I have that tell-tale accent, too, which my sister Janice, who lives here in Omaha, teases me about relentlessly every time I visit her. And by the way, my name is Alice."

"I'm Ed, and this young lady is Kristen," Ed said and extended his hand to Alice, which she gladly shook, and then Janice.

"You have family here?"

"No, we're just passing through on the way to Las Vegas."

"Shall I assume you have family there?" Alice said with an enticing smile.

"Not there, either. Actually, we're going there for Kristen's sake. She aspires to become a country singer," Ed said lightheartedly.

Kristen felt self-conscious and slightly wriggled. "Oh, come on."

"You're just getting started?" Alice said directly to Kristen.

"Yes."

Ed couldn't help extolling Kristen. "She's going to sing tonight at the Music Hall."

"I'd love to hear her; what time?" Alice said eagerly.

"We're not sure since the time will be determined when she signs up. It's a karaoke place, and they'll be others singing as well."

Alice turned to her sister. "Do you know the place?"

"Yes, it's one of Omaha's big attractions for wannabe singers, but I've never been there."

"Are you game?" Alice said with a nudging look.

"I've already told you—we'll do and see whatever you want."

"You have a cell phone we can reach you on?" Alice said to Ed.

"I don't, but Kristen does."

Once Alice exchanged numbers with Kristen, she looked over to Ed. "Guess you're from the 'old school' of simpler things, like me, with the exception, of course, that I have a cell phone."

"Women are more adaptable to new things. Just another advantage they have over men," Ed said with a grin.

"Finally, a man who admits to his shortcomings," Alice teased.

"What time do you and Kristen plan to be at the Music Hall?" Janice said to Ed.

"About nine so that we can get a table."

"A table for four, if you don't mind," Alice said and looked over to Kristen. "I really look forward to hearing you sing."

"Thank you."

"All right, sis, we've taken enough of Ed and Kristen's time, so let's get on over to the glass figurine place; maybe they'll have some adorable angels," Alice said, then turned to Ed. "We'll see you tonight, hopefully."

It was approaching four when Ed and Kristen returned to the hotel room, feeling a little worn out but happy for the experience. At Ed's insistence, Kristen had bought an arty blue-bead necklace, which he thought would complement her eyes and the top she was planning to wear.

"You know what I've deduced?" Kristen said as she tumbled onto her bed.

"What?"

"I think Alice has the hots for you, and we should have gone to the mall and got you a cell phone."

"And how does that relate?"

"Alice could call you directly and not be restrained by having to go through me."

"I'll probably never see her again after tonight, and besides, I've got you to worry about," Ed said good-naturedly.

"I think you're capable of dealing with more than one woman at a time," Kristen kidded.

"Someone in this room is getting impertinent and instead should devote her energy to rehearsing the song for tonight," Ed chided with a grin.

"I'm not sure which song to do. Any ideas?"

"Do a long and lively one. That way, they'll want to hear another like they did at Kelly's."

"I don't know that many long ones."

"How about the one you sang on the way here—think it was . . . 'Bobby McGee'?" Ed said with uncertainty.

"You mean 'Me and Bobby McGee.'"

"Yes, that's the one."

"I haven't done it enough to do it well," Kristen said hesitantly.

Ed glanced at his watch. "You've got at least three hours to rehearse."

"You'll get sick of hearing it."

"Are you going to give me a hard time?" Ed kidded.

"No, just don't want you to lose your mind," Kristen shot back.

"You know I never tire of hearing you sing."

"OK," Kristen said with a smile, appreciating Ed's solicitude.

"And by all means, do your gyrations to fill the gap when it's only music."

"That just comes naturally when I do a lively song."

"I should have known."

"Had a lot of practice when pole dancing," Kristen said forthrightly.

"No doubt," Ed said with a nod. "We'll have dinner in the room so you don't lose practice time."

"Yes, Sergeant Ed," Kristen quipped affably.

Music Hall was more impressive than any bar Ed had ever seen in terms of its size; the stage was large enough to easily accommodate a good-size band, with a profusion of overhead lights to illuminate the performers in various hues, including several strategically placed large spots. Kristen was unnerved by the sight and grabbed Ed's arm in a mild panic before they started for one of the handful of open tables near the stage. Most of the crowd was concentrated at the massive bar and surrounding high tables. Ed had no doubt Kristen was more than ready to do the new song, having rehearsed it a couple dozen times and seeming confident and poised afterward, but seeing her timid suddenly vexed him somewhat.

"At last, a table by the stage. They must have known you were coming," Ed kidded, hoping to loosen Kristen up.

"This place is bigger than the last two karaoke bars combined," Kristen observed as they removed their parkas and took their seats.

"You can handle it; just think of this place as your home and the crowd as immediate family," Ed encouraged.

"This time I really wish you could get up on the stage with me," Kristen said earnestly in a shaky voice.

"I will be in that heart on the chain around your neck—always know that," Ed proclaimed and squeezed Kristen's hand.

The attractive young waitress with pad and pen in hand stepped up to the table as Ed released Kristen's hand.

"My name's Judy, and I'll be your waitress for this evening. What can I get you?"

"A double Wild Turkey straight," Ed said, then glanced at Kristen "I'll have a Coke, and where do I sign up for the karaoke?"

"Are you entering the competition or doing it for fun?"

"Competition. What's the difference?"

"That will start after ten, and the winner, based on the applause meter, gets two hundred bucks."

"Where do I sign up?" Kristen asked, more upbeat.

"That would be Jesse Loomis; she's back at the bar and has the sign-up sheet and the song menu. What do you sing?"

"Country."

"Oh, that's great! Lately they're all singing the standard stuff, and I think the customers are ready for some good old country," Judy said encouragingly and left.

"I probably should have ordered double vodka without the Coke," Kristen, still unnerved, said half seriously.

"Not a good idea before you sing; it'll pass," Ed said reassuringly.

"Yeah, I guess," Kristen said, unconvinced, and glanced over to the stage.

"Just think of yourself as a grown-up and the audience as babes in soiled diapers," Ed said humorously.

Kristen chuckled. "Thanks, I'll do that."

"Also keep in mind what the waitress said—they're ready to hear some country, and you've rehearsed enough to do it great," Ed said forcefully.

"I wonder if Alice and Janice are coming?"

Ed glanced at his watch. "It's not quite nine yet, and they said they would call if they couldn't make it for some reason."

Judy was back with the drinks in record time, the song selection menu in hand. "Jesse had a couple of extras, so I thought I'd bring one for you to look at."

"Thanks," Kristen said, eagerly taking the thick song menu, which alphabetically grouped by type of music. "Has anybody signed up yet?"

"About half a dozen as of now, but I'm sure there'll be a heck of a lot more. There always is."

"I'll bring the menu back when I sign up if that's OK?"

"No hurry. Like I said, she has extras."

Ed, with wallet in hand, was ready to pay for the drinks. "What's the damage?"

"You don't want a tab?"

"No, I might have a heart attack and would hate to stick you with the bill," Ed joshed.

"You're a real gentleman, and in that case, it's sixteen bucks."

Ed handed Judy a twenty. "If by chance you see two lost mature ladies, please send them over to this table."

Judy chuckled. "Will do."

Ed once again glanced over at the door and, to his relief, saw Alice and Janice looking around.

He immediately stood up and waved, which they noticed and began the track through the maze of tables. Minutes later they reached the table with pleasant smiles and looking very urbane.

"Hello again! Sorry we're a little late. Janice couldn't get the car started, so we took a cab," Alice said as she and Janice removed their coats and draped them over their chairs.

"The karaoke hasn't started yet?" Alice asked, glancing at the stage.

"Not yet. The contest for the serious singers starts at ten, but there may be others before that who are doing it just for fun."

"Kristen, are you ready to compete?" Alice asked enthusiastically.

"I'm a bit overwhelmed by the size of this place," Kristen confessed.

"I spoke to my son on the phone earlier and mentioned we were coming here. He said he was here when they had the National Karaoke Championship and that this is the best karaoke bar in the country," Janice said knowingly.

"I guess they cater mostly to the younger crowd," Alice said, looking around.

"Yes, but I was told they do tolerate older folks," Ed cracked.

"Speaking of which, someone opened a senior bar a couple of years ago, but it went out of business in less than a year," Janice said.

"Whoever it was must have been young and didn't know seniors go to bed at ten," Ed joked.

Alice laughed the hardest, to the point of tears, and when she regained control, she looked admiringly at Ed. "You have a wonderful sense of humor."

"Now and then," Ed said nonchalantly and looked around for the waitress. "I guess Judy must be on a break."

"I'll get her," Kristen said, getting to her feet. "I'm gonna return the music menu and sign up."

"She's a doll. You must be so very proud of her," Alice said once Kristen had left.

"As Debby Boone once sang, she lights up my life."

"How long has she been singing?" Janice asked.

"Several years—but strictly for her own enjoyment. I suggested she go public."

"Does she have an extensive musical background?"

"Church choir as a youngster, and since then, she's being doing it for her own amusement."

"I can't wait to hear her sing."

"And you said she sings country songs?" Alice said.

"She loves country and thinks the words touch the heart."

"Are you also into country music?"

"Only of late. Been a huge Sinatra fan all my life."

"I love his music as well. My husband and I used to drive to Atlantic City and see his concerts at the casinos," Alice said, reminiscing.

"My wife and I did so as well. First time we saw him was at the Copa on our first date. It was really a memorable sight: they rolled him out on the stage with the lights out, atop a white piano; he had on a black tux, drink in hand. Of all the times we saw him after that, it's the image I always have of him."

"He was the ultimate showman, even into his later years," Alice said fondly.

"He and that upstart kid from Memphis," Ed kidded.

"Beg to differ with both of you, but as far as I'm concerned, Elvis was the ultimate showman," Janice declared boldly.

"Whatever," Alice said dismissively and focused on Ed. "I would guess you probably have a ton of Sinatra's albums."

"Sorry to interrupt, but I was told there are two ladies here who are dying of thirst," Judy joked, looking at Alice and Janice.

"A drink would be nice," Alice said congenially.

With orders taken, the waitress hurried off, and Ed glanced in the direction of the crowded bar. "Wonder what's keeping Kristen?"

"Perhaps she's in the ladies' room," Alice said thoughtfully.

"So how long do you and Kristen intend to stay in Las Vegas?" Janice asked.

Ed scratched his chin. "Not really sure right now since there are several things we'll need to check out, the foremost being a first-rate country music manager."

"Couldn't you have done it all in New York?"

"Country music in New York is kind of iffy, not many big-time managers. Las Vegas is the singers' mecca, with a concentration of experts in all the aspects of the music business, which might come in handy in case Kristen needs some help with her singing."

"That makes sense," Alice agreed.

"Enough about Kristen—you ladies haven't told me a single thing about yourselves."

"My husband died three years ago from a massive heart attack, and I have an unmarried daughter in Washington, DC, who works for the FBI, like her dad did," Alice said emotionally, then looked over to her sister to bail her out.

"I'm much more fortunate; my husband is alive, but he recently injured his back severely and is facing a long recovery. I have a single son who is in sales and, unfortunately, on the road forty weeks a year," Janice said with a dejected sigh.

The waitress, looking somewhat discombobulated, was back with the drinks. "Sorry for the delay; it's really getting a little hairy."

"We understand," Alice said graciously and reached for her purse.

"I've got it," Ed said promptly and handed Judy a twenty. "By any chance, have you seen Kristen back there?"

"No. She was talking to Jesse the last time I saw her, but she's not there anymore; she may have gone to the ladies' room," Judy guessed.

"Yeah, that must be it," Ed said with a nod.

"I'll check it out," Judy volunteered and hurried off.

"Well, no point having the drinks get warm," Ed said in jest and reached for his glass.

"We can wait," Alice said thoughtfully.

"I'm back," Kristen blurted as she hurried to the table. "Bathroom was a little busy."

Ed waited till Kristen was seated and raised his glass in a toast. "To Kristen's big night."

With glasses clicked and first swallows taken, all focused on the MC as she took the stage with mic in hand.

"Good evening and welcome to the famous Music Hall. I hope all of you had a great Christmas and got lots of presents. My name is Jesse Loomis, for those of you who are here for the first time. I'm the one who runs this gig and has the pleasure of introducing the for-fun and the serious wannabe singers. As is our custom, we allow anyone who has the guts to step onto this stage and give it their best shot with their chosen song. However, we do have the nightly contest for those who aspire to greater things and want to compete for the two-hundred-dollar winner's prize. The contest will start in about thirty minutes, but in the meantime, we have several brave souls who just want to sing for fun."

There were six young women who took the stage, and not one could carry a tune, but with the post-Christmas spirit, no one was booed off the stage, and they actually received smattering applause.

"I don't think I would have the guts to ever do that, no matter how many drinks I had," Janice declared after the last person left the stage.

"It's about forgetting your inhibitions and seeing it as a challenge," Ed said firmly for Kristen's sake.

"I can think of a thousand other things that would be more fun," Janice insisted.

"So how far down the list are you?" Ed said directly to Kristen, not wishing to dwell on Janice's negative comments.

"Number seven."

"Lucky number—good deal," Ed said positively and took a swallow of his drink.

The stage lights flashed in different hues as Jesse Loomis took center stage after a short break. "All right, folks, the magic hour you've been waiting for has arrived. It's showtime! We have a slew of contestants, and as I've already indicated, the prize money is two hundred bucks. So without further delay, let's welcome our first: Miss Cindy White, who will sing 'The Way We Were.'"

The four contestants who had sung so far were definitely several steps above the ones who had sung for fun, each with a more-than-passable voice and presentation, much to Ed's surprise; he'd expected less after the other two karaoke bars. It appeared that Kristen had serious competition, but Ed was encouraged because up to now, all the songs performed were slow and easy, and the contestants had been somewhat stiff.

Ed hoped the next two would be similar, but if not, he was confident that once onstage, Kristen would overcome her jitters and perform no worse than she did when rehearsing, which was definitely quite impressive. With the fifth contestant about to start, Kristen leaned over to Ed with a look of distress on her face and whispered, "I have to go to the ladies' room again."

"You've got time," Ed said calmly.

"Is she all right?" Alice said with concern once Kristen rushed off.

"A little case of the nerves, but she'll be fine once she gets on the stage."

Two contestants later, Ed grew uneasy and glanced over in the direction of the hallway leading to the restrooms. Alice noticed.

"Would you like me to go and check?"

"Let's just wait," Ed said, guessing Kristen was

probably still dealing with her issue and would miss her turn anyway.

With the last note sung, Jesse stepped back on the stage with the mic in one hand and a clipboard in the other.

"All right, guys and gals, let's hear it for Dani!"

Once the applause stopped and Dani left the stage, Jesse glanced at her clipboard and looked out at the crowd. "Our next contestant is Miss Kristen Cole, all the way from New York, so let's give her a special Omaha welcome."

Ed promptly stood up and yelled to Jesse, "She's indisposed right now."

"That's all right—I'll reschedule her. Let me know when she's back," Jesse hollered back, then called the next contestant.

Ed was relieved, and so were Alice and Janice, who, like Ed, didn't know if Kristen would get to sing after losing her turn.

"Thank goodness for that," Alice said.

A moment later, Kristen returned with her face flushed and eyes red, which Ed immediately noticed. "You OK?"

"I threw up. Did I lose my turn?" Kristen said with concern.

"Yes, but you can do your song next if you're ready."

"I am," Kristen said definitively.

When the contestant who took Kristen's turn finished and the applause ended, Ed stood up, waved his hand, and pointed to Kristen. Jesse noticed and motioned for her to come up.

"You can do this," Ed said firmly and hugged Kristen, then gently nudged her toward the stage.

Once onstage, Jesse introduced Kristen: "And the song Ms. Cole is doing, made famous by the great Janis Joplin, is 'Me and Bobby McGee.'"

Moments later, with the music cued, Kristen was in full control, and to Ed's amazement, she was doing it even better than when she had rehearsed. As the song progressed, so did Kristen's intensity—both vocally and physically—to the delight of the appreciative crowd. When she finished, the audience responded with thunderous applause, whistles, and howls. Alice and Janice were stunned, like most of the crowd, at the incredible performance. Jesse rushed to Kristen's side, clapping like everyone else and totally disbelieving what she had just seen. Minutes later, when the ovation finally stopped, Jesse turned on her mic and spoke to Kristen and the crowd.

"In all the years I've been doing this, I have never seen such an awesome performance,"

Jesse said wholeheartedly as a new round of applause erupted and continued for another minute.

"Ladies and gentlemen, with no disrespect to those who have already performed and those who will, soon take the stage, please accept my apology, but I think you'll probably agree that we have witnessed the birth of the next great country star."

When Kristen returned to the table, Ed was standing with open arms and tears in his eyes. He hugged her and kissed her on the cheek several times, with the patrons at the nearby tables enthusiastically applauding the affectionate gesture.

"There are no words good enough to say how proud I am," Ed whispered in Kristen's ear.

"You gave me courage when I had none," Kristen said out loud, then kissed Ed.

Alice and Janice took their turns, congratulating Kristen with hugs and words of admiration; both declared it was the best performance they had ever seen.

Jesse and the next contestant waited patiently for Kristen and others to take their seats and quiet down.

When at last the competition ended, there was no doubt in anybody's mind who deserved to take the prize. One by one, Jesse announced the contestants' names and made a note of the audience reaction on the applause meter. When she called out Kristen's name, the meter nearly broke. Minutes later, Kristen accepted the prize and acknowledged the impassioned pleas from the crowd for an encore with bows and thanks, but she politely declined, having discussed the response with Ed before taking the stage.

Numerous well-wishers stopped by the table to shake Kristen's hand and wish her a great career, whereas others asked her for selfies and autographs, to which she happily obliged. Shortly, Judy came with drinks, which puzzled Ed because he hadn't ordered any.

"Compliments of the house," Judy gladly announced and distributed the drinks.

"Please thank whoever sent these," Ed said appreciatively with a quizzical look.

"You can thank Warren yourself; he'll be by in a minute," Judy said, then turned her attention to Kirsten. "Where did you learn those sexy moves?"

"I guess it's just there," Kristen said with a shrug.

Judy reached into her pocket and withdrew a smartphone. "Do you mind if I take a selfie with you?"

"Not at all," Kristen said most agreeably and rose to her feet.

"When you're famous, I'll show it to the customers and say I served you drinks and we were pals---that is, if you don't mind me saying that.

"It may be a while before that happens, but yes, it's OK, my pal," Kristen said with a grin.

"No way," Judy said happily and headed back to the bar.

"Well, shall we toast the future country star?" Alice suggested.

"I totally concur," a barrel-chested, middle-aged man with thick head of hair and chiseled face said as he approached the table. "I'm Warren, one of the owners of Music Hall, and I have to tell you, Kristen, that was one hell of a performance."

"Thank you," Kristen said, doing her best not to burst from exultation.

"Are you visiting here?"

"No, we're just passing through."

"Will you be here another day?"

"No, we'll be leaving tomorrow," Ed readily answered.

"Shame—I was going to ask Kristen to stop in tomorrow night and do an encore performance, which of course, I would make worthwhile."

"Sorry, but we really have to get back on the road."

"Well, if that's the case, then have a safe trip, and Kristen, you are on your way to the big time, which I assume is your plan," Warren said, and with a nod to all, he promptly left.

Alice was equally disappointed to hear about Ed and Kristen's next-day departure. She had intended to invite them to her sister's house for dinner. "You really can't stay another day?"

"No, with the uncertainty of the weather this time of year, especially along the route we're taking, it could be a venturous drive."

Alice, greatly disappointed, was eager to find out if or when Ed and Kristen might be back in New York. "So is there a possibility that you may be back to Staten Island anytime in the near future?"

"There is a very good chance that I'll be back to meet with my lawyer to tie up some loose ends," Ed shared.

"Well, that's encouraging. Maybe if you've got time, we could get together?" Alice said eagerly.

"By all means—think you gave Kristen your cell phone number, right?"

"I have it," Kristen said promptly.

"Well, sis, I think we better call it a night. I promised Tim we'd be back before midnight, and you know what a fuddy-duddy he is," Janice said anxiously.

"You need to trade him for a younger husband," Alice kidded.

"We need to go as well," Ed said, glancing at his watch. "It was certainly delightful to have you ladies join us."

"Thank you for inviting us. And the very best of luck to you, Kristen. You are an incredible performer with a great career waiting for you," Alice said sincerely.

CHAPTER 7

E
d, still in bed, looked out the window at the dark-gray portending day and had second thoughts about leaving Omaha. To his surprise, overnight, Alice had wormed her way into his subconscious mind. After eight years of reclusive life, there were suddenly two people he cared about—one already solidly entrenched in his heart and the other with a foothold. He couldn't believe that in the space of just a few days, life had served up a lively menu, but unfortunately, it would soon be all in vain. There was no escape from what he had been dealt by fate, no matter how far he drove to escape it. Had it not been for Kristen in the room, he might have cursed and howled about it all. After having more than his share of pain and sadness already, he now faced the ultimate unfairness just when life suddenly held a promise of something splendid.

He was totally perplexed and unsure of what to do and how to handle it. For the first time in his life, he questioned his decision process. Throughout his entire adult life, he'd lived by a rule his dad had drummed into his head when he was young: "Once you make a decision, son, don't second guess yourself." And for the most part, that credo had served him well. One thing was absolutely certain: time was running out. With reluctance, he got out of bed to get on with the day and be ready for what-ever came. When finished with his morning ritual, he was pleasantly surprised to see Kristen wide awake, sitting up and gazing out the window with cell phone in hand. She looked over with a pleasant smile.

"Good morning! Looks like snow."

"Yes, better get ready soon as you can."

"Alice just called and wanted to speak with you."

"She say why?"

"No, but I think to see if you changed your mind about leaving today."

"Can you call her for me, please?" Ed asked as he approached.

"Sure," Kristen said and punched the dial key and handed over the phone, then headed for the bathroom.

"Good morning. You're up early," Ed said in a most pleasant voice.

"Good morning, Ed. Thank you for calling back," Alice said sweetly. "I wanted to reach you before you left."

"Something wrong?"

Alice sighed deeply then said, "I know last night you said you were definitely leaving this morning, but I want-ed to give it one more try and persuade you stay at least another day."

"It's very tempting, and believe it or not, I thought about it a great deal before getting out of bed, but I really think we need to head for Las Vegas since the weather is not looking good. According to what they said on TV last night, snow is coming in a big way."

"Well, isn't that a good reason to delay the trip?" Alice said wisely.

"Yes and no—we could be stuck here for several days, and there is some urgency, from my standpoint, in getting Kristen hooked up with the people who will help her get started."

"But will a couple of days' delay matter that much?" Alice pleaded.

"Please believe me when I say that there's a very good reason for seeing this thing with Kristen through in a very timely way," Ed said with all the sincerity he could muster. "If the circumstances were different, I wouldn't hesitate to stay and get to know you better."

Alice was surprised by the unexpected comment and momentarily was at a loss for a coherent reply. "I'm very flattered; that's the nicest compliment I've heard in quite some time."

"I'm sure someone as attractive and classy as you must hear it often."

"Are you toying with me?" Alice said dubiously.

"I never toy with people's emotions."

"In that case, I apologize," Alice said contritely. "So you have no definite date at this time when you'll be returning back to New York?"

"I don't want to mislead or give you false hope, but as it stands right now, I think it will definitely be soon. The things I have to take care of back home require prompt attention."

"That sounds promising," Alice said somewhat more happily. "I will be back the day after New Year's and will look forward to seeing you and Kristen when you return."

"Actually, she'll remain in Las Vegas."

"Ah, I see. You must be so very proud of her; she is an extraordinarily talented young lady, not only vocally but rhythmically as well. I have never seen such an incredible vocal and physical performance."

"She does put her heart and soul into it."

"And you said she never had any formal training?"

"No, it's just natural."

"Do you intend to manage her when she turns professional?"

Ed was relieved with the change in the line of questioning, having feared Alice would query him about Kristen's lineage.

"No, that'll require a pro and possibly an entourage."

"Will you travel with her?"

"I'm not sure right now."

"Well, as much as I hate to say goodbye, I'm sure you must be anxious to get on the road, so I won't take up any more of your time," Alice said gracefully.

"It was a true pleasure and my luck to have met you; please take care, and give my regards to your equally lovely sister."

"Will you call me from the road?"

"I will."

"Have a very safe trip, and I'll be thinking of you," Alice said with emotion.

Ed was deeply touched yet unsure if he would ever see Alice again. Suddenly, he felt a sharp pain in his gut and immediately walked over to the suitcase, pulled out a full bottle of Wild Turkey, and took a long swig. He replaced the bottle back in the suitcase just as Kristen stepped out of the bathroom and immediately noticed the pain on his face.

"You OK?"

"It just hit me like a bolt of lightning," Ed said through gritted teeth, a hand on his midriff.

"Did you have a slug of booze?"

"Just before you came out."

"Why don't you sit down and I'll get us ready—unless

you want to postpone the trip," Kristen said with a great concern.

"No, we're going to leave, no matter what," Ed said as he sat down on the edge of the bed and drew a deep breath.

"You have a nice conversation with Alice?" Kristen asked as she went about getting things ready for departure.

"Yes, it was mainly about you. She thinks you are a very special, talented young lady with an incredible future."

"I like her, too. She's a classy lady, and I'm glad we met her, mainly for your sake."

"Don't read too much into it; chances are I'll never see her again."

"Why not? She can come and visit us in Las Vegas or wherever we end up," Kristen said optimistically.

"We end up?"

"Yes, you're not going to pawn me off to a bunch of strangers. Like it or not, you're stuck with me for the rest of your life," Kristen said boldly.

"Well, if that's the case, then let's get going, consort," Ed said lightheartedly and slowly rose from the bed.

"I guess you're feeling somewhat better," Kristen said happily.

"It's starting to pass, and talking to you always helps."

Once they were out of Omaha and on Interstate 80, Ed pulled over on the shoulder, at Kristen's urging, to let her drive, even though he was capable of doing it now that the pain had subsided. There was very little traffic, and the road was mostly straight—an ideal time for Kristen to gain more experience. Even though it was midmorning, it seemed more like approaching evening, with the clouds dark and threatening. The meteorologist on the morning news report in Omaha had mentioned a significant cold-front moving eastward from the Rockies, which would definitely result in significant snow accumulation for at least a half dozen nearby states. With that possibility in mind, Ed had suggested before they left Omaha that they do some serious snack shopping.

"You really feeling better now?" Kristen said with a hopeful look.

"The Wild Turkey once again came through like a champ," Ed said in a kidding way, hoping to put Kristen's mind at ease since he felt bad about the burden he was placing on her.

"You always been a Wild Turkey man?"

"Got started on it in Vietnam and been a loyal customer ever since."

"You kill any Vietnamese?"

"Not at close range."

"Could you have?"

"Oh, sure. When the choice is your life or the other guy's, the prudent thing always is to save yours," Ed said with a grin.

"How'd you get shot?"

"There was a sniper hiding in a tree, and he got me and my two buddies as we were crossing an open field. I survived; they didn't. Later that day, we lost most of the platoon in an ambush not far from where I got shot. Guess I lucked out by getting wounded and taken back to the base, or I would have got killed with the other guys."

"What's it like getting shot?"

"It's definitely something to avoid at all costs. I

passed out right after the bullet hit me, and when I came to, I was in a field hospital under heavy sedation, with no idea what had happened to me, and I stayed that way for quite a while. The only thing that helped me withstand the pain was the morphine they pumped into my veins around the clock. It took nearly three months to wean me off the stuff."

Kristen shook her head and said sympathetically, "And here you are once again coping with that damn pain----just not fair."

"The only fair thing in life is that we all have to die," Ed said pontifically.

"I just made up my mind," Kristen said in a determined voice.

"What?"

"I'm going to make it big sooner than you think so that I can make a pile of money, and you know why?"

"So you can buy a yacht?" Ed cracked.

"No, so I'll have the bucks to find someone in this world who can get you out of this pain," Kristen said resolutely.

Ed was surprised by Kristen's good intentions. "I appreciate the caring thought, my precious little songbird, and I'm deeply touched, but as I've already told you, no one can get me out of this bind."

"I don't believe it, and I'll find that someone," Kristen said even more forcefully.

"After last night, there's no doubt in my mind that you will make it huge," Ed said with great delight.

"And you will get cured," Kristen reaffirmed.

Ed thought it best to let it be and get Kristen to think about something else. "OK, here's the plan for when we get to Las Vegas: First, we rent a condo, then get you your driver's license, and then seek out the best damn country music manager money can buy. Once that's done, I will have to make a trip back to New York and settle my affairs."

Kristen was puzzled. "Like what?"

"Make a new will and sell the house, then donate to charity what's in it and take care of whatever loose ends remain."

"Your house, your friends—you're giving it all up on my account?"

"I told you; it's all or nothing."

"It's so sudden and so much. Are you sure you want to do all that?" Kristen said unselfishly.

"There is no half measure when I do things."

"Why are you doing this?"

"I'll tell you one day."

Kristen shrugged, not wanting to pressure Ed. "You wanna hear our song?"

"Always," Ed said happily; he loved the words, which sounded like they were written specifically for him and Kristen. In the thousands of songs he had heard over a lifetime, not one had touched him the way this one did, especially when Kristen sang it—her heart and soul were in every word. He thought the song encapsulated what they meant to each other. Whenever Kristen finished the tune, she would pause to garner her emotions before being able to sing another, and he felt the same way listening to it.

"This may sound silly, but I always feel like our souls are joined when I do this song," Kristen said with deep emotion.

"Perhaps they are."

"You don't have a problem with that?"

"Why would I?"

"I mean, your wife and all."

"I think it's possible to have more than one," Ed said to gladden Kristen.

"You believe in heaven?"

Ed was slow to answer. "Honestly, I think it's just wishful thinking, but please don't let that dissuade you."

"What makes you think that?" Kristen pressed.

"People can't accept death as the ultimate end, so they desperately cling to the notion that life goes on in a different form."

"If you feel that way, then why'd you want to go to the Christmas Midnight Mass?"

"I guess it was to find out where I stand, but please, I beg you, don't you become like me," Ed said seriously, wishing he hadn't spouted off.

"Too late," Kristen kidded.

"I think you need a good spanking, young lady. The world doesn't need another heathen."

"At last, physical contact. When do we start?" Kristen joshed.

"All right, my little thrush, playtime is over, so let's get back to work and exercise those vocal cords."

The snow came down like an avalanche as they crossed the Colorado state line. Ed considered turning back to North Platte, Nebraska, where they'd stopped for gas and seen a nearby motel, but that was nearly fifty miles back and no closer than Sterling ahead, which also had a motel. He found himself in a quandary with no satisfactory choice. He regretted his unwise decision for not calling it a day earlier when they stopped, although he was not totally to blame; he'd taken the weather report on the radio as gospel truth, and it had turned out to be completely wrong. About the only positive thing he saw was that they had a nearly full tank of gas, fresh coffee in the thermos, and sufficient eats to last them a couple of days. Ed had seen several blizzards during his life, but this was the first on an open road. To make the situation even more foreboding, darkness had overtaken the snow, and he had not seen another vehicle in some time, not that it would have helped, other than to diminish the feeling of total isolation. He would have been less anxious had he been alone—then he wouldn't have to worry about Kristen, whom he'd exposed to danger with his foolhardy decision—but to his surprise, Kristen took it all in stride and actually thought it was a blast.

"Isn't this awesome?" Kristen said like a kid looking out the living room window in anticipation of canceled school.

"You're not concerned?" Ed said as he slowed the car to half the minimum speed.

"No, we're in good shape if we get stuck: plenty of snacks, hot coffee, a thick quilt and Wild Turkey to keep us warm, and you know what else?"

"I can't imagine."

"We get to cuddle for body heat," Kristen said with a naughty grin.

"I'm not sure about that."

"I don't know why not. It's not like we'll be in the raw, if that's your concern."

"My concern is that we may get buried in ten feet of snow. It does happen out here during blizzards, especially with this kind of drifting."

"You're just trying to scare me," Kristen said, not believing him.

Ed was amazed by Kristen's grit and did not want to break her spirit. "I'm glad you're taking this as a great adventure."

"It is, and look at all the stories we'll have to tell," Kristen said cheerily. "I thought you loved the snow."

"I do, in moderation."

"Moderation is totally boring and mostly practiced by stodgy people."

"Well . . ."

"You're not stodgy, and I'm not about to let you be. I'm gonna make you think and act young again."

Ed shook his head and could not deny that in just a handful of days, Kristen had indeed reawakened thoughts and feelings he had not known in decades.

"That we'll see," Ed said and slowed the car to a crawl since visibility was near zero now.

"Are we stopping?" Kristen said with a puzzled look.

"One, I can't see past the hood, and two, I'm not sure where the damn highway is."

"You want me to get out and guide you?" Kristen kidded.

"No, but that's exactly what I'm going to do—find the damn road and get us off on the shoulder, so get behind the wheel and very slowly follow me," Ed said and stopped the SUV.

"Can't we just stay where we are?"

"If we're still on the road, that would be very dangerous," Ed said as he climbed out of the car and put his parka on.

"OK," Kristen said, clambering over the console and into the driver's seat.

The snow was up to Ed's calves as he plodded through it with the headlights at his back and the wind-driven snow smashing his face. Several steps later, he noticed a speed limit sign off to the right side and motioned for Kristen to pull over just a few feet away from it. He hurried back to the warmth of the SUV, brushing the snow from the parka before getting in.

"It's really cold out there," Ed said as he slammed the door shut and settled in the passenger seat. "Think I'll have a little nip."

"You want me to keep the engine running?"

"Yes, few more minutes till I warm up," Ed said and reached in the back seat, pulling out a paper grocery shopping bag with the Wild Turkey and several snacks.

"Will we be able to restart it if I shut the engine off?" Kristen wisely asked.

"It'll be OK," Ed said reassuringly, sensing Kristen finally had some concern. "Are you hungry?" He eyed the snacks in the bag as he pulled out the Wild Turkey.

"Yes, and can I have a nip as well?"

Ed handed Kristen the bottle and set the bag on the console. "Damn."

"What?"

"We should have had dinner after we gassed up and just stayed overnight there—about the stupidest decision I've made in the last day," Ed said self-deprecatingly.

"I'm just as much to blame for encouraging you to go on."

"Well, let's make the best of it—since we have no choice—and hope this doesn't turn into a misadventure."

"I've got the cell phone, so we can call for help," Kristen said.

"I doubt it'll work with the heavy snow and being way out here."

"I'll give it a try after we eat."

Having filled up on the junk food, Kristen dialed 911, but as Ed predicted, to no avail.

"You were right," Kristen said with an unhappy shrug.

"We need to shut the engine and the headlights off, but before you do, I'll get out and clear some of the snow off the back of the SUV and make sure the taillights aren't blocked."

Kristen was puzzled. "Why is that?"

"Just in case we get lucky and have a rescue vehicle or any other come up behind us."

"I'll help."

"No, stay; just hand me the ice scraper that's on the floor by your feet."

The snow, driven by the relentless wind, had piled halfway up the passenger side of the door, forcing Ed to use all his strength to push it free. Once out, he forged his way to the back of the SUV and relieved himself, then cleared the snow off the taillights and a small area by the exhaust pipe. He then continued to the driver's side, where the snow was not nearly as bad, and pulled the door open.

"Climb back over to the passenger seat."

"I need to pee," Kristen said unabashedly.

"You can do it on the other side where I've left a path," Ed suggested.

Minutes later, they settled into their seats in total darkness with the engine off, listening to the sound of the wind and snow as it smashed against the SUV. It was ultimate isolation, which drew them even closer emotionally, beyond the bond they already shared.

"What'd you say we have a cup of joe and something sweet," Ed suggested once relaxed.

"Like me?" Kristen kidded.

"No, like one of those chocolate chip cookies if there's any left," Ed said and flipped on the overhead light, shaking his head at Kristen's suggestive teasing.

"I didn't eat them all," Kristen protested while searching for the cookies.

Minutes later, they both sipped the welcome hot coffee and nibbled, with relish, on the cookies.

"OK, here's the deal; when we finish, get the quilt since it's going to get quite cold without the heater running," Ed said tentatively. "I'll try to stay awake as much as I can and run the engine and the heater every now and then."

"We're going to cuddle under the quilt?" Kristen said happily.

"That's going to be hard with the console between the seats."

"You don't think I can squeeze onto the seat with you?"

"Not unless we both turn to broomsticks."

"But we won't generate enough body heat if we don't cuddle."

"I think we will."

"You don't want to try?" Kristen said, disappointed.

"All right," Ed said in exasperation.

Kristen immediately hopped over the console and squeezed tightly against Ed. "See, just like I said—we can do it."

"I'm not sure for how long," Ed said, jamming himself against the door.

"It's not fair for you to stay up all night, so please wake me and let me take a couple of turns," Kristen said thoughtfully.

"I may do that," Ed said and flipped off the overhead light.

"It's only eight thirty, and I'm not sleepy yet. You know any scary ghost stories?" Kristen said like a kid.

"Not a single one. Try the radio and see if you can get a station."

Kristen did as Ed suggested, but all she got was a lot of static. "Nothing—we might as well be on the moon."

"So much for fun and adventure," Ed teased.

"I'm having fun; aren't you?" Kristen fired back.

"No doubt about it, you are an absolute joy, my little thrush."

"I love that nickname—my daddy called me his little cupcake."

"You were his pride and great joy, no doubt," Ed affirmed.

"Guess I'll try to get some z's since I want to be ready to relieve you, but please do wake me."

"Good night and sweet dreams, my precious thrush," Ed said caringly.

"Good night, and please be sure to wake me so you're not doing it all night long," Kristen said and nuzzled tightly against Ed.

CHAPTER 8

The night was long and cold, even with the heavy quilt; Ed and Kristen woke repeatedly with chattering teeth and shivering bodies. Each time Ed would run the engine, they would eagerly wait several minutes for the welcome heat to come gushing from the vents. The snow throughout the night was steady and, whipped by the wind, piled up in a large drift against the passenger side of the SUV, totally covering the windows. Several times, Ed thought of getting out and clearing at least the windshield, but Kristen wisely talked him out of it, saying that it would be a wasted effort and that the cold would be too much to deal with.

Each time they ran the heat, Ed would wait for Kristen to fall asleep before shutting the engine off. He was amused by her ability to nod off as soon as she felt toasty warm, whereas it took him an excruciatingly long time to fall asleep, and at times, sleep never came. He would then wait till the cold got bad enough to start the engine once again. He remembered those youthful days when he also was able to drift off just by closing his eyes, even in the jungles of Vietnam, with swarms of mosquitos and exotic bugs that feasted on human blood.

Shortly after five, and totally exhausted, Ed fell off into an uneasy sleep, only to wake an hour later feeling like he had been covered in ice. He instinctively reached for the key and started the engine, which slightly hesitated before turning over. He glanced at Kristen, with her head resting on his shoulder and the rest of her scrunched under the quilt. He reached for her head and gently eased it against the seat, fearing that if she remained as she was, she would end up with severely sore neck. The only window not caked over with the snow was on the driver's side, but it was iced, blocking the emerging daylight. He attempted to lower it, but it didn't budge: frozen solid in its track. He tried the radio, but the reception was weak, and he didn't want to wake Kristen by increasing it to full volume. To top it all off, the pain in his gut was making itself known in a big way. He promptly reached for the paper shopping bag, which was now mostly full of empty wrappers, and pulled out the Wild Turkey; he hastily took a long swig, hoping that once again, it would smother the pain, which was on a steady increase. Once he placed the bottle back in the bag, he started the engine and turned on the car heater and the windshield defroster. The snow was slow to melt off the windshield because of the large accumulation, but the ice, to his joy, began to do so.

With the SUV warmed somewhat and Kristen still asleep, Ed decided to get out for a look-see and to relieve himself. He was surprised by how unevenly the snow had blanketed the road, with some areas covered by no more than a foot and others with significant drifts easily higher than most cars. Fortunately, their drift had enveloped just the passenger side of the SUV, but even at that, Ed figured driving out of the drift would not be an easy task without first clearing away some of the snow from the side and most definitely in the front, but of course, it would be to no avail until the road was plowed. With no immediate solution coming to mind, he began to brush away the snow from the windshield and then the rear window and taillights. Once finished and chilled to the bone, he got back in the toasty-warm SUV and saw Kristen's always-smiling face.

"Why didn't you wake me? I would have helped."

"Too cold for you to be out there, and you needed to sleep."

"It's not fair for you to be doing all this stuff alone."

"Not much you could have done anyway since we don't have shovels to clear away the snow."

"So what're we gonna do?"

"Hopefully when the plow trucks show up, they may have some shovels we can borrow. Maybe they'll even help."

"Does it look like we'll get more snow?"

"I don't know. Why don't you check the weather on the cell? It should be working now."

Kristen got right to it, and a minute later, she had the answer: "Only a slight chance since the front is moving away from the direction we are going."

"Great, let's celebrate. We have any coffee left?"

Kristen checked and shook her head. "Not a drop— guess we drank it all last night."

"Damn!"

"We got the booze," she happily suggested.

"Yeah, and it's full of caffeine," Ed cracked.

"You want some?"

"Yes, really got chilled out there."

"Can I have a swig since I gotta go out and take a pee?"

"Have it after you get back," Ed suggested and got out of the SUV, with Kristen right behind him.

"Where should I go?" Kristen said with a puzzled look, seeing the SUV snowed in on three sides.

"I guess in the back by the tailpipe, which I cleared somewhat, and don't take too long or you'll catch a cold down there," Ed said teasingly.

"Very funny," Kristen said with a chuckle and reached under the parka to unbuckle her blue-jeans.

"Wait till I get back inside," Ed said promptly, and with one swift motion, he was back in the driver's seat.

"I thought you'd stay and be my lookout to make sure nothing tries to bite me," Kristen hollered in jest.

"You'll just have to chance it," Ed hollered back.

Once Kristen was back inside and had her swig of Wild Turkey, she dug through the shopping bag for something edible and came up with a box of powdered miniature donuts.

"Better than nothing," she said with a shrug and held out the box for Ed to take some.

"That's what I call a first-rate breakfast," Ed said with a grin and took a few.

"Would you rather have a granola bar? There's one on the seat."

"No, this is fine," Ed said, indifferent.

"You want a Coke to wash it down?"

"I'll share one with you."

"Think they'll be plowing the road anytime soon?"

Ed shrugged. "After this splendid breakfast, call the Colorado DOT and ask them."

"Good idea," Kristen said happily.

"Still think this is a great adventure?"

"Yes, don't you?" Kristen said with a grin.

"It would be if we hadn't run out of coffee."

"At last, you are starting to think young," Kristen praised.

"At the rate you're indoctrinating me, I'll soon be half my age," Ed cracked.

"So glad to hear; then we can get intimate," Kristen said with a grin.

"After we have the donuts, maybe we can have a snowball fight," Ed joshed.

Kristen suddenly looked at Ed intently. "If I ask you something, will you give me an honest answer?"

"Haven't I up to now?"

"Had I met you when you were young, would you have wanted to marry me?"

"Is this a twenty questions game?"

"No, seriously, I'd like to know."

"What would have been the circumstance?"

"Let's say I was also working at the ad place, just like Ann, and I had not been tainted," Kristen said. "I'm sorry—that's so dumb, " she added, immediately correcting herself.

Ed guessed Kristen's reason for asking: having lost her father and been sidelined by her mother, then assaulted by her stepdad and cruelly used by her boyfriend—and all the while not knowing love. His heart broke for her, and since Ann was gone, whatever he said now wouldn't affect her one way or the other, but Kristen, on the other hand, could definitely be helped. He pulled her over close and held her face, with his eyes locked on hers.

"I would have been lucky and proud to have had you for my wife, and furthermore, you are not tainted," Ed said firmly and kissed Kristen on the forehead, "and you are very much loved."

The pent-up emotion in Kristen burst like a dam, and she sobbed uncontrollably as Ed held her and stroked her hair. When she finally stopped, she looked up at Ed with pure love in her eyes.

"Please don't ever leave me."

"As long as I live, that's a promise," Ed said and handed her a handkerchief.

Kristen stiffened and looked over her shoulder. "I hear a rumble."

"Let's hope it's the cavalry," Ed joshed.

With their eyes focused on the rear window, they waited with relief and giddiness as two plow trucks slowly cleared the snow, one onto the highway divider and the other onto the shoulder. Following the plow trucks was a large pickup with a pile of snow-related equipment.

"Maybe they'll have some coffee to spare," Kristen said optimistically.

"I'd gladly pay twenty bucks for a couple of cups," Ed said seriously.

"Be nice if they helped us with the SUV."

Ed turned on the flashers as the plow trucks neared. "Think I better get out and make sure they see us and don't plow more snow on us."

"You want me to come out, too?"

"No, stay inside. There's no point in both of us getting cold. Besides, your face is red as a beet, and it'll get chafed in the cold," Ed said thoughtfully, then got out.

The plow truck halted a few feet from the SUV, and the burly, unshaven driver in heavy snow gear made his way to Ed.

"You OK?"

"Yeah. Do you by any chance have any coffee to spare?" Ed asked eagerly.

"Got an extra-huge thermos and will be glad to give you some," the driver said genially.

"Really appreciate that, thanks," Ed said with great relief.

"How you doing on gas?"

"Got less than a quarter tank left."

"That should get you to Sterling, which is about thirty miles from here."

"Did you come across many others stuck on the road?" Ed said as the plow truck in the outer lane slowly passed.

"Two semis and a car; they'll be along in a while," the driver said, peering at the SUV.

"Looks like you gonna need some help getting the vehicle out of the drift."

"I'd be grateful for a helping hand," Ed said readily.

"No sweat—I'll get you some help. So where you headed?"

"Las Vegas."

"Planning to spend New Year's there?"

"Yes."

"Well, I better get going; there's a couple of guys in the truck behind me who'll give you a hand digging out. Get your container and I'll give you some joe."

"Thanks so much," Ed said and hurried off to the SUV for the thermos.

It took the two DOT men, who had pulled up in a pickup right after the plow truck left, several minutes to get the SUV freed from the snow.

"You can follow or wait awhile before getting back on the road so that the plow trucks can clear the snow ahead," the huskier man of the two said to Ed.

After thanking the two men, Ed reached into his wallet, pulled out a couple of twenties, and offered one to each man . At first they refused, but at Ed's insistence, they finally took it.

"Guess who called?" Kristen said teasingly as soon as Ed was in the SUV.

"I give up," Ed said, but he had a fairly good idea.

"Alice."

"She OK?"

"Yes, she wanted to know if we were. She saw on the news all about the blizzard and got quite concerned, especially when she couldn't reach us."

"That was very thoughtful of her; did she want me to call her back?"

"Yes," Kristen said with a grin. "You want some coffee before you call her?"

"You have to ask?" Ed quipped.

"Did you ask them how far to the next exit and some food?" Kristen said as she poured the coffee.

"About thirty miles, and I'm sure they'll be food."

"Can't wait to eat something warm," Kristen said as she handed Ed the steaming cup of coffee.

"Yes, and soon as you pour yours, would you please call Alice for me?" Ed said as he blew into the cup before taking a sip.

"I'll do it right now," Kristen said. A second later, she handed Ed the phone.

"Good morning, Alice. Kristen said you called," Ed said congenially.

"Yes, after hearing the weather report, I was very concerned about you two being stuck somewhere on the road. Tried to reach you late last night several times but couldn't get through," Alice said caringly.

"That was very sweet of you. Are you getting any of it?"

"Yes, watching it pile up as we speak."

"How much are you supposed to get?"

"They said about fifteen inches."

"See what would have happened had I stayed? Probably be stuck in the hotel till spring," Ed kidded.

"Who knows, you might have been here right now, sitting with me near the roaring fireplace," Alice said invitingly.

"That would have been my pleasure," Ed said guardedly, feeling somewhat ill at ease with Kristen listening.

"Kristen said it was a fun experience."

"That is up for debate," Ed said, shaking his head.

"So when do you expect to see Las Vegas?"

"Hopefully sometime tomorrow, depending, of course, on the road conditions and the weather."

"Will you please call me when you get there or even before?" Alice said pleadingly.

"I will. Stay warm and out of the snow."

"You two as well, and please be safe."

"Bye," Ed said and clicked off the phone.

"Guess she really cares about you."

"Both of us," Ed said affirmatively.

"You know what I think?"

"No."

"I really think she has the serious hots for you."

"I think she's just a very caring person."

"Nope, she's definitely got the hots for you," Kristen insisted.

"And I think you have a wild imagination," Ed said, shaking his head.

"OK, have it your way, but take it from me: she's not going to disappear. So where are we stopping for the night on this awesome day?"

"Denver."

"How long you figure it'll take to get there?"

"Depends how fast they clear the road, but at worst, I think we should get there by late afternoon. We'll hit the sack early and head for Vegas first thing in the morning."

CHAPTER 9

Assuming weather wouldn't be an issue, Ed figured it would take about fifteen hours driving at top speed and with minimum stops to reach Las Vegas if they left Denver no later than six. Even though he was growing weary of traveling, Ed felt like he was prolonging his existence, running from death on his heels, a reality that would catch him once he stopped. It was a childish and foolish game—the last he would play, and one swiftly coming to an end. It took every positive neuron in his brain not to allow the negativity to get the best of him and let Kristen down. She, on the other hand, was the driving force that kept him going emotionally, and he knew that without her, he would fold. He wondered if she had any inkling of what was really going on. At times, he felt like a total phony and a fraud for not being honest with her regarding his health, but he worried that if he told her, then everything would collapse. He thought Kristen was still much too weak and vulnerable to handle a major setback just as she was climbing out of her abyss. The time would come soon enough for reality to strike, but for now, Ed had to pretend to be a rock.

Kristen, not used to getting up in the dark of morning, was somewhat discombobulated as she went through the ritual of getting ready to hit the road. She was uncomplaining, though, knowing it was all on her behalf, with Ed settling for just her company and nothing else, even though she was more than willing, but he was a true gentleman, for which she admired him immensely. She had let him know numerous times, in teasing ways, that he could have her, but to her amazement, Ed dismissed the idea instantly, not even wanting to joke about it. It puzzled her since she had been approached by men Ed's age countless times after pole dancing and lustfully propositioned with offers of serious money. Shaking off the thought, she yawned, and as they approached a McDonald's within view of the interstate, she sleepily said, "We gonna stop for breakfast here before we hit the road?"

"Yes," Ed said as he turned in and drove right up to the menu post and placed the order.

Once on the interstate and a couple of bites into her egg and ham biscuit, along with several cautious sips of steaming coffee, Kristen snapped out of her sleepy stupor and was game for conversation.

"Are you ready for this trip to end?"

"Physically, yes; mentally, no."

"Funny, I feel the same way, and this might sound crazy, but I wish this car was a space capsule and we were traveling through the universe for all eternity, not burdened by physicality," Kristen said wistfully.

Ed took a sip of the coffee and momentarily contemplated Kristen's statement. "You'd miss out on some great life experiences waiting for you."

"Yes, along with the hurt and pain and other human deficiencies," Kristen said thoughtfully.

"It's hard to argue with that, but in your case, all the best now awaits you."

"What makes you so sure?"

"You've already had more than your share of the bad, and it's time for the good."

"So have you, but it still goes on, and that could happen to me as well."

"Not a chance," Ed said firmly, hoping to chase that thought from Kristen's mind. "I see your future being as bright as the summer sun, filled with all that you desire."

"And you at my side?" Kristen asked probingly.

"Hopefully."

"That doesn't sound very reassuring," Kristen said apprehensively.

"I'm not God."

"Please tell me truly, what are you getting out of this?"

"It's my last chance to do something worthwhile in this world; I've wasted so much time. So when you realize your dream, in a small way, that will be my contribution," Ed said faintly, holding his emotion in check with great difficulty.

Kristen was deeply touched and reached over and squeezed Ed's hand. "Yours is a lot more than a small contribution, and I'll make sure the world knows it, and that's a promise."

"Sorry, I didn't mean to sound pitiful."

"You're entitled to a little melancholy; it's not like you've had an overabundance of good things happen in your life," Kristen said tenderly.

"Perhaps not, but one thing is for sure: you coming into my life at this time more than makes up for all the nothing years."

"You have no idea how happy that makes me," Kristen said effusively. "For the first time in my life, someone needs me for something other than sex."

"Life certainly has not been easy for you," Ed said tenderly.

"You're more than making up for it," Kristen said cheerily.

"I truly appreciate you saying that."

"There's a song by Martina McBride that I want you to hear. It's called 'Till I Can Make It on My Own,' and since I haven't practiced it all, we'll listen to her sing it," Kristen said and promptly dialed it up on her cell.

Ed was amazed by the lyrics, which captured the very essence of his and Kristen's collaboration. "If I didn't know better, I would swear someone wrote this specifically for you and me—I'm deeply touched."

"Now do you see what you mean to me?" Kristen said fervently. "We have our song, but this one is strictly from me to you."

"Is there a reason you never sang it?"

"I think deep down, I resented it since there was no such person in my life."

"For whatever its worth, you've totally got me."

"I know you've got the medical issue, but maybe God will intercede and make you well, knowing how much I love and need you. He can't be that cruel and take you from me like he did my dad," Kristen said tearfully.

"That remains to be seen," Ed said faintly, with tears swelling.

"You sound tired and worn," Kristen said with great concern.

"Didn't sleep much," Ed said dismissively, not wanting to alarm Kristen more than she already was by telling her how bad the pain had gotten.

"I'll drive as soon as I finish the egg biscuit."

"Take your time. I'll snap out of it once I have some more of this black witch's brew."

"You're not hungry yet?" Kristen said, eyeing the egg and sausage biscuit in the bag on the console.

"I'll have it in a while," Ed said, even though he had no desire to eat.

"Have you decided where we're going to stay in Las Vegas?"

"No, might be a good idea for you to check out the room availability at the big casinos when you finish eating since New Year's Eve rooms are really hard to get."

"You don't want to stay at a motel or regular hotel?"

"Only if we have to. There's nothing more exciting than spending New Year's Eve at a big Las Vegas casino."

"Won't it be very expensive?"

"Yeah, but what the hell," Ed said freely.

"Are you rich?"

"No, but I want this New Year's Eve to be the best ever for both of us."

"What about the ones with Ann?"

"They were great, but this one will be the very special one," Ed said honestly.

"And you don't mind spending it with me?"

"There's no one I'd rather spend it with."

"Not Alice or someone else you know?" Kristen asked.

"No," Ed said firmly. "I just hope you don't mind spending New Year's Eve with a worn-out old man."

"I will do all I can to make it great and help you feel like a young man."

"I'll try to be one," Ed kidded and handed Kristen his wallet with the credit card. "Say you're my personal secretary and ask for the best suite they have; that way, it'll put them on notice that I might be a big-time gambler, which they give preference to."

"Which casino should I start with, and how many days?"

"Any of the major ones, and make it open ended."

Kristen hurried to polish off her biscuit, then started the reservation process, which turned out to be quite exasperating, with the suites and even rooms in short supply. But luck was onKristen's side when she called the Venetian since someone had just canceled their suite reservation, and Kristen was all over it till she heard the price.

"How much?" she gasped.

Ed smiled and murmured, "It's OK—whatever it costs."

Once finished, Kristen shook her head and exclaimed, "I don't believe it."

"What?"

"One night is more than a month's rent for the apartment we had in New York."

"Yeah, but you probably didn't have room service twenty-four-seven," Ed joked.

"No, but we had roaches," Kristen countered.

"Hope you charged them rent," Ed cracked.

"You gamble?"

"Not seriously."

"Did you ever win?"

"Sometimes. Why?"

"Maybe you should do it to help offset the cost of the suite."

"We'll give it a shot."

"We?" Kristen said with a puzzled look.

"Sure, who knows—you might have beginner's luck."

"I've never gambled."

"That's a plus," Ed kidded.

"Are you trying to go broke?"

"No, just making up for living parsimoniously for the last several years."

Kristen scrunched her face, "You've lost me."

"Sorry, frugally."

"You know, this will be the first time in the last three years that I won't be grinding on the stage, gripping a pole, on New Year's Eve and being pawed," Kristen said disdainfully.

"The last eight New Year Eve's, I got sloshed and fell asleep way before the ball dropped," Ed confessed.

"We have much to make up for, then," Kristen said buoyantly.

"Yes, we do, and we're going to do it up to the hilt," Ed said emphatically.

After nearly sixteen hours of breakneck driving with stops only to refuel, take a bathroom break, and grab snacks to eat along the way, the Las Vegas skyline finally came into view like a giant reddish mushroom top glowing in the cold black night. Ed slowed the SUV down to the posted speed limit, now certain they would make the midnight check-in deadline at the Venetian, where a suite with two queen-size beds awaited them, along with around-the-clock staff to fill their needs. At this point, Ed didn't give a damn what it cost to be treated lavishly. He made up his mind to go out like a blazing star and give Kristen a taste of the good life, so she would know what to expect when she made it big. He smiled, thinking how radically he'd changed his outlook in just a few short days, and it was all because of Kristen. He had prepared himself to leave the world quietly and donate all that he owned to charities, but now that was not about to happen, and much to his surprise, he felt no guilt or regret for the self-indulgence.

CHAPTER 10

Saturday morning, soon as Ed awoke, he got on with the things to be done. With Kristen still soundly asleep, he ambled over to the huge, lavish bathroom and began the morning ritual with the pain in his gut steadily growing. He hurriedly shaved, showered, and dressed, then rushed out to the dresser and retrieved the fifth of Wild Turkey and returned to the bathroom. He sat down on the plush chair by the makeup desk, poured half a glass, and took a double swallow, then reached for the phone and dialed Ted Stevens, his longtime friend and an attorney in Staten Island. He hoped Ted was home and not in Vermont skiing, which he often did on long holidays and some weekends.

"Good morning," Ted answered cheerfully.

"Good morning, it's Ed, and a belated Merry Christmas," Ed said, feeling guilty for not calling before.

"Same to you, and I'm so glad to hear from you, buddy. How you doing?"

"Hanging in there," Ed said boldly.

"How was the trip to Illinois?"

"You won't believe this, but I'm in Vegas."

"You're in Vegas?" Ted said disbelievingly.

"Yeah, got here last night."

"What the hell are you doing there?"

154

"It's a long story, but I'm going to give you the short version so you don't charge me an arm and a leg," Ed said humorously.

"When have I done that?" Ted said defensively.

"Just kidding, anyway, I need you to change my will, effective immediately, and do a few other things."

"What's going on?"

"Well, on my way to Illinois, I picked up a hitchhiker at a gas station in Pennsylvania who was going to Las Vegas, so I drove with her to Moline and decided to drive her there after my stop."

"Ah, a *she* hitchhiker, but go on," Ted said with a dubious tone.

"I felt sorry for her after she told me her story, and there was something that drew me to her," Ed said and was interrupted immediately.

"How old is she, dare I ask?"

"Twenty-two."

"I don't believe it," Ted said incredulously.

"Are you doing her?"

"Are you out of your fucking mind? She's a kid," Ed said in a raised voice.

"So what's the deal?"

"She's one hell of a country singer, and I think she can really make it big, so I'm gonna make it possible for her."

"I don't believe it," Ted said in exasperation.

"Why the hell not?" Ed said forcefully.

"Since when in the hell did you become a country aficionado; you're a lifetime Sinatra guy."

"Still am, but there is something really special about the classic country music, especially the way Kristen sings it. You have to hear her to understand."

"So that's the reason you want to change the will?"

Ed felt slightly edgy, knowing how foolhardy it all must have sounded. "Yes."

"You thought this all out thoroughly?"

"Yes."

"So how much you want to leave her?"

Ed cleared his throat timorously. "Whatever is left after this undertaking."

There was a gasp and a brief silence. "You really serious?"

"I'm as serious as my goddamn cancer," Ed said peevishly.

"What's the motivation? I just don't get it," Ted asked sincerely.

Ed gathered his thoughts momentarily, then said calmly, "When a man faces death, he reflects on his life and what he's done, and as far as I can see, I haven't done one goddamn thing that means anything."

"So how does this girl fit into your contribution to this fucked-up world?" Ted said sarcastically.

"Her singing will be my indirect contribution since I'm making it possible."

"OK, I can see you helping her get started, but I don't get why you're leaving her everything."

"Well, I'm not sure how much there will be left after she gets started, and besides, she's just as worthy as my charity, maybe even more."

"But if she's as good as you think, she'll be a millionaire, and you leaving her what will be left of your worth might be diddly shit."

"I believe she will be big, but maybe not overnight, and if I should suddenly croak, she might need the dough to see it through."

"As your attorney and longtime friend, I have to advise against it," Ted said with true concern.

"It's my dough and my call," Ed said evenly.

"Yeah, it is. Are you planning to come back at all?"

"Yes."

"When?"

"First thing next week—if you've got time to see me."

"Great, it's slow this time of the year, so by all means," Ted said encouragingly.

"I'll catch a flight Monday and see you Tuesday morning at your office if that suits you?"

"I'm wide open," Ted said sprightly. "Listen, I'm having a New Year's party as usual, which you've not been to since Ann died, so why don't you catch an early flight tomorrow and join us?"

"Thanks, but I can't do it for two reasons: I don't want to leave Kristen alone for New Year's Eve, and second, I want to spend this last one here, where it's the greatest."

"So her name is Kristen?"

"Kristen Cole; remember it because she's on her way to big-time fame."

"Country, huh?" Ted said curiously.

"You should hear her."

"Guess I will if she's that good," Ted said deliberately. "So where you staying?"

"The Venetian."

"First class," Ted cracked.

"All the way," Ed quipped.

"Well, my good friend, I wish you the best New Year's Eve ever, and I'll see you Tuesday morning."

"You and Marci have a great one, too, and give her my best," Ed said thoughtfully, then hung up the phone just as Kristen pushed open the door.

"I have to pee."

Ed started to rise from the chair.

"It's OK, you can stay; the commode is enclosed, as you see. Were you on the phone?"

"Yes, with my attorney."

"Anything important?" Kristen asked as she made a beeline for the toilet.

"I'm going to New York Monday to close the old life."

"Am I going, too?"

"I need you to stay here and get us set up in our new domicile."

"Which will be what and when?" Kristen said as she emerged from the toilet and headed for one of the double sinks to wash her hands.

"What's your preference: a furnished condo or a house?"

"A house would be nice; that way, we wouldn't have to put up with loudmouth neighbors and all the crap that goes on. Done that, and it's no fun, especially for you since you've lived in a house most of your life," Kristen said thoughtfully as she dried her hands.

"A very good point. We'll get a hold of a rental agent and have her find us something no later than Monday, and that's why I need you to stay."

"How long will you be gone?"

"Couple of days, and believe me, it's not something I want to do, especially leaving you," Ed said regrettably and with great concern.

"You'll call me?"

"I'll get a cell phone today and call you every hour," Ed kidded.

"Good, I'll teach you how to use it so you don't fail to call me," Kristen said with a perky smile.

"There is one more thing we have to do today."

"What?"

"Get you a driver's license. So with all that's on our plate, we better get a move on."

"We're not going back to bed?" Kristen teased.

"Not this morning or any other," Ed said, shaking his head.

"I didn't mean in the same bed," Kristen countered smartly with a flirtatious grin.

"I'm sure you didn't," Ed said dismissively and rose from the chair.

"I guess I won't have time to take a bath," Kristen said with a nod toward the large, lavish Roman tub.

"You can take one after we get back."

It was nearly five when Ed and Kristen returned to their Rialto Suite, both exhausted but happy with the day's accomplishments. Cell phone for Ed, a temporary driver's license for Kristen, and a meeting with a house rental agent who was able to show them a handful of furnished homes—one less than twenty minutes from the Strip. Ed was most anxious to get the house issue resolved before he left because Kristen seemed somewhat overwhelmed by the whole Las Vegas scene. He suddenly realized that in the few days they'd been together, she had grown overly attached and too dependent on him, and he hoped Morgan would help out in that regard.

"You might want to get hold of Morgan and let her know we're here," Ed suggested as he poured himself half a glass of Wild Turkey, hoping to get some relief.

"I'll do it while I take a bath if you don't mind, unless you've got something else for me to do," Kristen said as she plopped down on her bed and kicked off her boots.

"Enjoy your bath."

"How much time have I got?"

"As long as you want—just don't fall asleep," Ed teased.

"Then you better come in the bathroom with me and be a lifeguard," Kristen teased back.

"Are we starting that again?"

"Yes, because you love it," Kristen said with a knowing grin, "and see how much fun I bring to your life?"

"That you do, my little thrush," Ed said fondly and stepped over to the mini bar and poured himself a substantial drink.

Kristen no longer questioned Ed about the pain and just assumed he was having a bad pain attack when he resorted to the booze. "You mind if I have some while I soak?"

"Help yourself, but just one. We can't mix the singing and the booze."

"No way you have to worry. I would ever jeopardize my singing," Kristen said with certainty and poured only two mouthfuls.

Figuring Kristen would be soaking in a tub for a while and feeling worn, Ed decided to stretch out and considered taking a nap since the pain had kept him up a good part of the night. Even though he told Kristen he would try to figure out how to use the smartphone on his own, he decided to eliminate the certain frustration and wait for her to show him how. He decided this would also be a good time to play some Sinatra music on the portable CD player, which he hadn't listened to at all yet. As he lay in bed immersed in the soothing music, he wished Sinatra was still alive and performing in Las Vegas so that he could take Kristen to see his stage presence and interaction with the audience. He wanted to give Kristen every opportunity to ensure her success in the shortest time possible. With the pleasant thought and feeling mellow, Ed drifted off to sleep, only too soon feeling a tugging on his shirt. Forcing his eyes open, he saw Kristen wrapped in a large bath towel, handing him her cell phone.

"Someone wants to talk to you," she gushed.

Ed propped himself up on one elbow and said wearily, "Who is it?"

"Alice," Kristen mouthed the name and headed back to the bathroom.

"Hi, Alice," Ed said groggily.

"Are you OK?"

"Just a little tired. We had a very busy day. I was actually going to call you in a little while on the cell phone I finally bought . Kristen needs to activate it and show me how to use the damn thing," Ed admitted freely.

"Yes, she just mentioned it. So glad you bought one. Now I won't have to bother Kristen and interrupt her calls."

"I'm sure she didn't mind; otherwise, she wouldn't have answered," Ed assured Alice, sensing she felt bad.

"She also said you were rental hunting?"

"Yes, we saw a couple today and will see more tomorrow."

"I hope you don't mind me asking, but are you planning to live there permanently?"

"Yes, this is where she needs to be to accomplish her goal."

"You must love her extraordinarily to make that kind of commitment."

"She's all I've got."

"So will you be coming back to New York soon like you said?"

"I'm planning to fly back Monday, which I was going to let you know."

"Will I get to see you?"

"If you're still so disposed."

"Why would you think I wouldn't be?" Alice said hurtfully.

"Sorry, I would like very much to see you."

"When?" Alice asked eagerly.

"I'll call you Monday when I get there and we'll decide the time and place."

"So Kristen is definitely not coming?"

"No."

"You don't mind leaving her alone?"

"She won't be; she has a girlfriend from New York who lives here now, and besides, it'll only be for a couple of days."

"I'm very much looking forward to seeing you when I get back to New York as well."

Ed was surprised. "You're still at your sister's?"

"Yes, I thought I had mentioned that when you were here. I'll be leaving late Monday morning. It's a shame we couldn't be on the same flight back."

"You could come here for New Year's Eve—then we could."

"I'd love to, but it would break my sister's heart if I wasn't here for New Year's Eve since it's a kind of family tradition," Alice said. "When my husband was alive, we used to alternate locations."

"I understand, but think about it," Ed said enticingly.

"So what are your plans for New Year's Eve?"

"I'm not sure yet, but it will be grand."

"Let me think about your suggestion and call you back."

"Fair enough, take care."

"Bye," Alice said congenially.

Ed clicked off the phone and stretched out again, thinking about the conversation he'd just had. He suddenly felt a sense of dishonesty that he was leading Alice on a short-lived, hopeless journey. He thought of calling her back just as Kristen emerged from the bathroom in a plush robe, hair wrapped in a towel.

"Conversation over?" Kristen asked.

"Yes," Ed said pensively and sat up.

"Something wrong?"

"My dysfunctional brain," Ed said sarcastically.

Kristen walked up to the side of the bed and sat down next to Ed. "You want to talk about it?"

"Not right now," Ed said dismissively and forced a smile. "Did you soak enough?"

"I could have stayed longer."

Ed glanced at his watch. "Why didn't you?"

"Once I got out to give you the phone, I didn't feel like getting back in, so I've just been doing little things to get ready."

"You should have told Alice I would call her back and not gotten out."

"She sounded like she really needed you."

"I offered to have her come here for New Year's Eve and pay the expenses."

"Is she going to?"

"She'll let me know. Did you talk to Morgan?"

"Yes, she can't believe we're staying at the Venetian and would love to get together for lunch tomorrow."

"OK, let's do it. We'll have lunch here at the Venetian."

"But I thought we were going to look at more rental homes?"

"We'll do it in the morning and meet her here for lunch."

"I'll let her know. Oh, I also checked out the karaoke scene, and they have a slew of them, even one that is strictly country music."

"Great, you feel up to going there tonight?"

"You have to ask?" Kristen said with a grin.

"That's my girl. We'll have dinner at one of the choice restaurants, then do the karaoke bar."

"Which song should I practice?"

"The one that got you the incredible reaction," Ed said without hesitation.

"'Me and Bobby McGee'?"

"Yes."

"How much time have I got?"

Ed glanced at his watch, "Couple of hours."

"Good," Kristen said happily and hopped off the bed.

After a sumptuous dinner at the Black Tap restaurant, one of many at the Venetian, Ed and Kristen took a cab to Gilley's country karaoke bar. Being a Saturday, the place was jammed, and the country-star wannabes were already on stage doing their songs. After listening to a couple while waiting to find a place to sit, Ed had a strange feeling this was going to be Kristen's biggest night yet. There was a passion and fire in her unique voice while she practiced that he had not yet heard. It took nearly twenty minutes before Ed spotted two vacant chairs at a four-person table halfway between the bar and the large stage. With Kristen in tow, he made a beeline for it. Once there, the two young women occupying two of four chairs congenially welcomed Ed and Kristen to join them. After the introductions, they focused their attention back on the stage and the wannabes, some of whom sounded like they'd been at it for a while rather than first-timers who were doing it on a dare or after one too many drinks. While waiting for a waitress, Ed suggested Kristen go see whoever was in charge at the bar and sign up. Minutes later, Kristen returned, shaking her head.

"You're not gonna believe this, but it might be quite a while before I get a chance to sing."

"That's a new one. Well, it'll give you a chance to acclimate and assess the competition," Ed said effusively.

"Your first time here?" one of the two young women at the table said.

"Yes," Kristen answered.

"You a serious singer?"

"Yes."

"Tell you what, I'm doing it for the first time and am scared out of my mind, so when they call my name, I'll let you take my place."

"Thanks, I'll owe you one. What's your name?"

"I'm Debbie, and she's Sandy."

"And I'm Kristen, and that's Ed," Kristen said with a nod.

"The drinks will be on me whenever the damn waitress shows," Ed said, looking around.

"Somebody refer to me disparagingly?" the waitress said humorously as she approached from Ed's blind side.

"My apologies," Ed said with a grin.

"I'm Sissy. What can I get you?"

After everyone order their drinks, they all once again focused on the stage, where the next couple of performers were being drowned out at times by some patrons who were cheering wildly as brave young women attempted to ride the mechanical bull in another part of the bar.

Ed was confident that once Kristen started, she would garner full attention even from the rowdies by the mechanical bull.

"You guys been to the other karaoke bars?" Kristen said when the performer finished.

"Several," Debbie said.

"Are they as rowdy as this place?"

"Nothing like it," Debbie said critically, shaking her head. "Bunch of wild cowboys here."

"Of the one's you've been to, which would you say is the best from the singer's point of view?" Ed asked.

"Money Plays—it's off the Strip."

"If you're strictly into rock, then the Rock Bar is the place," Sandy said.

"You ladies local?" Ed guessed.

"After a year, everybody in Las Vegas is a local, including the illegals," Sandy said with a grin.

"How's this for prompt service?" Sissy said proudly when she reached the table with the four drinks.

After Ed paid the bill and Sissy left, Ed raised his drink in a toast. "Down the hatch and not the nose."

Several performers later, Kristen was starting to feel somewhat discouraged about doing her song because the crowd noise was growing louder by the minute and nearly drowning out every performer on the stage. In some ways, it reminded her of her days as a pole dancer and dealing with the loudmouths and their vulgar comments. She made up her mind, as she did then, that this crowd was not going to get the best of her. With that thought, she took a swig of Ed's drink and decided to take them head-on.

"Our next singer is Miss Debbie Vogel, so let's put our hands together, and I don't mean to pray," the splendidly built middle-aged MC dressed in western attire cracked.

Debbie rose promptly to her feet and hollered, "Kristen here is going to take my place if it's OK."

"Not a problem," the MC said indifferently. "Come on up, Kristen."

Kristen weaved her way between the tables to the large stage.

"I'm on the list but way down," Kristen said to the MC once on the stage.

"I see it: Kristen Cole," the MC said, looking at her clipboard, "and you're doing 'Me and Bobby McGee'?"

"Yes."

"OK," the MC said and turned to the audience. "Listen up! Kristen Cole is taking Debbie's spot and doing 'Me and Bobby McGee.'"

With mic in hand and an open stance, Kristen blasted off into the song, instantly stopping the loud chatter and, just like in Omaha, making her presence known in the most decisive way. Weaving and grinding across the entire stage like a roused tiger, she not only conquered the stage but the rowdies as well, in an indomitable way. When she finished the whooping and applause erupted and continued for several minutes, with all hollering for Kristen to do another song. After catching her breath, she glanced at the MC, who nodded encouragingly and asked what tune to cue up.

"'Help Me Make It through the Night,'" Kristen hollered over the din and promptly combined her soulful words with the music. When she was done, the audience gave her an ovation worthy of a megastar. Many bows later, Kristen returned to the table and was greeted not only by Ed but also a throng of well-wishers eager for autographs and selfies. Several minutes later, Kristen was finally able to take her seat.

"That was awesome," Debbie and Sandy gushed simultaneously.

"Thanks, glad you liked it," Kristen said breathlessly.

"Now all we need is some fresh drinks to celebrate," Ed said, looking around for the waitress, who, to his surprise, was on the way.

"Ready for more drinks?" Sissy said jovially once she reached the table.

"Please," Ed said congenially.

"Let me add my kudos to your incredible performance," Sissy said directly to Kristen. "I've been working here several years and have never seen anything remotely similar to what you did and that kind of audience response."

"Thanks," Kristen said with an appreciative smile.

"You are on your way to the big time," Sissy said and glanced at the four empty glasses. "More of the same?"

"Yes, please," Ed said with a nod, "three of the same and a Coke."

It was approaching eleven thirty, and after many more handshakes and good wishes, Ed suggested to Kristen they call it a night, which she gladly agreed to, especially since the MC announced a thirty-minute break. On their feet and ready to leave, they were halted by the MC.

"So glad I caught you before you left," the MC said to Kristen. "By the way, I'm Madge. I've been doing this for nearly fifteen years and have never seen such a performance and response from the crowd. You're the best I've ever seen here."

"Thanks," Kristen said appreciatively.

Madge glanced over to Ed. "I assume you're her granddad and/or manager?"

"More or less," Ed acknowledged with a nod and a grin.

"I think Kristen is incredibly talented and can make it big with a first-rate manager if that's your plan."

"Most definitely," Ed said eagerly.

"I keep an eye out for exceptional talent as a favor for a good friend of mine who's in the music business. Over the years, he's developed a number of big-time country singers. His name is Sid Greene, and I'll gladly put you in touch with him."

"Thanks, that'd be great," Ed said happily.

Madge pulled out a business card from her pocket and handed it to Ed. "This is Sid's card. He's in Vail, Colorado, for the holidays and will be back Monday. I'll most likely speak to him tomorrow and give him heads-up about Kristen. Then when you call, he'll know who you are and take the call. Oh, and for your information, Sid just concluded his contract with a too-big-for-her-thong bitch and is looking for a new young face."

"Thanks so much," Kristen said jubilantly and hugged Madge.

"Can I buy you a drink before we leave?" Ed said gladly.

"You can do it next time you're here with this sure-to-be country megastar," Madge said with a wink and started back to the stage.

CHAPTER 11

I t was nearing noon when Ed and Kristen viewed the last rental house, which, like the others, Ed had nixed; he then asked the agent to take them back for a second look at the house they saw the day before. It was twenty minutes from the Strip, which Ed thought was a plus, and had been totally renovated and was also furnished. The one feature that Kristen went bonkers over was the sparkling pool in the backyard. The entire property was shielded with a six-foot-high wall, which Ed considered a great plus, anticipating Kristen's celebrity status and need of privacy. Ed and the rental agent were at the front door ready to leave, but they had to wait as Kristen dashed from room to room like a ten-year-old, loving the spaciousness of the house after living in a cramped three-room apartment. When she finished, she raced over to Ed and mightily hugged him.

"I guess you approve," Ed said with a grin.

"I just love it, and can't believe I'm gonna live in it," Kristen said exuberantly.

Ed anticipated the rental agent's possible wonderment and promptly said, "Your mother did the best she could."

"I assume you want it," the agent guessed with a grin.

"Yes, yes," Kristen blurted before Ed could answer.

"Can you have the lease ready for signature by this afternoon?" Ed said sprightly.

"Not a problem—the owner is anxious to rent," the agent said and pushed open the front door just as Kristen's cell phone chimed.

"It's Alice," Kristen said, viewing the phone and handing it to Ed as they proceeded to the car.

"Yes or no?" Ed asked curiously.

"Sorry for not calling you sooner, but my sister had a mishap with a knife this morning and cut her hand severely. We had to rush her to the emergency room—she needed twenty stitches."

"I'm truly sorry to hear that; please give my best regards," Ed said thoughtfully.

"Just so you know, I was leaning toward coming to Las Vegas, but in view of what's happened, I just can't," Alice said with an extended sigh.

"I understand, and I don't blame you a bit," Ed said congenially. "Listen, we're with the rental agent right now and about to get in the car; let me call you back in a couple of hours."

"I'll be looking forward to it. Bye," Alice said warmly.

Morgan, in skintight blue jeans and a hot-pink sweater that emphasized her abundant breasts, was waiting by the hostess stand at the Venetian Burger & Brew sandwich shop when Ed and Kristen got there.

"Hope you haven't been waiting long," Kristen called out as she rushed over and hugged Morgan.

"About two years," Morgan cracked and, once released, looked over curiously to Ed.

"Morgan, this is Ed, my guardian angel," Kristen said affectionately.

"So nice to meet you at last. Kristen has bragged so much about you," Morgan said gladly and extended her hand.

Ed couldn't believe Morgan was only three years older than Kristen; had he not known, he would have guessed she was thirtysomething rather than twenty-five. It also seemed to Ed that her bodacious body perfectly matched her pert, roundish face.

"I'm glad to meet you as well, and don't believe half of what Kristen told you; I'm no angel," Ed said with a grin.

"Which do you prefer, table or booth?" the hostess said to Ed, menus in hand.

"Booth would be good."

"I can't believe you guys are staying in this fabulous place," Morgan said once they were seated.

"You should see our suite," Kristen bragged.

"I'd love to."

Kristen looked over to Ed at her side. "Do you mind?"

"Take her up after lunch; I've got some things to take care of," Ed said most agreeably.

"Are you some kind of millionaire?" Morgan said to Ed.

"No, just a spendthrift," Ed kidded.

"Kristen, my good friend, you have really lucked out. I'm so very happy for you."

"Maybe some of my luck will rub off on you," Kristen said encouragingly, sensing her friend needed a boost.

"I sure could use it," Morgan said dispiritedly.

Even though Morgan came across as somewhat tough, Ed felt there was a certain goodness about her and said encouragingly, "Who knows? The new year may have something good in store for you as well."

"It'll be the first," Morgan said dismissively. "So did you guys find a house?"

"Yes, about twenty minutes from here," Kristen said cheerfully. "It's like new—fully furnished, and it has a swimming pool."

"Awesome! When you moving in?"

"Hopefully Monday," Kristen said, looking over to Ed for confirmation.

"I'm signing the lease this afternoon."

"You intend to stay in Vegas permanently or just till Kristen gets off the ground?"

"Permanently," Ed said without hesitation.

"I'm very happy for you guys; I think you'll love it here."

"Here comes the waitress. Guess we better look at the menus," Ed said, reaching for one in the middle of the table.

"Hi, I'm Mimi. Are you guys ready to order?"

"Give us a sec," Ed said and motioned for Kristen and Morgan to look at the menus.

Once everyone ordered and the waitress left, the conversation resumed, with Morgan asking Kristen about her potential singing career. Ed was pleased with Kristen's enthusiasm and absolute commitment, which were buoyed by her previous night's success at Gilley's. He also noticed a certain sadness in Morgan's face, even though she did her best to conceal it and instead shared in Kristen's happiness. Now that he'd met her, Ed was even more inclined to help her, regardless of her dubious life. He felt that under her tough facade was a remnant of a little girl who, through no fault of her own, was forced into adulthood way before her time. Seeing the two of them get along so grandly also eased his mind about taking the trip.

Nearly an hour later, Ed suggested they better leave since there were several people by the hostess stand waiting to be seated.

"Ladies, I enjoyed your company immensely and look forward to doing this soon again."

"Thank you for a wonderful lunch," Morgan said with an appreciative smile, "and yes,

I would love to join you again."

"You're including me, I hope," Kristen joked.

Once outside the restaurant, they paused, and Ed extended his hand to Morgan. "It was nice to have met you, and I hope to see more of you when I get back from New York. I would appreciate very much if you watched out for Kristen while I'm gone. Perhaps you might even stay at the house."

"I'd be happy to," Morgan said eagerly with a glad smile.

"Kristen, why don't you take Morgan up to the suite now; I should be done in a couple of hours, so it'll give you time to get caught up."

"Sounds great," Kristen said and hugged Ed.

"Morgan, since I might not see you when I get back, I wish you a very happy New Year and good things in the coming year.

"I wish you one, too, and have a safe trip," Morgan said most congenially and, surprisingly, hugged Ed.

It was nearly four thirty when Ed returned and found Kristen curled up, sound asleep, near the end of her bed, looking very much at peace. Not wanting to wake her, he quietly walked over and placed the Barney's box at her side then poured a drink and sat down in the plush chair facing Kristen. Many thoughts rushed through his head as he sipped the drink, but the most prominent was that he hoped to live long enough to see Kristen well on her way with the singing career. Engrossed deeply in his thoughts and gazing out the window, he was startled when Kristen suddenly awoke and called out

"Been back long?"

"Just few minutes," Ed replied readily and motioned to the box.

"For me?" Kristen asked excitedly.

"Go ahead and open it."

Kristen sat up, removed the top of the box, and gasped. "It's beautiful. You bought it for me?"

"Who else?" Ed said with a smile.

Kristen pulled out the dress, hopped off the bed, and pressed the emerald designer dress against her. "It's perfect. How'd you know my size, and what's this for?"

"After forty years on Madison Avenue and dealing with models, I developed a pretty good eye for women's sizes. And as to why: I can't have you looking less than gorgeous on New Year's Eve."

"You got a reservation?" Kristen said disbelievingly.

"Yes, at the Stratosphere."

"How in the world did you manage that with all the hot spots booked for months?" Kristen said in wonderment.

"You'd be amazed what a few C-notes in the right hands will do."

"You bribed someone to get us in?"

"It's the Vegas way," Ed said with a grin.

Kristen, clutching the dress, dashed over to Ed and kissed him on the lips. "I know, I know—you don't want me to do that, but that's the very least way I can show my appreciation."

"I'll forgive you this time," Ed kidded.

"Should I try it on?"

"Might be wise just in case I've lost my eye for women sizes," Ed said with a grin.

Moments later, Kristen walked out of the bathroom looking even better than Ed had envisioned when he bought the very expensive dress.

"Stunning," Ed exclaimed.

"And a perfect fit," Kristen said glowingly as she slowly turned for Ed to have a full view.

"No one will outshine you tonight," Ed said happily.

"You really think so?"

"Without a doubt."

"Wish Morgan could see me," Kristen said as she whirled.

"Let's take a picture with the cell and send it to her," Ed said thoughtfully.

Moment later, Ed snapped a couple of pictures, which Kristen promptly sent; almost instantly, she received Morgan's text.

"You know what Morgan said?"

"You look gorgeous."

"Yes, and that you are an incredible man."

"That's very nice of her to say."

"I think she's got a thing for you," Kristen teased.

"And I think you need to soak in the tub and scrub your brain," Ed said, shaking his head.

"OK, OK, I know when I'm being admonished. How long can I soak?"

"Not too long. I made you a reservation at Raffino's for six."

"Seriously?" Kristen said with mouth aghast. "The beauty salon where the very affluent go?"

"Want you looking like a megastar."

"That's a little premature."

"Not at all—you are on your way, and nothing is going to stop you."

"You're just biased."

"I speak the truth."

"You're overwhelming me," Kristen said, starry-eyed.

"So happy to hear it. Now off with you to the tub, and don't fall asleep."

"And what are you going to do?"

"Think I'll take a nap since it's going to be one hell of a long, incredible night."

"Good idea, get your rest, cause I'll expect you to dance me off my feet," Kristen teased.

"Maybe just a swirl or two," Ed said evasively.

"I'll settle for that," Kristen said happily and rushed off.

Ed wasn't sorry at all for laying out nearly a grand for the last-minute reservation at the Stratosphere; the Top of the World restaurant, famous for its five-course gourmet dining and incredible view of Las Vegas from a hundred eight stories high, was exquisite. It was filled with well-heeled celebrants, including many celebrities. The females dressed to kill, but no one was more stunning than Kristen, Ed thought. Down below on the Strip was a giant block party in full swing, being celebrated by more than three hundred thousand so-called "close friends" well on their way to getting sloshed. For those wanting to dance, there were several live bands alternately shown on the gigantic LED screen, which, at midnight, would show close-ups of the world famous fireworks spectacular. New Year's Eve was the one time when all the casinos worked conjointly to wow the visitors and the locals.

Kristen, looking no less than a movie star, caught everybody's eye, greatly helped by Ed, who'd arranged for one of the house photographers to take countless photos of her throughout the night. Several of the tipsy celebrants, thinking Kristen was, in fact, a celebrity, came up to her and asked for her autograph, which she hesitantly signed. Ed considered the night not only a New Year's Eve celebration but also Kristen's coming-out party. He wanted to make this night one she would never forget and set no limit on how much she drank, short of wipeout.

Just before midnight, the champagne glasses were filled; noisemakers, horns, and streamers passed, and the lights dimmed for the big moment. With fifteen seconds to go, Las Vegas grew dark, and the count began in the hotels and out on the Strip. Kristen, feeling mellow and quite amorous, thought this was the perfect time to plant a full-mouth kiss on Ed's lips and didn't care what anyone thought. Much to her surprise, Ed for once did not object, and she thought he actually enjoyed the fervid kiss; had they not been interrupted by the well-wishers next to them, Kristen would have kissed him again.

The view from the Stratosphere tower of the Grucci fireworks extravaganza at the stroke of midnight was breathtaking and something nowhere else to been seen. The oohs and ahs were overwhelming with each new volley as they burst with colors more vibrant than the ones before. Kristen, very much like a little girl, clung to Ed's arm at times and jumped with joy, much to his amusement. He felt doubly glad for spending the money for this once-in-a-lifetime special evening. Finally, with the fireworks concluded and spectators catching their breath,

Ed decided it was an opportune time to leave. He had danced with Kristen just as he promised, and nothing further would be gained by staying. Kristen had garnered more than her share of attention, and anything subsequent would be detrimental to her image since she was approaching her alcohol limit.

When they were finally back at the Venetian after a painfully slow cab ride through side streets filled with half-stewed celebrants, Ed sensed Kristen was more clear-headed than he thought and not quite ready to call it a night, so he decided to let her do a little gambling. It was also to give her more exposure and attention and let people wonder who the young beauty was. The casino was jammed, and just like at the Stratosphere, Kristen caught more than her share of admiring and wanton looks. She was thrilled when Ed told her to choose a game, which, much to his surprise, was blackjack. She told him she used to play it with the girls at the skin bar between pole dances to pass the time.

The blackjack tables were all jammed, but when Kristen approached, magically, room was made for her to sit with the mostly male players already seated. Before she sat down, Ed discreetly placed twenty hundred-dollar bills in her hand to buy the chips and told her to have fun and not worry if she lost. After losing the first few hands, Kristen's luck suddenly changed, and she got on a big-time winning streak, with the players and the spectators cheering her on with each winning hand. Ed wasn't a hundred percent certain, but he suspected someone in management might have signaled the very dexterous female card dealer to help Kristen win. It was done by the casinos all the time for publicity and goodwill, and this being New Year's Eve, it was a perfect time to do it.

An hour later, with her luck starting to change, Kristen wisely called it quits, greatly disappointing her vocal male supporters. She had won nearly five grand and was about to burst with joy; it was the most she had ever possessed. After tipping the card dealer, she handed the winning chips directly to Ed to cash in. Even though it was nearly two thirty, you couldn't tell it by the crowd. The celebration was still going strong, and the gambling in the casino was smoking hot. It would continue well into daybreak for those who were able to shut off their body clocks.

CHAPTER 12

Monday, New Year's Day, things were back to normal for the casinos, and most locals took it as just another day. For Ed and Kristen, it was a busy day—checking out of the Venetian and moving into the rental house, which they were both happy to do after living in motels and hotels for nearly two weeks. The other major thing that they suddenly realized needed to be done a shopping trip for food and kitchen essentials, which Ed viewed as a nuisance but Kristen saw as a great joy. This was the first house she was going to live in since having run away from home, and she was really looking forward to it.

With drink in hand while sitting at the kitchen table, Ed was amused as he watched Kristen stock the refrigerator and the cabinets with all kinds of foodstuffs with great joy, like a little girl playing house.

"Are you having fun?" Ed said with a grin when Kristen turned from the cabinet.

"I love it, and I love this house—so glad we moved in before you left."

"I'll be gone two days, so have a ball."

"Will that give you enough time to take care of all you have to get done?"

"It'll have to do since I've got to be back in time for

our meeting with Sid on Friday and need a day to prep you for it.

"What do you think of Sid after talking to him?"

"He definitely knows the entertainment business inside out, but we'll find out more when we see him."

"Did Madge tell him much about me?"

"He said she told him you're the best she's ever seen."

Kristen scrunched her face. "Hope I can live up to that."

"You'll be fine. Just focus on that star you're reaching for and nothing else."

"You're not going to quit looking after me if Sid takes me on, right?" Kristen said tentatively.

"I'll be there for you; please don't fret."

"Forever?" Kristen said in a puerile tone.

"That, my precious, I can't promise," Ed said and took a swig of his drink.

"Is there something you're not telling me?" Kristen said with concern.

"You know I'm dealing with this damned pain, which is getting worse by the day."

"Yes, but I just have this uneasy feeling there's a lot more to it than you're telling me."

"I've already told you all about it," Ed said dismissively.

Kristen shook her head deliberately and leaned against the counter. "While you're gone, I'm gonna find out who's the best doctor in Las Vegas, and we'll go see him when you're back. I'll pay for the visit, now that I've got some money from the gambling."

"That's very sweet, but I'm going to see my doctor on Staten Island while I'm there, and speaking of your money, first thing tomorrow morning when the banks open, get an account and deposit it. I hate to even think about all that cash in the house with me not here."

"I'll stash it somewhere before you leave."

"Hide it in the back of the freezer," Ed said half seriously.

"You're so smart—see why you can't ever leave me? I'd be lost."

"So what's the deal with Morgan? Will she be able to stay with you?"

"Yep, starting tonight. She's taking a couple of days off and is going to help with the house. Besides the food and kitchen stuff, we still need all kinds of other things."

"I'm very relieved she'll be staying with you; I hated the idea of you spending the nights all alone," Ed said gladly. "I owe her."

"Are you going to see Alice?" Kristen said with slight jealousy in her voice.

"You don't want me to?"

"I just wondered."

"We made a tentative date for tomorrow evening."

"Taking her to a fancy restaurant?"

"No, she wants to make dinner at home."

"Sounds to me like she's got more in mind than just a dinner," Kristen said with raised eyebrows.

"She's too much of a lady to have such an iniquitous motive."

Kristen shrugged. "A what?"

"Immoral."

"Well, just the same, be prepared," Kristen warned.

"I think your imagination is running wild, and besides, I wouldn't cheat on you," Ed said with a straight face but holding back the urge to grin.

"You mean that?"

"Absolutely, I'm a one-woman man."

"If you're serious, then I'm honored, even though we've never made love," Kristen said fervidly.

"I'm waiting for you to get older," Ed said, tongue-in-cheek.

"Yeah, right," Kristen said skeptically.

Ed was relieved when his cell phone on the table buzzed, saving him from flirtatious conversation.

"Hi, are you home?" Alice asked.

"Yes, Kristen and I were just talking about you."

"Nothing bad, I hope," Alice said genially.

"Definitely good," Ed said firmly.

"I'm glad. So did you move into the house?"

"Yes, Kristen is the process of putting all the food away."

"Are you helping?"

"No, she insists on doing it without my help."

"Were you able to get a flight?"

"I managed to get one that gets me to La Guardia rather late."

"That's too bad; otherwise, I could have picked you up, and you could have spent the night at my house. It would have given us more time together, but I don't feel comfortable driving to the airport that late."

"I wouldn't want you to."

"Will you be renting a car?"

"Really haven't made up my mind. I just might settle for the cabs and avoid the city-driving aggravation."

"That's true, but it'll get expensive."

"Renting a car isn't cheap."

"A valid point—has Kristen spent any of her winnings yet?"

"Not so far. I suggested she put it all in the bank tomorrow."

"Oh, that's right. Today is a legal holiday, so the banks are closed."

"How's the weather there?"

"Actually, not bad—thank God, no snow," Alice said happily.

"Yeah, I'm good on the snow for a while, too," Ed joked.

"Yes, you two had quite a snow adventure," Alice said with a chuckle. "Oh, before I forget, did you and Kristen get together with the music agent?"

"No, I spoke to him on the phone; we're meeting Friday."

"Kristen must be thrilled."

"Yes, she is, and also a little nervous, especially after we found out yesterday that he's handled some of the biggest country stars in the business."

"Well, I'm no expert in country music, but after hearing her sing, I have no doubt she's on her way to becoming a huge country star."

"It won't be for lack of determination," Ed said laudably.

"Has the pain eased up today?" Alice said deliberately.

Ed was surprised by the question since he hadn't mentioned it when he spoke to Alice the day before. Actually, he really never told her much about his medical condition at all. "Yes, how'd you know?"

"Kristen mentioned it when I spoke to her yesterday while you had gone to get something from the car."

"That little snitch—I'll have to ground her," Ed said humorously and winked at Kristen as she suddenly turned with a surprised look on her face.

"Don't be hard on her; she loves so you very much

and is concerned," Alice said kindly.

"What else did she tell you?" Ed said playfully.

"What an incredible person you are and how you take care of her."

"She's exaggerating."

"Not from what I saw," Alice said admiringly.

"I appreciate your overstated praise."

"Not at all, and before I forget, would you mind taking some pictures of the house? I'd love to see it."

"I'd be happy to."

"Oh, and by all means, please don't forget the pictures of Kristen from New Year's Eve."

"Glad you reminded me. We got them hand-delivered just a little bit ago."

"So what's your schedule for tomorrow?"

"A meeting with my fried and attorney Ted on Staten Island, which might take some time since we've got lot of ground to cover."

"After that, are you coming straight to my house?"

"As fast as I can."

"Good, I can't wait to see you." Alice paused and drew a deep breath. "Would you like to spend the night?"

"You sure about that?" Ed asked, totally surprised.

"I'd be thrilled," Alice said with great relief, having dreaded to ask.

"I'll give you a call before I head your way, just in case you changed your mind," Ed kidded.

"Don't you even think that in jest, and you really don't have to call."

"Well, then, I'll see you tomorrow, and please don't go overboard on my account."

"Till tomorrow. Bye."

Kristen placed the box of cereal in the cabinet and,

with a large grin, made a beeline for Ed.

"I hope you didn't mind me staying and listening to your conversation."

"I have no secrets from you," Ed said and, with his foot, pushed a chair for Kristen to sit.

"Well, maybe I stopped you from having a sexy conversation," Kristen teased as she plopped down in the chair.

"Don't you know us older people don't have such conversations," Ed said with a smile.

"That's not what I saw at the skin joint; the older guys made just as many lewd comments as the young ones, maybe even more."

"Don't think I'm sticking up for them, but just so you know, the mind doesn't age the same way the body does."

"Well, if that's the case, do you ever think of me in a sexual way?" Kristen said forthrightly. "And be honest."

"You're really asking way too much," Ed said firmly.

"Didn't you tell me way back when that we could talk openly about any subject?"

"Yes, I did, and I should have known better," Ed grumbled, shaking his head.

"So are we?"

"Not at this time," Ed said firmly.

Kristen sensed she was pushing Ed too hard and wisely backed off. "OK, OK, I'll get back to what I was doing, but before I do, can I have a sip of your drink?"

"You're turning into a little boozehound," Ed said congenially and handed her the drink.

"Not to worry—I've been doing this for a while and know when to stop, thanks to Mom," Kristen said resolutely.

"Just as long as it doesn't impede your singing," Ed

said seriously.

"Whew, I was afraid you were going to ask me to stop," Kristen said and mockingly wiped her brow. "And be assured, there is nothing I would ever allow to jeopardize my singing."

"I'm glad to hear that, and by the way, have you given any more thought to the song you were writing?"

"I'm trying hard, but I just can't get the words to mesh perfectly."

"Can I help? I have some experience in meshing words."

"Wish you could, but it's about you, and it has to come from me alone."

Ed was really curious. "Can you at least tell me the title?"

"I don't know," Kristen equivocated. Then she reluctantly acceded, "It's called 'You Were There for Me.'"

Ed was sincerely moved. "I'm touched and honored, and if by chance you can't finish it, just having you tell me that is the greatest gift you could ever give me."

"You really think it's all gonna happen that soon?"

"Yes, and you've got to believe and act that way," Ed asserted.

"It's such a long leap for someone unknown and with no musical experience other than karaoke."

"You have a natural gift, which is worth more than any amount of musical background, and when Sid signs you on, you'll be on your way to reaching stardom. With his knowledge of the country music business, it'll be a cinch," Ed said to reinforce Kristen's confidence.

"But what about the 'pay your dues' thing?"

"Only losers pay the dues; you're a winner, and you're going to the top like a rocket."

Kristen dashed to Ed with open arms and face aglow.

"You really do believe that."

Ed rose from the chair and hugged her. "With my heart and soul."

"I love you so much," Kristen affirmed and kissed Ed on the cheeks repeatedly.

"I love you, too, in a most special way, and always remember that no matter where or how far I am, in spirit, I'm right with you in that heart on the chain.

"That sounds ominous."

"I didn't mean it to," Ed prevaricated, knowing how critical this time was for Kristen to believe in herself.

"So what would like me to fix for dinner?"

"Whatever is easiest for you and not extravagant since my flight leaves at six forty."

"You'll probably find it hard to believe, but I'm a pretty good cook—had to be since money was scarce when I lived with that crud."

"When I get back you can fix a chef's meal."

"It's a deal, but I'll expect you to eat it all, not like you've been doing."

"I'll give it my best shot," Ed said with a grin.

"You better do more than that," Kristen playfully warned.

"C'mon, I'll give you a hand putting the stuff away."

"Why don't you just sit and finish your drink?"

"I need to get on my feet for a little while since I'll be on my duff when flying tonight."

"How many hours is it?"

"About four and some change, depending on the headwinds."

"I'm really going to miss you," Kristen said tenderly. "We've been nonstop together for almost two weeks."

"I'll miss you, too, my little thrush."

"You're not tired of me yet?" Kristen said uneasily.

"How can you even think that?"

"I just want to make sure that I don't annoy you."

"You're my absolute joy, and I get such a kick out of everything you do, especially when you tease."

"I was afraid that you might not like it, but I didn't want to say anything."

"I'll let you know when you do, and in turn, you do the same."

Kristen giggled. "We sound like a married couple."

"Yeah, we do."

"Do you mind if I ask you a kind of personal question?"

"Shoot."

"Have you not dated since your wife died?"

"Why do you ask?"

"Because you are still a very attractive man—like Cary Grant when he was your age—and I'm sure you caught the eye of many women, just as you did with Alice."

"Cary Grant, that's really a far stretch," Ed said, shaking his head, "but since Ann died, I've been pretty much an anchorite."

"A what?" Kristen said with a puzzled look.

"A recluse."

"I find it hard to believe, especially since you worked in advertising all those years and no doubt interacted with hundreds of beautiful women."

"I guess I'm just a one-woman man, like I said," Ed said wittingly.

"Until now," Kristen teased.

"Yes," Ed said in jest.

"Did you not see all the looks you got New Year's Eve from some of those gorgeous women?"

"I think they were looking at you with jealous eyes."

"I'm not really beautiful," Kristen said self-critically. "They were looking at the gown."

"You are more than you think," Ed said decisively, "and it doesn't matter what you wear, including blue jeans and a sweatshirt, which doesn't diminish your beauty."

"You're just prejudiced."

"I have a huge request."

"I'll do anything you ask."

"End all your self-doubts by the time I get back," Ed said congenially. "I know you can do it when you make up your mind."

"I'll try," Kristen said affirmatively.

"Good, I'll drink to that," Ed said with a grin and took a swig of the Wild Turkey, then, without thinking, handed the drink to Kristen.

CHAPTER 13

Ted Stevens met Ed at the door since the office was officially closed for another day and the secretary had the day off.

"Great to see you," Ted said vociferously with an extended hand and then a hug.

"Likewise," Ed replied with equal vigor as he shook Ted's hand.

"Have a good flight?"

"Bumpy as hell."

"They usually are this time of year," Ted said as he guided Ed through the reception office into his, then motioned to one of the two red leather high-back chairs in front of the massive desk.

"Been a while since I've flown, and I forgot that's part of the deal," Ed said as he settled in the chair.

"When'd you get in?"

"Landed about midnight at La Guardia. Got to the house just before two."

"You must be exhausted as hell. We could have met a little later."

"Not too bad," Ed said dismissively. "I've never slept more than five or six hours max."

"I've got coffee brewing," Ted said and motioned to the coffeepot on the credenza.

"Never turned down a drink or a cup of joe," Ed said with a grin.

"So tell me about this girl who's turned your life upside down."

"Like I told you on the phone, I met her at a gas station in Pennsylvania; she was hitching a ride. It was a miserable night, with ice and snow, and it didn't look like she was going to have any luck going any farther, so I offered to drive her to the nearby motel. To make the story short, they only had one room left, so I couldn't let her sleep in the freezing car, which she wanted to do, so I asked if she wanted to stay in my room since there were two beds."

Ted shook his head. "That's how all this got started?"

"Yeah," Ed said with a nod.

"How old is she again?" Ted said with a querying face.

"Twenty-two."

"So how in the hell did she talk you into driving her to Las Vegas?"

"She didn't. I wanted to for two reasons: I felt sorry for her after she told me her sad story, especially with it being Christmas and all, and second, I thought she had a great voice and the potential to be country star. I'm giving her that chance, and what better place than Las Vegas, the center of world entertainment?"

"Did you accomplish what you wanted in your hometown?"

"Yeah," Ed said dismissively.

"Does she have any experience as a country singer?"

"No, it was strictly my idea."

"You're kidding?" Ted said disbelievingly.

"I'm dead serious."

"How in the hell did you conclude that she could be a star?"

"Listening to her sing," Ed said with a quizzical look.

"Don't take this personally, but what the hell do you know about country music?"

"Squat, but that's not the issue; it's all about her voice and style."

"Has she done any public singing at all?"

"Some," Ed fibbed, not wanting to look like a total fool. "She also did several karaoke gigs on the way to Vegas and received an unbelievable audience response at each place."

"I don't know much about karaoke, but isn't that like pretend singing?"

"It's for real; you get the music and provide your voice, which she does audaciously."

"And that's it?"

"Yeah, wherever she sang she knocked them dead, including the biggest hot spot in Omaha. They had national competition there last year, and they wanted her to stay longer and do several paid performances," Ed said boldly. "She blew the audiences away, not only with her voice but her stage presence, which is not dissimilar from Elvis and Tina Turner combined."

"But she's had no professional voice training?"

"No, she's a natural, and with a good country music manager, she'll make it big."

"You really believe that?" Ted said with raised eyebrows.

"Yeah, a hundred ten percent," Ed said unequivocally.

"Where's she from?"

"For the last five years she's lived in New York, but originally Albany."

"Aside from the minor singing experience, a New York girl becoming a country singer—somehow it's hard to grasp," Ted said with a skewed look as he rose from the chair and headed for the coffee pot."

"They all don't come from Nashville, you know," Ed said dismissively.

"So you're into country music now after a lifetime of Sinatra?" Ted said with a smirk.

"Only the classy stuff, which is what she sings, and not the redneck shit."

"Just don't see you as country man," Ted said wryly as he poured the coffee.

"I'm expanding my field of music appreciation," Ed said with a grin.

"Well, OK. What would you like in your coffee?"

"Black will do."

"And you're willing to spend all your dough on her?" Ted said as he headed back with two steaming mugs.

"Every dime if that's what it takes," Ed said firmly as he took the mug.

"You're not serious?" Ted said, shaking his head as he eased into the chair.

"Serious as my goddamned cancer," Ed said briskly.

"So you want me to change the will to what?"

"Make her the beneficiary of all I'm worth," Ed said firmly and blew into the steaming coffee before taking a sip.

"Are you really sure about this?" Ted groused.

"Like I said before, when a man faces death, he wants to know if he's leaving anything worth a damn," Ed said reflectively. "Kristen's music will be my contribution."

Ted shrugged. "I don't know what to say."

"Just change the will and accept it," Ed said simply.

"OK, if that's what you want," Ted said with finality.

"You may not believe this, but in less than two weeks,

this girl has brought more joy to my life than I can tell you."

"And you're not banging her," Ted said skeptically.

"I told you no before," Ed said peevishly.

"Well, looks like you've made up your mind, so I won't try to dissuade you," he said.

"Don't get me wrong—I do appreciate your concern as a really caring friend. You've been there for me at the most critical times in my life, but this is something I want to do."

"I'll do the will exactly as you want," Ted affirmed and took a slug of coffee.

"She's young and may be given bad advice or tempted to spend the money foolishly, so I would like you to be her guardian and make sure that doesn't happen."

"I'd be glad to do that."

"Thanks."

"So how long you going to be in town?"

"Flying out late Wednesday afternoon."

"I assume you'll be selling the house?"

"Yeah, I'll need a realtor."

"S. I. Realty, which I do business with, has an office on the ground floor in this building; if you want, I'll get you an agent I've been using."

"That'd be great. What's the real estate market like right now?"

"Houses in your neighborhood sell very quickly."

"The sooner the better," Ed said emphatically.

Ted was reluctant to ask the next question and cleared his throat a couple of times. "How much time have you got?"

"About four months if I'm lucky," Ed said straight out.

"Are you in pain?"

"Yeah, I'm controlling it with the booze as long as I can, but it won't be much longer before I have to use the fentanyl."

Ted shook his head and said, "I'm truly sorry."

"Who knows? I may die of cirrhosis instead of cancer," Ed joked sarcastically.

Ted drew a deep breath. "Does Kristen know?"

"I'm trying to hold off telling her as long as I can since I don't know if she'll be able to handle it and go through with her singing."

"And what's the game plan for that?"

"We're meeting with a top country music manager Friday."

"Any idea how much dough you will need upfront?"

"I'll find out Friday."

"I wish you luck, and I truly mean that."

"Thanks. I'll need it since time is of the essence."

"Let me give the realtor a jingle and have her come up if that's agreeable," Ted said and reached for the phone on the desk.

"That'd be great. So how the kids doing?"

"Thought I mentioned it when you were here last— Jason is in Boston with an investment bank, and Dawn is in Hollywood trying to get in the flicks."

Ed chuckled. "If it all works out, you might be dealing with two showbiz kids."

"Wouldn't that be a kick," Ted said humorously, "an actress and a country singer."

Ed suddenly winced in pain and grabbed his gut. "Goddamn."

Ted snatched Ed's mug and set it on the desk.

Ed took several deep breaths and wiped his brow. "You have any booze?"

"Yeah," Ted blurted, then made a beeline for the credenza behind the conference table. "Got Jack Daniels and Johnnie Walker; which do you prefer?"

"Jack Daniels will do."

Ted returned with the bottle and a glass, which he filled halfway and handed to Ed. "Hope it helps."

Ed nodded and took a long swig, then once again wiped his brow.

"So this is what it's like," Ted said sympathetically.

"Yeah, except this one was a real fucking doozy. Never had one this bad."

"You have the pain pills with you?"

Ed shook his head. "No."

"You want to call the doc and have him call in a prescription?"

"I'm planning to see him while I'm here."

"Good idea since he doesn't know about your move to Vegas."

"Listen, I need you to do me another favor. Can you arrange for the Salvation Army to get all the stuff in the house?"

"You're not taking anything to Vegas?"

"Probably a couple of paintings—the house I rented is fully furnished, and I really don't want any reminders of the past."

"I'll handle it."

"I've got a whole bunch of tools, electronics, and other stuff; you might want to take a look and see if you can use it before Salvation Army gets it."

"Thanks, I'll do that."

"Is there anything more you need from me?"

"Can't think of a thing right now," Ed said with a shrug.

"You up to seeing the realtor?" Ted said with concern.

"Yeah."

After wrapping up the business affairs and having lunch with Ted and the real estate agent, Ed took a taxi to Alice's house, still not sure if he should tell her of his circumstances. For now, he was grateful the pain had eased and he was able to think clearly. Just before he got to the door, he glanced up at the darkening sky and shook his head, wondering what the forecast was. He rang the doorbell and waited a moment for Alice to answer.

"So sorry—I was on the phone with my sister," Alice said breathlessly.

"She doing OK?"

"Yes—healing nicely."

"You look like a million bucks," Ed said admiringly.

"Thank you. Do come in," Alice said graciously with a welcoming smile and shut the door. "Let me take your coat, and you can leave your bag here for the time being."

Once that was done, Alice took Ed's hand and guided him into the living room, gesturing to a comfy-looking couch in front a brightly burning gas fireplace.

"Perfect touch, very homey," Ed said gladly, glancing around.

"Thank you. Let's sit and talk for a while," Alice said invitingly.

Ed noticed several photos of Alice and her deceased husband on the fireplace mantel and nodded in their direction. "A very handsome couple."

"Thank you—obviously taken a long time ago."

"You are still an extremely attractive woman."

"You're being very kind, and I can say the same of you as a handsome man."

"Now that's a stretch," Ed said humorously. "What did your husband do in the FBI, if you don't mind me asking?"

"He was in the white-collar crime division."

"Must have been a very smart man," Ed said affirmatively.

"He had a law degree and attended never-ending symposiums to expand his knowledge."

"Did you always live in the New York area?"

"Yes, except when he was at the academy. We met at NYU—Frank was two years ahead of me, and we got married not long after I graduated. Once he got his law degree and finished training at the academy, they assigned him to New York: white-collar crime division, focusing on Wall Street and the banks. We bought this house not long after we moved back."

"You had the house renovated recently?" Ed said, looking around.

"Just before Frank died; he was going to retire the following year and wanted it out of the way so that he could relax and not have to deal with it after," Alice said with a sigh. "Speaking of houses, did you list yours?"

"Yes, I did."

Alice couldn't hide her disappointment and shook her head. "Might have been wise to wait awhile in case you change your mind about living in Las Vegas."

"Las Vegas is the best place for Kristen to be; there's a whole colony of big-time entertainers living there."

"That reminds me, I hope you remembered Kristen's New Year's pictures and the rented house."

"I have her pictures in the bag if you'd like to see them now."

"Yes, I'd love to," Alice said eagerly.

Ed went over to the entrance foyer and retrieved a manila envelope and a small white box from his travel bag and handed both to Alice when he got back.

"What's this?" Alice said, peering at the box. "I was only expecting pictures."

"A belated Christmas present," Ed replied.

"That's not fair," Alice protested.

"Please open it."

Alice removed the box top and the tissue paper from the object in the box and was stunned. "It's beautiful, a crystal Lismore Angel. How'd you know?"

"You probably don't remember, but when we were at the art gallery, you had mentioned that you collect angels and shopping for one."

"I don't know what to say or how to thank you," Alice said emotionally and kissed the figurine and then Ed on the cheek.

"Glad you like it," Ed said happily.

"I feel so badly since I don't have anything for you," Alice said contritely.

"But you have—inviting me over for a home-cooked dinner, which I haven't had in quite some time."

"That reminds me, I better put the pot roast in the oven, and when I return, maybe we can have a predinner drink," Alice said buoyantly.

"That sounds great."

When Alice returned, she headed straight to the liquor cabinet and retrieved two glasses and a bottle of Wild Turkey. "I've been wondering what it tastes like; when Frank would have a drink, I would always have a sip, but I think it would be most inappropriate to ask of you."

"I don't mind, and how sweet of you to remember what I drink," Ed said with a nod at the bottle.

"I appreciate your offer, but for now, please pour me just a mouthful," Alice said congenially.

"I can already smell the pot roast," Ed said as he unscrewed the bottle top and poured a little more than a mouthful for Alice and a third of glass for himself, then raised the drink in a toast. "To those not with us anymore but who forever live in our hearts."

"That's a lovely toast," Alice said and took a tiny sip. "Oh my, that's strong."

"I'm sorry—I should have warned you."

"Kristen had mentioned that you were badly wounded in Vietnam and that you're experiencing some serious pain."

"It comes and goes," Ed said dismissively, glad that at least it was now in the open.

"So many young men were hurt and died needlessly," Alice said, shaking her head.

"Like all wars—young men die while old men talk and grow rich."

"You have medication for the pain?"

"Not yet. I'm trying to hold off since it's addictive and has some serious side effects."

Alice sensed it was a topic Ed was uncomfortable with and promptly switched. "So you think this manager you're meeting Friday will really do what you want for Kristen?"

"I'm certain from the way he sounded on the phone, and I found out he has handled some of the biggest female country singers in the business."

"Kristen must be so excited. And to think, you made it happen," Alice said admiringly. "Will you still be involved once he's in the picture?"

"Very minimally, if at all."

"Are you going on the road with her?"

"Most likely not since it's a grind and more suitable for the young."

"I'm sure it is," Alice said and reached for the envelope with the pictures on the coffee table. "Been dying to see these."

"I think you'll like them."

"Oh my, she's gorgeous, looks like a movie star, and the dress is absolutely fabulous.

Did you choose it?"

Ed nodded. "She wears things well."

"You certainly have an eye for enhancing a woman's visage," Alice said admiringly.

"Something I picked up along the way working as an ad man on Madison Avenue."

"You worked on Madison Avenue?" Alice said with bright face.

"Yes, about forty years."

"Well, no wonder," Alice said. "Did you go clothes shopping with your wife?"

"Just for party dresses, and she had to twist my arm," Ed said with a chuckle.

"Are there any pictures of you and Kristen?" Alice said as she viewed them closely.

"There's a couple at the bottom of the stack."

Alice hurried to see them. "Oh, I love it—you and Kristen dancing."

"The beast and the beauty," Ed cracked.

"You are still a very attractive man in a Cary Grant way," Alice said like a woman who was emotionally invested.

"Funny, that's what Kristen said."

"Don't you know that men are still attractive going into their seventies, unlike women?"

"Some lucky few, and actually, there are many very attractive older women; I'm looking at one."

"That's very sweet of you to say," Alice said with a full smile.

"I apologize for part of that comment by putting you in the older category."

"No apology needed since I am," Alice said and stuffed the pictures back in the envelope.

"And where are the pictures of the house?"

"They're on my cell phone," ED said and pulled it out from his sport coat pocket and brought the pictures up.

"The house looks new and the furniture very classy."

"The rental agent told us it was totally renovated; the furniture was selected by a professional decorator."

"It certainly shows," Alice said approvingly.

It was approaching eleven, and the long day was catching up with Alice and Ed as they sipped the brandy and began winding down their get-to-know-each-other conversation. They had laughed at times and were sad when recalling the events leading up to the loss of their mates. Alice was much more emotional and open, whereas Ed was more reserved, not wanting to look unmanly and weak. In the course of the evening, they'd learned more about each other than most know before they get married. The light falling snow, clearly visible through the windows, and the warm, glowing fireplace created a perfect atmosphere to be romantic. It was greatly enhanced by the drinks, but neither Alice nor Ed made a move, and actually, Ed was glad Alice held back, thinking of his circumstances and not wanting to mislead her.

"There's something I need to tell you in all fairness so that I don't disappoint you," Alice said reluctantly. "At this stage, let's just start with being good friends and not rush into an amorous relationship. Frank's been dead just three years, and I'm not ready to fall in love again or have an affair, and please forgive me if that's not what you had in mind. But having said that, I hope you know I am very attracted to you."

"I understand perfectly and admire your honesty. And since you've stated how you feel, I should do the same." Ed paused, drew a deep breath, and winced slightly. "I have pancreatic cancer."

Alice turned pale, as if suddenly drained of life, and said disbelievingly, "Oh my God, are you serious?"

"Wish I weren't," Ed said solemnly.

Alice shook her head. "That can't be, not after you lost your son and wife."

"Life's not fair sometimes," Ed said with a shrug, trying hard to maintain his composure.

"So what are they doing for you?"

Ed wanted to sound encouraging but felt that would be misleading and give Alice false hope. "There's not much they can do at this stage."

"Oh God," Alice cried out and burst into tears.

Ed pulled her close, letting her head rest against his chest as she sobbed, her fingers clutching his arm. He was suddenly lost for words and couldn't think of any way to ease the devastating news. It seemed to Ed like an eternity before Alice finally stopped and pulled back, her eyes swollen and her face beet red. He reached into his pocket and handed her a handkerchief, which she readily took.

"Does Kristen know?" Alice whimpered.

"No, it would absolutely devastate her; I don't want to tell her when she's at this very critical stage in pursuit of a singing career."

"But doesn't she suspect something is badly amiss with you being in pain and relying on the alcohol?"

"I told her it's because of the war wound."

"I hate to ask this since it may sound so awful," Alice said reticently.

"Go ahead."

"How much time have you got?"

Ed drew a deep breath and said faintly, "Not a lot."

Alice, with tears flowing once again, locked her arms around Ed's neck, then pulled him to her and kissed him repeatedly on the face. "I'm so sorry, I'm so very sorry . . ."

"I am, too, for getting caught up in the moment and not letting you know back in Omaha; maybe it'd be best for me to leave."

"Don't you dare," Alice said forcefully. "What kind of a woman would I be to turn my back when you need someone, at the worst time of your life? Yes, I know you have Kristen, but it's not the same."

"I don't want you to go through hell again; you've paid your dues once already," Ed said with all the sincerity he could muster.

"I just wish you were here and not so far away so that I could be there for you every day."

Ed nodded and smiled faintly, looking directly into Alice's distraught eyes. "Just you saying that is a great comfort."

"When are you going to tell Kristen?"

"I'm hoping to hold off till she's on her way."

"I'll pray for that as well," Alice said solemnly.

"I have a huge favor to ask of you," Ed said uneasily.

"Anything at all," Alice said firmly.

"Could you stay in touch with her and be her friend in a kind of motherly way?"

"I'd be happy to for as long as she wants."

"She thinks the world of you."

"And I do of her."

"I just wish I had more time to make sure she's got the right people around her when I'm gone," Ed said pensively.

"Maybe God will intercede and help you live longer than you think," Alice said encouragingly.

"Perhaps," Ed said for Alice's sake.

"How much more have you got to do tomorrow?"

"Just a couple of things and some goodbyes. Shouldn't take me long."

"Good, it'll give us more time together before you leave," Alice said gladly.

"You want me to come back?"

"Yes, of course," Alice said forcefully.

"This might be the one time you'd be wise to walk away."

"I've already given you my answer," Alice said definitively.

"I just want to spare you needless grief."

"I'm a lot tougher than you think," Alice said with a determined look.

"You are truly an extraordinary woman; I wish I had met you a few years ago."

CHAPTER 14

B ecause of the number of people Ed had to see, Alice convinced him to use her car instead of relying on taxis. Ed reluctantly agreed, feeling somewhat anxious about driving in the New York City traffic, which he hadn't done since he'd retired. He was greatly relieved when he reached Dr. Nelson's office in Staten Island without mishap, and to his surprise, he didn't have to wait to see him.

"How are you doing?" Dr. Nelson said warmly, rising from his chair with an extended hand and motioning for Ed to take a seat as he did as well.

"Hanging in there," Ed said wryly.

"And how is the pain?"

"Significantly increasing."

"Are you using the pain pills yet?"

"No, but I'm getting there."

"Have any of the other telling symptoms we talked about surfaced yet?"

"Lack of appetite," Ed said reluctantly and did not want to enumerate some of the other ones.

"That's a tough one to overcome, but try to force yourself to eat whatever you can tolerate, and don't go by any preset times."

"Well, at least I haven't lost my appetite for booze," Ed joshed.

"Whatever works at this point; I'm not going to tell you to give it up, but just don't drive," Dr. Nelson said agreeably.

"You think I might lose my life?" Ed joked.

"Glad you haven't lost your sense of humor."

"About the only thing I haven't lost," Ed said offhandedly.

"Oh, before I forget, have you filled out the Directive for Health Care Agent form?"

"I have not."

"In view of you having no kin, I'd gladly be the agent."

"I appreciate that, but I don't think you can—I've moved to Las Vegas."

"What?" Dr. Nelson said disbelievingly. "When did this happen, and why?"

"It's a long and complicated story, so I won't waste your valuable time; I just came back to take care of some loose ends and say my goodbyes."

"You have someone in Las Vegas?" Dr. Nelson said with a querying look.

"Yes."

"But you have longtime friends here who I'm sure will want to be there for you."

"No doubt," Ed said with finality to avoid further words.

"I don't know what to say other than to offer my best and suggest you find an oncologist in Las Vegas without delay."

"I will," Ed said with a nod. "Oh, can you write me a new prescription since I've misplaced the one you gave me? Then I can have it filled before I leave."

"Certainly," Dr. Nelson said and reached for the prescription pad.

"Thanks for seeing me without much notice and being a caring friend."

Dr. Nelson walked around the desk and hugged Ed. "I'm truly sorry the treatment failed, and if you need to talk, please don't hesitate to call, day or night."

"Don't blame yourself; it just wasn't to be," Ed said dismissively, then proceeded to the door with quick steps, doing his best to stay composed.

After saying goodbyes to a couple of his oldest friends, Ed decided he'd had enough of the morbid and headed to Saint Mary's Church in reverence to Ann, who loved it so. He made his way slowly to the front of the church and knelt in the second pew, staring at the life-size Jesus on the cross behind the altar on the wall. It was the first time he had returned to the church since that final parting with his beloved wife. After a couple of minutes on his knees, he sat down on the bench and stared blankly at the cross, totally unaware of Father Connelly's approach.

"Ed Goff, is that you?" Father Connelly called out.

Ed was startled as he peered at the frail old man ambling toward him. "Father Connelly, you're still here? Thought you would have retired by now."

"Been some time since you've been here. I just recently heard the bad news about your cancer, and I'm truly sorry," Father Connelly said with an extended hand.

"Stuff happens, most times not of our choosing," Ed said with a shrug as he shook Father Connelly's bony hand.

"I'm also sorry that you've stayed away from the church since Ann's demise," Father Connelly said with regret. "I tried to reach you many times—left messages on your answering machine and even stopped to see you in person, but I guess you were out or didn't want to see me."

"Sorry about that, but I just wasn't in the mood for ethereal conversations."

"I hope you haven't totally lost your faith," Father Connelly said poignantly.

"Lost it when I watched Ann pass," Ed said bitterly. "Just stopped here for a minute in her memory."

"Can we talk?"

"If you like," Ed said indifferently and slid somewhat sideways to make room for Father Connelly to sit.

"I hate to ask, but how much time have they given you?"

"About four months."

"Oh my," Father Connelly said empathically, shaking his head. "You must be in great deal of pain."

"I'm getting there."

"What medication they have you on?"

"Fentanyl."

"Never heard of it. Is it potent?"

"They told me very, but I really don't know since I haven't taken it yet; as a matter of fact, I just had the first prescription filled this morning."

"I'm surprised you've held off this long."

"The stuff is a hundred times more potent than morphine, and the side effects are from hell," Ed said bluntly.

"So up to now, you haven't used anything at all?"

"Oh yeah, my longtime friend: Wild Turkey," Ed said extemporaneously.

"It helps?" Father Connelly said with a curious face.

"Up to now, it's made the pain bearable, but it's losing its effectiveness."

"Father Connelly shook his head. "I will say a special Mass for you on Sunday, and I hope you will attend."

"I appreciate the thought, but I won't be here."

"You're taking a trip?

"I've moved to Las Vegas few days ago."

"Las Vegas?" Father Connelly said with an astonished look. "You don't have anyone there."

"I do have someone, and it's best that way."

"Isn't that rather drastic in view of what you're facing?"

"I suppose, but what difference does it make where I die? The end game is the same. You die alone no matter where you are."

"But you have people here who care about you and will be there for you, including me," Father Connelly said kindly. "This has been your home for most of your life."

"The deed is done, and besides, I'll spare people unnecessary grief and wasted time," Ed said dismissively.

"What about the house and all your possessions?"

"I put the house up for sale yesterday, and all the stuff is being donated to the Salvation Army."

"Wish I would have known; I have some needy parishioners that could use furniture and other household things."

"Sorry, I didn't know, but if that's the case, you can send them over to Mrs. Conti, the next-door neighbor. She has the key to the house, and they can have whatever they need. I'll call her and let her know."

"What about the Salvation Army?"

"They can have what's left," Ed said with a shrug.

"It'll be greatly appreciated by the needy parishioners. I'll ask them to pray for you."

"They don't have to—it's a waste of time."

"You don't believe in God?"

"It's a myth and a fabrication."

Father Connelly was taken aback and shook his head in dismay. "You don't mean that, Ed."

"It's nothing more than wishful thinking," Ed said deliberately. "People refuse to accept the finality of death and have created a fantasy."

"You believe in hell?"

"Oh yeah, there's a hell, all right."

"You believe in hell but not heaven; isn't that a contradiction?" Father Connelly said poignantly.

"Not at all: everything doesn't have two sides—circles and the balls."

"Well, it seems you have pretty much made up your mind, so I don't think what I say will change that," Father Connelly said with a disappointed sigh. "I will pray that you return to God, and I'll still say the Mass for you on Sunday."

"Sorry I've caused you consternation," Ed said sincerely. "So when are you going to retire?"

Father Connelly shrugged. "As you probably know, with all that's being going on with the Catholic Church and the massive resignations and forced departures, there is a severe shortage of priests, so it looks like I'll be here till my last breath, but I really don't mind; I love this church and what I'm doing."

Ed rose to his feet and extended his hand. "I wish you the very best; you are truly a holy man."

Father Connelly's eyes swelled with emotion as he shook Ed's hand. "That's the nicest compliment you could have given me, and I will pray for you, even though you don't believe."

It was nearly two when Ed pulled into Alice's driveway just as large wet snowflakes began to fall. He got out of the car and made his way to the front door, which Alice flung open as he was about to ring the bell.

"I'm so glad you're back early," Alice gushed.

"That makes two of us; now tell me about this white stuff coming down—how much are they predicting?"

"About ten inches," Alice said hesitantly, anticipating Ed's intent.

"First time in my life that's not what I want to hear," Ed said as he entered the foyer and removed his coat, which Alice took and hung in the closet.

"Let's go in the kitchen; I have a freshly brewed pot of coffee—have you eaten lunch?"

"I didn't want to waste time getting here."

"How very sweet. I'll fix you a sandwich; please have a seat."

"Looks like I'm going have to change my travel schedule," Ed said reluctantly as Alice started on the sandwich.

"I was afraid you were going to say that as soon as I heard the amount of snow," Alice said dejectedly. "Any chance you can reschedule the appointment with the man in Las Vegas?"

"This is really more like an audition rather than a business meeting. We're lucky he's even seeing us since he's managed some of the top country singers and just became available."

Alice was heartbroken and was unable to hide her disappointment. "I was hoping we'd have some intimate time together before you left."

"I'm truly sorry, but as you know, time is not on my side, and I have to make sure Kristen has someone who can take her to the top, and I think this man will."

"I apologize. I must sound very selfish," Alice said as she approached with the sandwich and a mug of coffee.

"Not at all, I promise we'll get together very soon, whether here or in Vegas, if you're still willing."

"Yes, of course," Alice said gladly and sat across from Ed.

Ed forced the sandwich down, and as soon as he'd finished, he called the airline. After several minutes of waiting, he made the reservation. Alice listened attentively to Ed's side of the conversation and tried hard not to show her disappointment and the tears in her eyes.

"I'm afraid it doesn't leave us much time," Ed said as he clicked off the phone.

"Just enough for you to finish the coffee," Alice said brokenheartedly.

"You mind calling a cab while I finish?"

"I'll drive you," Alice said without hesitation.

Ed shook his head. "No, not with this snow. And I'm sure by now the traffic to the airport must be hell."

"Do you want me to call Kristen for you after the cab?"

"I'll do that on the way to the airport; our last moment right now is more important."

Alice acknowledged his kind words with a nod and a forced smile. "You'll call me as soon as you get to Las Vegas?"

"It might be late."

"It doesn't matter; otherwise, I won't be able to sleep wondering if you got home all right."

"I will call you, then," Ed said and squeezed Alice's hand as tears filled his eyes as well.

CHAPTER 15

Once off the plane, Ed, good to his word, made his way to the deserted passenger waiting area just outside of the exit doors and reached for his cell phone.

"It's Ed—hope I didn't wake you."

"No, I'm watching the eleven o'clock news with one eye and all the snow coming down with the other," Alice said downheartedly.

"You OK?"

"Since you left, I've been miserable and crying, thinking we got robbed of our time."

"Yes, we did, but there's still time, if you're willing, for us to make one hell of a splash," Ed said to buoy her spirits.

"What'd you have in mind?"

"You'll have to come to Las Vegas for it to happen."

"I'll gladly do that," Alice said without hesitation. "Kristen must be happy to have you back."

"I haven't seen her yet. I just got off the plane and wanted to call you before it got any later, but I spoke to her on the way to the airport, and she sounded awful."

"What happened?"

"I asked what was going on since I've never heard her sound so bad, but she said she wouldn't tell me until I got home. I didn't want to press her with the audition coming up and get her even more upset."

"You poor man—just what you need, two women in distress," Alice said sympathetically.

"Not so bad. It's like old times at the ad agency," Ed said sportingly.

"How long before you're home?"

"Still got to take the shuttle train and then a cab, so it'll be at least an hour."

"Will you please call me if it's something really bad that Kristen is dealing with?"

"Yes. So what's the snow situation?"

"You got out just in time; they've closed down all the airports in the New York area and increased the predicted amount of snow by a couple more inches."

Ed chuckled. "It's unbelievable; since we met, there's been nothing but snow everywhere."

"Unfortunately, we don't get to enjoy it together," Alice said sadly.

"Winter's just begun, and with our luck, we may see a lot more, and if not, I know a place where the snow is guaranteed up to April."

"Where?" Alice said eagerly.

"Lake Tahoe."

"Let's decide on that when I'm there."

"By all means," Ed said easily.

"You've made me feel so much better," Alice said with a glad sigh, "and with that said, let's hang up so that you can get home and see what's going on with Kristen. But if it' something bad, promise to call me tonight."

"I'll do that; otherwise, I'll call you first thing in the morning. Good night and pleasant dreams."

"You as well, and I'm sorry for being such a pain," Alice said sweetly and clicked off the phone.

It was just past nine when Ed rang the doorbell, feeling somewhat anxious but most eager to see Kristen. He hoped there was no major problem since the last two days were highly draining and he needed some respite. He was about to ring again, but the door opened, and Kristen, with arms outstretched, flew at him.

"So happy you're back," Kristen gushed, then hugged Ed with all her might.

"I take it you missed me," Ed said, relieved to see Kristen physically unhurt.

"Let me take your bag," Kristen volunteered once she released Ed.

"So tell me, what's going on?" Ed said as he followed Kristen into the living room and removed his coat, then tossed it on a stuffed seat.

"Would you like a drink first?"

"Do I need one before you tell me?"

"I'm not sure," Kristen said hesitantly.

"Think I could use one anyway. Been a hell of a two days, including the flight home," Ed said as he eased tiredly onto the sofa in front of the brightly burning fireplace.

It took Kristen no time at all to rush to the kitchen and return with the drink, which she sipped before handing it to Ed, something which was fast becoming a ritual.

"So tell me."

"You promise not to get mad?" Kristen said as she sat down next to Ed.

"Have I ever?" Ed said calmly and took a drink.

"Last night after Morgan finished her gig at the Pink Pony—"

"Pink Pony—her gig?" Ed immediately interrupted with a puzzled look.

"Pole dancing at a strip joint," Kristen said uneasily.

"I thought she was working at the Golden Nugget as a cocktail waitress and training to be a blackjack dealer?" Ed said with a querying look. "That's what she said when we had lunch, or did I not hear right?"

"No, you heard right, and please don't get mad at her for lying," Kristen pleaded amiably. "She was too ashamed to tell you what she was really doing."

Ed took another swallow of the drink. "Go on."

"Some creep followed her out to the parking lot and to her car, and when she opened the door, he rushed over and shoved her inside on the back seat and violently raped her," Kristen said emotionally.

"Christ, how awful!" Ed gasped. "How is she?"

"She's bruised, especially down there, and badly shaken," Kristen said tensely.

"Is she in the hospital?"

"She was, but they released her late this afternoon, so she's here," Kristen said with a strained look.

"I'm proud of you."

"You're not upset?"

"Of course not," Ed said calmly.

Kristen mockingly wiped her brow. "I'm so relieved."

"What time did this happen?"

"Around midnight last night."

"And when did you find out?"

"Not long after. The cops called me and said she was on the way to the hospital; Morgan gave them my number."

Ed shook his head angrily. "Don't they have security in these parking lots?"

"I guess not."

"They give her something to relax her and calm her down?"

"Yes, she's been asleep since I got her here, but she's having terrible nightmares and wakes up screaming. So I thought it would be best to have her in my bed; that way, I'll be there to calm her down, and hopefully she won't wake you during the night."

"That's very thoughtful, and don't you worry about her waking me. I'll sleep on this couch," Ed said as he patted the seat.

"So how was your time with Alice?"

"She's a very classy lady—wish I had met her a couple of years sooner."

"Then you and I wouldn't have met," Kristen teased. "But actually, you've lucked out; now you have me and her as well."

"And the way things are going, I may even have Morgan now," Ed said lightheartedly.

"For real?" Kristen said with a questioning look.

"I had mentioned that possibility when we were driving and you told me about her situation; now, ironically, the opportunity has manifested."

"Opportunity?" Kristen said with a puzzled look.

"Yes, she's here and needs help for a reason not of her making."

"You are one incredible man. No wonder I love you so much."

"And I love you as well, my little thrush."

"Are you thinking of letting her move in with us?" Kristen asked eagerly.

"Yes—otherwise what I have in mind won't work. She needs to change her life completely, just like you did."

"It won't be easy for her," Kristen warned.

"I'm sure it won't, but maybe after this horrible experience, she'll be ready," Ed said optimistically.

Kristen shook her head. "You are really something else—first me and now Morgan."

"We're not there yet, and with that said, would you mind doing my drink again?" Ed said with a pained look.

"Is it bad?" Kristen said with deep concern.

"It's getting there."

"I'm so sorry; I would forgo the singing career if your pain went away," Kristen said earnestly.

"I would never want you to do that, no matter what my circumstance. Your destiny is to be a great country singer, and no one or anything can stand in the way, including me."

"Maybe you should take a pain pill."

Ed forced a smile to calm the distress on Kristen's face. "It'll ease up once I have another drink."

"I'll get it right now," Kristen said, then grabbed the empty glass and rushed out.

CHAPTER 16

With dawn approaching, Ed felt like he could finally sleep; his pain had eased, and Morgan's screams had ended from the hellish nightmares of the brutal rape. Throughout the night, he could hear Kristen consoling Morgan each time she awoke from her own outcries. More than once, Ed was tempted to rush upstairs and comfort both the girls since he knew Kristen must have been overwhelmed and no doubt roused from an uneasy sleep. But he thought better of it, considering that Morgan might be alarmed even more by the sight of a man she hardly knew. His thoughts once again turned to the degenerate who perpetrated the brutal rape, and he wished he could meet him with a gun in hand and blast his crotch all to hell. He always felt that short of killing, there was no more hideous crime than rape, and he never understood why a castration law hadn't been enacted, especially with all the women in politics. It suddenly occurred to him how vulnerable Kristen would be going public, no doubt attracting all kinds of sexual predators. With that thought, he decided to buy a handgun without delay. Satisfied with his decision, he finally drifted off to sleep.

Three hours into the uneasy slumber, Ed was suddenly woken by the buzzing cell phone on the coffee table.

Bleary-eyed, he groped for the phone and clicked it on once in hand, and groggily uttered. "Hello."

"Did I wake you?" Alice said meekly.

"What time is it?"

"Ten thirty," Alice said and immediately corrected herself. "No, it's seven thirty your time in Las Vegas."

"Can't remember the last time I slept this late," Ed said, shaking the cobwebs from his foggy brain, saturated by the nearly half a bottle of Wild Turkey he'd consumed during the long night.

"I'll hang up and let you call me when you're ready," Alice said apologetically.

"No, please stay on. I need to get up and tell you what happened, which I promised to do first thing this morning."

"Are you sure you're up to it right now?"

"Yes, and the reason you caught me still sleeping is because it was a horrid night."

"Kristen OK?" Alice said anxiously.

"Yes, it's her friend Morgan, who is here and had nightmares the entire night."

"What happened?"

"She was raped the night before, in a parking lot."

"Oh my God, how horrific," Alice gasped. "In a parking lot?"

"Yes, she was going to her car and this creep followed her, and when she opened the door, he shoved her in and attacked her viciously."

"There was no one else there?"

"No."

"Is she badly bruised—I mean, other than the obvious?" Alice said uneasily.

"I haven't seen her yet—she was in bed when I got home—but I imagine she probably is."

"I assume she's been medically checked?"

"Yes, in a hospital. I think they should have kept her for a couple of days, but she doesn't have insurance, so they released her."

"How absolutely heartless. Any chance she'll be able to identify this animal?" Alice said angrily.

"As I said, I haven't seen or spoken to her yet."

"You poor man. With all that you're dealing with, now you have another issue."

"Not so bad. I won't have time to think about myself, and maybe I can make her life a little easier. From what Kristen has told me, the poor girl has really had one hell of a life so far."

"You are such a caring man. I've never known anyone quite like you."

"Please don't give me too much credit; I'm just trying to make up for my egocentric, wasted life."

"I don't believe that."

"I appreciate you saying that; I just hope I'm around long enough to see it all through."

"I'll pray that God grants you enough time and maybe even changes his mind about calling you in," Alice said encouragingly.

"I think my end game has already been decided," Ed said without rancor.

"You don't believe in miracles?"

"Miracles happen only to the ignorant and in the movies."

"You do believe in God?" Alice said fretfully.

"I once did."

"What changed your mind?"

"I've seen too many hideous things—the latest being what just happened to Morgan."

"Yes, unfortunately, things do happen that shake our faith and raise doubt," Alice said with a heavy sigh.

"Please don't let me influence you negatively," Ed said thoughtfully and decided to change the subject. "So is it still snowing there?"

"It stopped about an hour ago after nearly thirteen inches; it's a good thing you got out when you did, especially in view of what happened to Morgan."

"Yeah, some kind of luck on both counts," Ed said casually.

"Or a divine intervention," Alice said reverently.

"No, definitely luck; I don't have any of those."

"Are you teasing me?"

"Just having some fun," Ed said affably.

"I think with all that has come your way, you have held up remarkably well."

"That remains to be seen; the worst is just around the corner."

"I have no doubt about your resolve, but let's talk about something more immediate, and that's Morgan and Kristen," Alice said thoughtfully to get Ed away from the morose.

"You're right; Morgan has certainly added to the load, which I hope doesn't distract Kristen from what she has to do tomorrow."

"And you don't want to reschedule the meeting?"

"As I mentioned, I'd like to but can't take a chance of him going with someone else before we even see him—we lucked out that he's free and even willing to see Kristen."

"Well, at least you've got today to get Kristen relaxed and primed, and I have no doubt she'll do just fine. After all, look who she's got for a coach?" Alice ribbed.

"Who?" Ed teased back.

"Oh, the doorbell—think the man must have finished plowing the driveway and is looking to get paid. Please call me when you have a handle on it all, and I'm anxious to know how Morgan is."

It was approaching ten, and Ed was on his second cup of coffee at the kitchen table, totally immersed in an issue of *Billboard* magazine, when Kristen ambled in wearing an oversize 'I Love Vegas' pink T-shirt.

"Good morning, bright eyes," Ed said humorously as he looked up from the magazine.

"Good morning, and you certainly can't mean me," Kristen said when she reached Ed and kissed him on the forehead.

"On the contrary, you look bright and lively, and with that said, how is Morgan?"

"She'll be out shortly; she's washing up. She bled a bit during the night and is very sore down there," Kristen said empathetically and glanced at the magazine. "Anything interesting?"

"As a matter of fact, yes: they have an article on Sid Greene. It says that over the course of thirty years, he's made five country singers into big-time stars, but the next will be the biggest of all since it'll be his last."

"Oh God, that makes me even more nervous now," Kristen said pensively.

"Put that thought out of your mind; you're going to do great," Ed said firmly and took the last swallow of his coffee. "Can you please get me a refill?"

Minutes later, Kristen returned with two steaming mugs of coffee and sat across from Ed. "Did you sleep at all last night?"

"Couple of hours, but no big deal," Ed said dismissively and looked at Kristen with admiration. "I'm very proud of how you took care of Morgan."

"She would do the same for me," Kristen said without hesitation.

"I'm glad to hear that since it coincides with what I'm thinking," Ed said and took a sip of coffee.

"What'd you have in mind?" Kristen said eagerly.

"Since you two are so close, we should have Morgan move in without delay, and when you start your tours, she can be your tour companion and social manager," Ed said thoughtfully. "You'll need someone you can trust to keep the parasites away and be a close friend you can turn to when you have doubts or needs."

"What about you?"

"The pain's increasing daily, and even if it wasn't, I'm too old to handle concert tours. You really need a female close to your age."

Kristen choked up and shook her head. "There is no one who can look after me like you."

"I'll try to go on the first tour if it's soon; after that, it'll be strictly Morgan, which I'm counting on her agreeing to. Meantime, what's left of today, we'll need every minute so that I can get you ready for the meeting tomorrow morning."

"Besides the questions, do you think he'll ask me to sing?"

"I'm certain he will, so pick a couple of songs that you love, and rehearse them after I prep you."

"Good morning," Morgan said weakly as she gingerly made her way into the kitchen, wearing Kristen's bathrobe.

Ed's heart broke seeing Morgan so pallid and her right cheekbone fairly swollen.

"Good morning. Glad you're here just in time to join us for coffee and some plans."

"I apologize profusely for all the screaming during the night, which no doubt kept you up," Morgan said contritely when she reached the table and slowly eased into the chair.

"No need to apologize, and don't' feel badly; you certainly couldn't help it," Ed said kindly. "Ready for some coffee?"

"Yes, I could use it," Morgan said and started to rise from the chair.

"I'll get it," Kristen blurted and motioned for Morgan to stay seated.

"I won't keep you up another night; just give me few more hours and I'll be out of your hair."

"You can forget that. As a matter of fact, I have a proposal that I hope you'll accept," Ed said and waited a moment for Kristen to return with Morgan's coffee. "Here's the deal: Kristen and I would like you to move in with us permanently."

"You want someone like me living in your house?" Morgan said disbelievingly. She then reluctantly added, "Kristen tell you what I do?"

"Yes, trying to survive any way you can," Ed said thoughtfully. "And furthermore, I want you to be Kristen's personal assistant, which she also wholeheartedly wants."

Morgan was bowled over and glanced at Kristen. "For real?"

"Yes," Kristen exclaimed.

"When she starts touring, you'll be the one she can totally trust and also keep the parasites away," Ed said seriously. "And to that end, I'm buying a gun and having you trained to use it. For all of that, you will, of course, be fairly paid."

Morgan no longer could contain her tears and let them flow. When she finally regained her composure, she looked at Ed and shook her head. "Kristen told me you were her guardian angel, and now I see she wan't exaggerating; How do I thank you?"

"I'm far from it, but I appreciate the thought. So I assume you accept and will move in with us as well?"

"Will tomorrow after your meeting be OK?"

"Yes," Ed said with a glad nod.

"Welcome to the team," Kristen happily exclaimed. "How about I do breakfast?"

"I'll help," Morgan happily volunteered.

"Just relax and get acquainted with your guardian angel," Kristen teased and rose to her feet.

Not even the persistent pain dampened Ed's positive feelings about the day. He had rehearsed and pumped up Kristen to the point of excess, and when finished, he let her rehearse her songs, which she did with heart and soul. It was as if her life depended on attaining the end result, which was Sid becoming her manager. Even Morgan was surprised by Kristen's prodigious effort, something she had never seen in the three years they'd spent together in New York. Ed was also delighted by the way Morgan encouraged Kristen, which affirmed his belief that she would have Kristen's back. To celebrate the eventful day and to the delight of the girls, Ed suggested they order out because of Morgan's condition—a Japanese feast and two bottles of sake to wash it down.

It took them nearly two hours to fill up with the sumptuous meal and the two bottles of sake, heated perfectly in the Japanese style.

"Ladies, I can't remember when I enjoyed an evening

as much. I thank you both, and with that said, let me excuse myself and give Alice a call."

"Will you be back?" Kristen said.

"Probably not, and I suggest you two call it a night as well; tomorrow's the big day."

"Good night," both the girls chimed.

CHAPTER 17

Just before entering Sid Greene's office, Ed turned to Kristen and hugged her mightily. "You can do this."

"I won't let you down," Kristen said, even though she felt weak-kneed.

"That's my girl," Ed said intently and pushed open the door.

"Good morning. You must be Mr. Goff and Miss Cole," the attractive middle-aged secretary said warmly. "Mr. Greene will be with you momentarily; he's on the phone. My name is Donna."

"Good morning," Ed and Kristen replied simultaneously as they paused halfway to her desk.

"Would you care to sit?" Donna asked politely, motioning to the chairs near her desk.

"If you don't mind, I'd like to have a closer look at the vinyl album covers on the walls," Ed said, looking around.

"They represent the gold and platinum albums of the country stars Mr. Greene has managed through his thirty-year career," Donna said proudly.

"Quite a collection," Ed said as he walked over for a closer look with Kristen at his side and nodded his head approvingly.

"I can't believe all these," Kristen said in awe as she gazed at the autographed albums.

"Hopefully in the not too distant future, they'll have to make room for yours," Ed said with a wink at Donna.

"That won't be for a while; first I have to pay my dues," Kristen said astutely.

"If Mr. Greene decides to take you on, that is something you won't have to do if you're as good as Madge said," Donna declared.

"I'm off the phone; please send them in," Sid hollered through the partially open door.

Ed and Kristen promptly turned and made their way into Sid's office, which was adorned with individual autographed photos of most of the big country stars, along with an array of candid ones. Sid, a slender man of average height with an angular face and head, topped off with a black western hat, smiled and rose from the plush leather chair.

"Good morning, I'm Sid Greene, and I love western wear, as you can see, including the boots," Sid said amiably and stuck out his hand, which Ed and Kristen gladly shook before settling into the chairs across from the desk.

"Thanks for seeing us," Ed said forthrightly.

"You came highly recommended by Madge; as a matter of fact, in all the years I've known her, she has never bragged so much about a karaoke singer," Sid said, looking directly at Kristen.

"It was very kind of her to say that," Kristen said with a nervous smile.

"I detect a slight New York accent."

"Not when I sing," Kristen said defensively.

Sid noticed Kristen tighten up and wanted to put her at ease. "I'm not criticizing; it's just a simple observation. Please, tell me about yourself."

Kristen took a deep breath to recall her well-rehearsed

story, which Ed had meticulously concocted for her with a smidge of fabrication.

"I was born in Albany, and the day after graduating high school, I left for New York City, where I hooked up with a musician the first day I got there. He had a three-guy band that played mostly at cheesy clubs and sports bars. After four years of getting nowhere, I broke up with him just before this Christmas and, finally, after many years, decided to look up my uncle Ed on Staten Island. He told me he was driving to Las Vegas for the holidays and asked if I wanted to join him, which was exactly what I was thinking of doing since my girlfriend moved here a year ago and said I might have better luck with my singing in Las Vegas than New York. So here I am."

"A country singer in New York," Sid queried.

"It was closer than Nashville, and I didn't have enough of money to get me there."

Sid chuckled. "And why does a New York girl choose country music above all the others?"

"Country songs tell soulful stories that touch the heart and soul," Kristen said with deep feeling.

"That's a very astute observation," Sid said with an approving nod.

"May ask why you chose it?" Kristen countered eagerly.

Sid grinned. "Truthfully, I got into it because of Dolly Parton. I was a stagehand at MGM, where she performed, and I fell in love with her and the whole country scene. In case you're wondering, I don't sing or play an instrument."

"And I don't read sheet music," Kristen confessed humorously.

"No big deal—that you can easily learn," Sid said casually. "The important thing is how well you sing."

"Would you like to hear me?" Kristen said enthusiastically.

"Not just yet," Sid said and turned to Ed. "So how do you fit in with Kristen's quest?"

"I'm totlly committed to her singing career and will do whatever it takes financially to have her succeed."

"How do you mean?"

"Getting her the best pros in the business to teach her whatever she lacks, like reading sheet music or anything else."

"That's quite a commitment," Sid said admiringly, "but if she's as good as you and Madge say, she won't need any major help—the voice is the thing."

"She has that and a bit more," Ed soundly declared.

"You'll be staying in Vegas permanently?"

"I've already rented a house."

"You mind telling me what you did before retiring?"

"I worked on Madison Avenue for forty years."

"I'll be damned—I had a feeling you were in the publicity business. I may ask you to help out if you're game," Sid said enticingly.

"By all means. Anything to help Kristen."

"Good to know," Sid said with an approving nod. "And for your info, I'm fifty-six. A couple of months ago, my contract with Holly Spring ended. My next client will be my last, and I intend to make this the biggest country star I've managed. After nearly two months, I still haven't found anyone who impressed me, and I've seen quite a few."

"Look no more," Ed said boldly.

"With that said, are you ready, Kristen, to warble few notes?" Sid said lightheartedly.

"Yes, sir," Kristen said snappily.

"Just one more thing so that you both know right

upfront: when I take on a singer, I push them to the hilt and will settle for nothing less than their very best at all times." Sid proclaimed, then rose to his feet. "Let's head to the music chamber."

Ed and Kristen followed Sid through the padded door and into a large soundproof room with several folding chairs scattered about in front of a stand-up mic and two large floor speakers. Off to the side were all sorts of electronic gear, including a karaoke machine. Along one wall were shelves stacked with vinyl albums and CDs. On the far side of the room was a seventy-two-inch TV screen, and below it, there was a long table with stacks of DVDs.

"Ed, why don't you grab a chair while I get Kristen set up, and then I'll join you," Sid said and guided Kristen to the mic and karaoke machine.

"So what're you gonna sing?"

"I'll start with 'Help Me Make It through the Night' and follow with 'Me and Bobby McGee,' if that's OK?"

"Love 'em both," Sid said cheerfully and keyed them up on the machine. "Just push the 'Play' button after I take a seat, and then grab the floor mic and do your thing."

When Kristen finished the song, Sid applauded vigorously, along with Ed, and loudly exclaimed, "Very moving—I'm impressed."

Kristen acknowledged his praise with a bow, then reached over and cued the karaoke machine for the next song. When it started, she changed her stance from demure to brazen and her tone from soft to rugged and bold. Minutes later, with the last note sung, Kristen was spent.

Sid rose to his feet and bellowed, "Awesome! Bravo!" He then turned to Ed, who was also up on his feet, and declared, "She's a combination of Elvis and Tina Turner."

Kristen, breathless, smiled and replaced the mic in its stand and waited.

"Come and join us," Sid urged.

Kristen hastened over, heartened by Sid's positive response.

"Pull up a chair," Sid said forcefully.

"Thank you for the enthusiastic response," Kristen said happily and sat down.

Sid wore an ear-splitting grin as he shook his head. "You have one hell of a voice range, and the way you move is something else—thought I was watching a more dynamic Tina Turner and Elvis Presley. Where'd you learn to move like that?"

"It just comes naturally when I get into a rowdy song."

"I owe Madge whatever she wants," Sid boasted.

"I owe her, too," Kristen said jubilantly.

"Here's what I have in mind. I know the manager at Drai's, one of the hottest nightclubs in Las Vegas, and also the band that's performing there right now. I'd like you to do the two songs you just did for me. Madge said you brought the roof down with 'Me and Bobby McGee.' I wanna see if it happens again."

"Tomorrow night," Kristen said, full of disbelief.

"Yes," Sid exclaimed. "Here's what I'd like you to wear: a black short dress and a pair of Jessie Western boots." Then turned to Ed. "They're about twelve hundred bucks."

"Not a problem," Ed said coolly.

"Oh, let me mention a couple of things to consider, Kristen: Always wear black panties when wearing short skirts or dresses, and don't wear silks since they don't do well with perspiration. Also, no carbonated sodas or big meals—and absolutely no booze before you perform,"

Sid said firmly and rose to his feet. "If it wasn't for this previously scheduled lunch date, I would invite you to have one with me."

"Thanks for the thought and for seeing Kristen," Ed said once on his feet.

"I'll call you Saturday and fill you in on the details," Sid said warmly and shook their hands, then guided them to the door.

Ed decided they would celebrate Kristen's monumental day with champagne and exotic snacks, which they got before coming home, only to find Morgan in the kitchen, leaning against the counter and looking distressed.

"What's wrong?" Ed said, setting the bags of goods on the kitchen counter couple steps from Morgan.

"The sheriff's office called and said I have to come down to the station and look at pictures of recently arrested rapists."

"Well, that's not about to happen," Ed said boldly. "Do you know who you spoke to, and do you have his number?"

"Yes, it's on my cell phone," Morgan said, holding it in her hand.

"Call him and let me speak to him," Ed said firmly.

Morgan did exactly as told and handed the phone to Ed, whispering, "Sergeant Dunn."

"I'm Ed Goff, and my niece Morgan Phelps tells me you told her that she has to come in today and look at pictures of pervert rapists."

"I know it's repulsive, but she needs to do it while it's still fresh, and if she IDs him, that's one more rapist we can get off the street and prosecute."

"She's just starting to get over the trauma and in no

condition to do that yet. We'll call you when she can," Ed said decisively and clicked off the phone.

"Thank you so much," Morgan said with utmost feeling.

"For what?"

"Sticking up for me."

"Glad to do it," Ed said easily. "Tell you what, if you're up to it, let's go over to your apartment and get your stuff; then we'll celebrate Kristen's great news and you starting a new life. And tomorrow, I'm taking you both to buy some rags and whatever else you need."

"You're including me?" Morgan said disbelievingly.

"Yes, of course—you're part of the team. We're going to Drai's tomorrow night for Kristen's big blowout, and I want you both looking chic."

Morgan rushed over to Kristen and hugged her. "Oh my God, you're going to perform at Drai's. That's the hottest nightclub on the Strip."

"That's what Sid said."

"So he's going to manage you?" Morgan said excitedly.

"He didn't say that, but he sure acted like he is."

"It's as good as done," Ed said confidently.

"I'm so happy for you," Morgan said joyfully and hugged Kristen.

"And you know what? You'll be with me all the way," Kristen said happily.

"All right, ladies, what do you say we saddle up and get Morgan moved, then celebrate?"

CHAPTER 18

I t was a Saturday from hell that Ed could not believe, between his pain and Kristen's nerves. Several times he seriously considered taking a pain pill, but he knew it would impede his thinking and his ability to snap Kristen out of her major stage fright, which began right after breakfast. He could see it as she ate with deliberation and, shortly after, dashed to the bathroom; when she finally returned, she was pale, and her eyes were bloodshot.

"Did you heave?" Ed said with deep concern.

"Yes, maybe it's the flu," Kristen said.

"I think it's more like a case of really bad nerves, which is understandable and happens even to most experienced pros. We need to get your mind to focus on something else, like us going shopping, which we have to do," Ed said and winked at Morgan, who got the message.

"Yeah, that sounds great! Come on, Kristen—let's get dressed and do it," Morgan said encouragingly and rose to her feet.

"After we finish shopping, we'll stop over at Cromwell Hotel and check out Drai's," Ed said deftly.

"Why?" Kristen said with a perplexed look.

"The best way to overcome fear is to take it head-on and kick its ass," Ed said lightheartedly. "That's what I used to do."

"You did that?"

"Yes, when I had to pitch our firm to new clients and at other large functions."

"You were nervous like me?"

"Sometimes worse," Ed fibbed and glanced over to Morgan for reinforcement.

"This is a piece of cake compared to what you used to do," Morgan said, taking the hint.

Kristen looked at Morgan with a questioning look. "When?"

"Pole dancing, you twit."

"Yeah, I guess," Kristen said with a sigh.

"Don't you remember? We used to kid about it and say we were performing for a bunch of slobbering baboons."

Kristen chuckled. "And most of them were."

"Glad you ladies reminded me; please, whatever you do, don't bring up pole dancing in front of Sid."

"Hope he's never been to the Pink Pony or some of the other strip joints," Morgan said uneasily.

"He probably wouldn't recognize you with your clothes on," Kristen joshed.

"Maybe I shouldn't go," Morgan said seriously.

"Nonsense—he'll be seeing you a lot of you once Kristen goes on the road, so we might as well get it over with if, in fact, he's seen you before," Ed said calmly.

"You really think he's going to sign Kristen?"

"After her performance tonight, he'll be begging her to sign," Ed said confidently.

"Not if he sees me all shaken up," Kristen said apprehensively.

"I'm sure he's seen it many times before with his performers and others; it goes with the territory."

"I bet Dolly Parton was never like this."

"When she started she was," Morgan said.

"You're just saying that."

"It's true; I read it in a magazine," Morgan insisted, even though she hadn't.

"Well, I guess I better pull myself together," Kristen said, more upbeat.

"That's my girl," Ed said proudly.

As prearranged, Sid met Ed and the two girls near the entrance to Drai's; he was wearing a black western suit with red piping, a light-pink shirt, and a black string tie, and on his head was a dressy, custom-made black Diamante Stetson.

"Wow," Sid exclaimed as Kristen and Morgan approached just ahead of Ed. "Kristen, you look absolutely fantastic in that outfit; it's exactly as I had hoped. Ed wasn't kidding when he told me, 'Wait till you see her.'"

"You don't think the dress is a little too short?"

"Not with those legs, and by the way, the boots look great."

"They should, for what they cost," Kristen said with a glance at Ed.

Sid then turned his attention to Morgan, who looked stunning in a designer gold plunging-neckline dress, amply exposing her voluptuous breasts.

"I'm Sid, and you do justice to that exquisite dress," Sid said with an extended hand.

"I'm Morgan. Nice to meet you, and thank you for the compliment, which Ed should receive since he picked it out," Morgan said as she shook Sid's hand.

"Ed, you certainly have an eye for what beautiful women should wear."

"Had lot of practice doing it at the ad agency," Ed said humbly.

"Maybe you should open a consulting business—teach these showbiz broads how to dress efficaciously," Sid said with a grin.

"I had all I could stand dealing with those boors for forty years," Ed said sardonically.

Sid glanced at his watch. "We've got time for some drinks before Kristen goes on."

"Great idea," Ed said with a nod and motioned to the girls to follow Sid.

As they weaved their way through the crowded tables, some of the men passed sexy remarks at Kristen and especially Morgan, who acknowledged them with an eat-your-hearts-out look. Once they were all at the table, Sid ordered a round of drinks for everybody except Kristen, who had to settle for a glass of orange juice.

"You know, we stopped by here earlier today for a preview, but it looks so much different with this huge crowd and those incredible lights on," Ed said, looking around.

"It was designed by Victor Drai, and besides the lights, it has great acoustics as well. Don't be surprised to see showbiz types and big-time jocks. They come here after gambling and other joints to really party it up," Sid said buoyantly. "And if you want a breath of fresh desert air, there's a terrace out there with a panoramic view of the Strip and the Bellagio Water Show."

"Definitely impressive," Ed said, glancing up at the infused LED lights over the dance floor, which gave it surreal appearance.

"Just about everything in Vegas is; that's why I live here," Sid said with a grin. "Kristen, make sure to take advantage of the sound system; it's the very best."

Kristen nodded. "I'll do that; I just wish I could take the stage right now."

"It'll come soon enough, so in the meantime, absorb the atmosphere; it'll help to calm your nerves."

"A drink would help," Kristen joshed.

"You know my rule," Sid said unequivocally.

After the second round of drinks and numerous requests by eager young men asking Kristen and Morgan to dance, which they both declined, Sid glanced at his watch, then Kristen. "Are you ready?"

"Yes," Kristen said bravely.

Ed smiled and squeezed Kristen's hand. "Go knock 'em dead like you did everyplace else."

Once she was backstage, Kristen's nerves seriously got the best of her, and she started to hyperventilate, prompting Sid to take immediate action. He pulled a brown paper bag out of his jacket pocket and handed it to Kristen.

"Breathe into the bag repeatedly."

Minutes later, Kristen's breathing normalized, and she handed the bag back to Sid with an appreciative smile. "Thank you—thought I was going to pass out."

"It's something I've had plenty of experience with, so don't think it's just you," Sid said with a relieved look and stuck the bag back in his pocket.

"I feel like such a wuss," Kristen said dejectedly.

"It'll get better as your confidence grows," Sid said in a calming voice. "Now continue to breathe deeply."

"I'll be all right once I'm on the stage and the music starts," Kristen said.

"This is your moment in life. Go for it with all you've got," Sid said with an encouraging grin and a pat on her back.

Kristen nodded with a forced smile. "This is for Ed as well; I can't let him down.

"When you do 'Help Me Make It through the Night,' close your eyes and pretend you are singing to your lover. Then, when you do 'Me and Bobby McGee,' let it all hang out like you did at audition and use the entire stage."

"You're gonna watch me from back here?"

"No, I'm going back to the table, unless you want me to stay here?"

"No, I'll be OK."

"I believe in you, just like Ed," Sid said confidently.

"Thanks."

"He's taken you a long way in a hurry," Sid said thoughtfully.

"More than you'll ever know," Kristen murmured and glanced over at the very fit middle-aged man approaching.

"Sid, my pal, what're you doing, guarding the goods?"

"Yeah, from the likes of you," Sid said lightheartedly and extended his hand. "Good to see you, Doug."

"So this your new discovery?" Doug said, eyeing Kristen.

Sid nodded with a gratifying grin. "Kristen, this is my good friend Doug Collins, the Las Vegas wolf who made this possible."

"Nice to meet you, and thanks," Kristen said appreciatively and held out her hand, which Doug grasp and kissed in a gentlemanly way.

"Now that I've met you, I'm doubly glad Sid talked me into doing this, and please disregard Sid's fallacious comment."

"I'll pretend I didn't hear it," Kristen said with smile.

"Is this your first public appearance?"

"I've done others, but nothing like this."

"Audience-wise, I'm sure."

"That and the place."

"You nervous?"

"I was very nervous, but Sid talked me down."

"What songs are you doing?"

"'Help Me Make It through the Night' and 'Me and Bobby McGee.'"

"Great country songs," Doug said.

"There's the cue song," Sid said as the music wound down. "Doug will introduce you, so take a few more deep breaths to steady yourself."

"Have a great performance," Doug said and hurried onto the stage.

"Knock their socks off!" Sid said fervently.

"Ladies and gentlemen, we have a special treat for you tonight, courtesy of Mr. Sid Greene—his new discovery in country music. Let's put our hands together and welcome her the Las Vegas way: Miss Kristen Cole."

Kristen bolted onto the stage and dashed directly to the floor mic, which she removed and then acknowledged the applause with a bow. Once Doug left and the room quieted, she closed her eyes as Sid suggested and began 'Help Me Make It through the Night,' totally oblivious of the crowd. A few bars later and more confident, she opened her eyes at well-timed moments and focused on a nearby table and an attentive young couple. When she neared the end, the applause broke, and she bowed repeatedly, then turned to the band and nodded for them to start her blockbuster song. In an instant, she transformed herself from a nearly motionless stance to an exploding, spicy bombshell, with the voice to match. Within moments, the audience was caught up in Kristen's bodacious performance and went crazy as she wildly traversed the stage in perfect sync with the music and the words. When she finished, she was breathless and totally spent. Holding the mic in hand with a wide stance at the edge of the stage, she smiled and looked out at the audience, which exploded in thunderous applause, whistles, and chants of "One more." She bowed slowly and repeated, "Thank you."

Sid, like everyone else, was totally stunned and on his feet. "Holy Christ, she took a page from Tina Turner and amplified it. No one has ever done that in country music. She's dynamite!"

Ed smiled and said humorously, "She's really a reserved girl."

"I can vouch for that," Morgan chimed in.

"Ed, I owe you big time; we'll discuss it all later. Right now, let's watch Kristen enjoy the biggest night of her life."

After numerous bows, Kristen climbed down the stage stairs and hurried back to the table, but she was repeatedly stopped along the way by the people wanting to shake her hand and showering her with accolades. When she finally reached the table, she stepped directly into Ed's open arms, followed by proud hugs and cheek kisses.

"I never thought I'd get a chance to be part of something this great," Ed said in a choked voice. "Thanks so much."

"I hope to give you many more such occasions," Kristen said only for Ed to hear.

"Kristen, you knocked the ball out of the park, and it's still traveling through space," Sid said to Kristen after the hugs and once all were seated.

"Thanks so much for giving me the chance."

"It's not only your movement, but you also amped up your voice, from mellow to bodacious, when you did the second one."

"The song just does that to me."

"If that's the case, then we'll have to find more songs like that or write them for you,"

Sid said enthusiastically.

"Either way, I'm game," Kristen said happily and gently nudged Ed's leg under the table with her foot, hoping he caught the message as well.

"Kristen, congratulations—that was one hell of performance and needs to be celebrated," Doug said vociferously when he reached the table with two waiters in tow: one with two buckets of iced champagne and the other with five glasses on a tray.

"Thank you so much. Glad you liked it."

"Liked it so much that I want you to do an encore tomorrow night."

"Sorry, pal, one performance is all you're going to get," Sid said outright, "and with that, let me introduce you to Ed and Morgan."

Once done shaking hands, Doug pulled up a chair next to Morgan and instructed the waiter to pour the champagne, then turned to Morgan.

"You look sensational."

"Thank you," Morgan said cordially.

"You're Kristen's friend?"

"Yes."

"Don't know why, but I feel like I know you," Doug said with a scrutinizing look.

"We've never met," Morgan said firmly but suddenly felt her worst fear coming true, thinking Doug may have seen her at one of the strip joints.

"Well, maybe not," Doug said dismissively and raised his glass with a nod at Kristen. "Here's to the next country megastar."

All acknowledged the toast with agreeable comments, and some of the people at the nearby tables even joined in the accolades. Doug was most anxious to know all about Kristen and peppered her with questions, which she guardedly answered. With the champagne having been quickly consumed by all except Kristen, Doug ordered more, and Sid took over on the joviality front, delivering rapid-fire risqué jokes, pausing at times to give the others a chance to catch their breath from the gut-splitting laughter. A while later, finally spent, Sid took a well-earned break.

"Sid, my man, you have really outdone yourself with this find," Doug praised.

"Thanks to Ed—a perfect congruence of all the right components."

"Well, it's been a blast," Doug said and rose to his feet. "Kristen, not long from now when you're a megastar, please come back and do an encore."

"I will," Kristen said agreeably.

With Doug's departure, Sid got down to business and pulled an envelope from his jacket pocket, then handed it to Ed. "No doubt you know what this is."

"I have an idea," Ed said with a knowing nod.

"It's Kristen's contract; read it over and see an attorney Monday morning. If it's acceptable, let's get together at my office in the early afternoon and have Kristen sign it," Sid said gladly. "And just to ease your mind, it's fairly straightforward, no fancy legalese or hidden clauses—not my way."

"Thanks," Ed said and extended his hand.

"Just so you know, I made the decision after Kristen did the first song yesterday," Sid said with a wink and grin.

"Thank you so much," Kristen blurted happily.

"You've more than earned it, and Ed, now I would suggest you might want to get the ladies home. Otherwise, they're going to be hit all night long, and we have to be mindful of Kristen's image from now on."

"You're right about that," Ed said most agreeably and motioned to the girls to get ready to leave.

CHAPTER 19

It was little after nine Sunday morning when Ed's cell phone buzzed. He thought it was Alice, but to his surprise it was Ted Stevenson, his attorney.

"Hope I didn't wake you," Ted kidded, knowing Ed's sleeping schedule very well.

"I'm on my third cup of coffee, washing it down with a glass of Wild Turkey," Ed said tepidly.

"Pain getting worse?" Ted asked with true concern.

"Yeah, the booze is just not working like it did before, and very shortly I'll have to start on the fentanyl, but on the positive side, I have accomplished what I hoped for Kristen."

"That's fantastic; tell me about it," Ted said eagerly.

"Sid Greene, the country-star-maker extraordinaire, as of last night agreed to manage Kristen after she brought the house down. As a matter of fact, I was going to call and ask you to review the entertainment contract, which I've looked at and is fairly simple; I'll fax it to you for a glance if you don't mind."

"Congratulations, that's awesome. Kristen must be floating on cloud nine—wish I could have seen her perform," Ted said earnestly. "I can certainly take a look at the contract."

"I still can't believe all this has happened so quickly, and of course, neither can Kristen. To think it was just a whim when I told her to pursue a singing career. Now in just weeks, she's about to sign a contract with a big-time manager. The Drai's entertainment director totally agreed that Kristen's on her way to megastardom."

"So what's next?"

"We'll find out Monday when we get together to sign the contract. I'm sure there's a hell of a lot to do before she starts performing."

"You still going to be involved?"

"My job is done. I'm just about at the end of the road on both counts."

"A goddamn shame," Ted said glumly.

"Hey, at least I'll be leaving something worthwhile behind."

"From the sound of it, it's more than just something," Ted said encouragingly.

"So listen, you call me for any particular reason?"

"Yeah, a very good one—your house is sold as of a couple of hours ago. And get this, there were three buyers bidding, and it sold for ten grand more than you had asked," Ted said proudly.

"I'll be damned, what a weekend," Ed said wryly and poured himself another drink. "When do they want to close?"

"Just as soon as possible; they're already mortgage preapproved. You've got some serious money coming your way."

"Yeah, to enjoy in my retirement," Ed said sardonically.

"I wish to Christ I knew what to say," Ted said uneasily.

"Sorry, I must sound pitiful, and that's the last goddamn thing I ever want to do."

"You're not. Now getting back to the house closing, the good news is that you won't have to come."

"Why not?"

"You gave me full power of attorney and I can do it on your behalf."

"That's great; I'm not in the mood to take another trip back there," Ed said with relief. "Listen, I'll fax you copies of the entertainment contract, so I'll need your number."

"Got a pencil?"

A moment later with the phone number written and goodbyes said, Ed settled back in the kitchen chair and took a long swig of the booze. He felt a sense of relief, having the house sold and no further constraints. He gazed about his new and final place of residence and thought it unreal—sharing a house with two young women he met by chance and, even more bizarre, leaving Kristen his life's worth and quite possibly Morgan as well. He shook his head with a slight chuckle and wondered what Ann would have thought. His introspection was suddenly halted by the buzzing cell phone once again.

"Good morning, Ed," Alice cheerfully said. "Hope I'm not interrupting anything."

"Good morning. And you're not—just having a third cup of coffee and some Wild Turkey," Ed confessed, figuring Alice probably would have guessed by the sound of his voice. At this stage he was past trying to act as if he didn't drink.

"I had a Mass said for you this morning, but I guess so far it hasn't helped," Alice said, sounding disappointed.

"I appreciate that very much, but at this stage, it's way too late even for God, but on a much happier note, Kristen had an incredible night, topped off by Sid agreeing to manage her."

"That's marvelous! I'm so happy for her and you as

well. Just can't believe it's really happened. Is she with you now? I'd like to congratulate her," Alice said excitedly.

"No, she's still asleep; we had some drinks and got home somewhat late."

"Wish I could have seen her."

"Morgan recorded some of Kristen's performance on her cell phone.

"I'll ask my daughter if there is a way to send it to my cell phone or computer; she knows a lot about that stuff."

"I hope there is a way, and you've just given me idea—think I'll buy a couple of laptops for the girls; they'll probably need them for things I can' even think of," Ed said lightheartedly.

"I'm sure they will, and we'll be able to video conference," Alice said thoughtfully.

"Wish I had thought of it sooner."

"You've had a lot on your plate," Alice said kindly.

"Well, it's all winding down," Ed said reflectively.

Alice felt the sadness in those words and promptly countered, "I have some great news, too; Mickey is moving back to New York and will live with me."

"That's great. How soon?" Ed said enthusiastically.

"Next weekend if she can arrange it all," Alice said happily.

"Did you have any inkling?"

"She vaguely hinted she might after Frank died, but I really didn't think she would since she was solidly settled in DC and in her position there."

"There's nothing like having your own flesh and blood nearby in your later years, and now your sister won't be pressuring you into moving to Omaha," Ed kidded.

"Wish we could celebrate both our great news."

"Most definitely," Ed said with a mock toast and took a swallow of the booze.

"How soon, you think, before Kristen has her professional performance debut?"

"I really don't know since there's quite a bit to be done. Are you by chance thinking of seeing her perform?" Ed said hopefully.

"Yes, I'd love to if it's in Las Vegas, which would go in stride with what you mentioned."

"It'll be my treat—I mean you flying here," Ed said promptly.

"That would be unfair of me," Alice said reticently. "You've already spent some money on me with that expensive angel."

"I sure as hell can't take it with me."

"Well, you certainly had an eventful weekend. Which reminds me, how is Morgan?"

"She's physically recovering well and actually went with us to the nightclub; of course, I don't know how she's doing mentally, but that recovery will likely take a lot longer."

"So she's going to live with you and Kristen permanently?"

"Yes, we already got her stuff."

"Just remember what they say about two women under one roof," Alice teased.

"No problem—it won't be for long anyway."

Alice winced. "Let's concentrate on all the good news, please."

"You're right. I apologize."

"She's so lucky to have you and Kristen."

"Actually, I'm the one who's lucky; I can't imagine what my life would have been alone at this point."

"And we wouldn't have met."

"I'm not sure you gained very much."

"That's a terrible thing to say," Alice chided.

"I'm sorry. What I meant is that you don't need the grief," Ed said and took another swig.

"I know it's not for me to say, but maybe you should start taking the pain pills instead of the Wild Turkey since it sounds like it's not helping," Alice suggested weakly.

"The problem is, once I start, there's no going back, not even a day."

"But you're in so much pain."

"I'll get through it for a little longer."

"Maybe I should let you go, and you can call me when you're not in so much pain."

"I'll do that for certain," Ed said positively.

"Please don't give up," Alice murmured.

"I haven't so far, bye."

CHAPTER 20

At Sid's request, Ed and Kristen got to his reporter-filled office at two o'clock, which was no surprise since Sid had called Ed midmorning and let him know they would be there. He'd assured Ed they would not be obnoxious since he knew them all well. Many of the older ones had been there when he introduced his other country stars. To ensure their cordiality, Sid treated them to a catered luncheon in the music room, with no limit on drinks, of course. Ed was quite aware of how it all worked since he had extensive experience in doing the same over the years at the ad agency when pursuing new clients.

"Ladies and gentlemen, there she is, my last and soon to be greatest country star: Miss Kristen Cole," Sid announced vociferously, making his way to the doorway to take Kristen's hand and guiding her back to his desk, where he motioned for her to sit in his chair while he stood at her side.

"Now before your questions, I would like you all to witness Kristen signing the contract, which will make our association good for as long as she wants," Sid said grandly.

With the contract signed and pictures snapped, Sid helped Kristen out of the chair and had her sit on the corner of the desk, exposing her well-toned legs half-way up the thighs, which the male reporters lapped up; the camera shutters clicked away. Even though Ed was not pleased with the stunt, he knew very well what Sid was doing; the tactic had been developed long ago on Madison Avenue. Once the photo frenzy stopped, Sid announced that Kristen would answer questions, which she did fairly well, and whenever she started to stumble, Sid immediately jumped in and helped her answer. Twenty minutes later, Sid raised his hands and thanked everyone for their insightful probes and bid them a good rest of the day. When all had left, Sid helped Kristen off the desk, then pulled out a bottle of Jack Daniels from a drawer and three glasses, two of which he amply filled, giving Kristen a single sip.

"To a great, rewarding association and your super-stardom," Sid said directly to Kristen with the glass held high.

"I'll do my best to live up to your expectations."

"I have full confidence you will," Sid said propitiously and clinked Ed and Kristen's glasses.

Once they were seated, Sid pushed his hat slightly back and looked directly at Ed. "I noticed a disapproving look on your face when seeing Kristen expose her legs, but being an ad man, you know why."

"Yeah, I do," Ed conceded. "Guess I'm being overprotective."

"In this business, it's all about the buzz, and Kristen has created a firestorm. I've lost count of the number of calls from casino entertainment bigwigs wanting Kristen to perform as a warm-up for their headliners, but that's not about to happen. She will do nothing less than top billing right from the start," Sid said forcefully.

"I'm with you on that a hundred percent," Ed said staunchly. "So what's next?"

"The band. I've already hired five top country musicians, so Kristen can start rehearsing with them starting Wednesday morning. Oh, one of them writes country songs, which she'll need, and he'll also teach her to read sheet music. We'll also need sound equipment and a tour bus; that aside, the choker will be the initial promo expense for the tour."

"What'd you have in mind?"

"Local radio, plus TV in the tour cities."

"What's the bottom line?" Ed said eagerly.

"At least two hundred grand—probably more," Sid said.

"I can handle it," Ed said coolly.

Sid was bowled over. "Seriously?"

"I just sold my house, which will more than cover it."

"Tell you what," Sid said thoughtfully. "Why don't we split it and add to it if we need more: I believe in Kristen as well."

"I appreciate the offer on both counts," Ed said readily.

"Just one more thing: To what extent do you plan to be involved?"

Ed glanced at his watch. "As of an hour ago when Kristen signed the contract, I relinquished my charge into your most capable hands."

Kristen looked over to Ed and said pathetically, "You're just walking away from me?"

Ed smiled kindly. "I'll always be there for you, but Sid is the man who will take you to the very top now; I just got you started."

"Will you go on the tour with me?"

"If I were in good health, of course I would, but you know my situation."

"Is there something I don't know?" Sid said with a querying look at Ed.

"Yeah, I'll fill you in after we finish with Kristen."

"Well, more or less that just about does it, unless you have questions."

"Where are you thinking of taking her on the tour?"

"Texas: the land of country music."

"I thought that was Tennessee?" Ed said ignorantly.

"Nashville popularized it; Texas lives it."

"That does it for me, question-wise," Ed said with finality.

"Kristen, why don't you get together with Donna and go over the rehearsal schedule and the photo shoot?"

Once Kristen left, Sid focused on Ed with a scrutinizing look. "So what's the issue with your health, if you don't mind me asking?"

Ed's face hardened. "I've got stage four pancreatic cancer and not much time."

"Oh Christ, I'm so sorry—Kristen know?"

"No, I was wounded in the gut in Vietnam, which I told Kristen is causing all the pain; I've been holding off telling her till she got her break."

"So that's why all this hurry," Sid said keenly. "And there's nothing that can be done about it?"

"Unfortunately not," Ed said with a shrug.

"What a goddamn lousy break," Sid said and emptied his glass. "When do you plan to tell her?"

"I'm hoping to hold off till after her tour."

"I'll do my best to get her ready as quickly as I can," Sid said kindly. "I'll have to push her to the limit with the rehearsals, just so you know."

"She'll do it, knowing it's probably because of me since she's getting suspicious that it's something more than the wound."

"Is she the only family you have?"

"Yeah," Ed said dismissively to halt further conversation about it.

"So did the New Year's Eve in Las Vegas live up to your expectations?" Sid asked, changing the subject.

"More than I even imagined."

"Lucky for me, you wanted to spend it here; otherwise, you'd probably have gone to Nashville—that's where most wannabe country singers go."

"It was fate," Ed said wryly.

"You're probably right," Sid said with a grin.

"Oh, one thing more that concerns Morgan: I'd appreciate it if you would put her on Kristen's payroll since she's her close friend, and Kristen will need her when I'm gone."

"Makes good sense, and I'll even up it: when we're in Vegas, she can help Donna in the office; that way, she'll have a full-time job."

"Thanks, she really needs a break."

"I'm surprised. She's an attractive, well-endowed girl. I thought she was probably a chorus dancer or had something to do with the showbiz world."

"It's a long story; maybe she'll tell you one day," Ed said and rose to his feet with an extended hand. "Thanks so much for taking Kristen on."

"And I thank you for bringing her to me." Sid countered with a warm handshake and walked Ed to the door.

When Ed and Kristen got home, they found Morgan pacing the kitchen floor, looking nervous and dismayed.

"What's wrong?" Ed asked earnestly.

"The sheriff's office called a while ago and asked me to come as soon as I can to view a lineup," Morgan said nervously. "Last night they arrested some lowlife animal for an attempted rape a couple of blocks from where I was attacked. This time he went after the wrong woman; she was a plainclothes cop on an assignment, and they think it might be the same guy who raped me."

"You want me to go with you?"

"You don't mind?"

"I'd be glad to," Ed said sprightly.

Morgan relaxed and looked at Kristen. "So how did it go?"

"Like I can't believe," Kristen said cheerfully.

Morgan perked up. "Tell me!"

"I start rehearsals Wednesday with a five-piece band, and you can be my travel liaison on a salary, and when we're in Vegas, you'll be helping Donna in the office."

"For real?" Morgan said excitedly.

"Yes, starting Wednesday, same as me."

Morgan rushed over and hugged Kristen. "I'm so happy."

"You owe Ed a hug as well since he's the one who came up with the idea."

Morgan turned and warmly hugged Ed. "Thank you so much. I just love you."

"I do you as well."

"So how soon is the tour?" Morgan said eagerly.

"When Sid says I'm ready, which I intend to be a lot sooner than he thinks," Kristen said confidently.

"I have no doubt," Morgan said supportively.

Ed glanced at his watch, then Morgan. "Are you ready?"

"Yes."

"I'll fix dinner while you guys are gone," Kristen announced.

"On the way back, we'll stop and get some wine and dessert," Ed said and started for the door with Morgan at his side.

Once they were in the car and on the way, Morgan grew silent and fidgety, which puzzled Ed. "What's up?"

"This is really a waste of time," Morgan murmured, disgruntled.

"But he might be the one," Ed said with a puzzled look.

Morgan made a sour face and shook her head. "The only way I can identify him is if they make him show his prick since the guy was hung like a horse and did me from behind. I didn't even see his face."

Ed was stunned by the revelation and momentarily speechless. "Did you tell the cops that when they interviewed you?"

"I'm not sure what I said," Morgan grumbled.

"That's understandable," Ed said sympathetically. "You need to tell them now."

"If by chance I do identify him, what will happen then?"

"There'll be a trial, of course, and you'll have to testify."

"I'll be grilled?"

"That's for sure."

"They'll ask about my past?"

"Yes."

"And I'll have to tell them about my sordid life?"

"I'm afraid so."

"So I'll be publicly ridiculed and labeled a slut," Morgan brooded.

"Perhaps by some," Ed said uneasily.

"Then this new beginning you arranged will be shot to hell."

Ed knew where Morgan was coming from and struggled with giving her advice, but he desperately wanted to ease her mind. "From what you said, there is no way you could positively identify the lowlife creep other than by his prick, and I doubt they'll have the guys drop their pants, so perhaps it might be wise not to do this."

"I'm so glad you see it that way, too," Morgan said with relief.

"Are you open to some advice?"

"Yes, if it's from you."

"I suggest from now on that you be more selective with your men. Believe it or not, there are some good ones out there."

"But no one like you," Morgan said tenderly.

"Are you messing with me?"

"That was sincere, but I will if you want," Morgan teased.

"I'll be ready," Ed said and grabbed his gut.

"Bad pain again?" Morgan said with deep concern.

"It's a goddamn bitch."

"Kristen told me the pain comes from a wound you got in Vietnam, but now she thinks it's something more serious than that."

"If I tell you, will you promise not to tell her?"

Morgan hesitated momentarily and reluctantly nodded. "OK, but she should know."

"I'll tell her after the tour."

"I understand. So what is it?" Morgan asked uneasily.

"I've got stage four pancreatic cancer."

"Oh, God no," Morgan screamed out and grabbed Ed's arm.

"One of life's little gifts that some get," Ed said un-emotionally and took several deep breaths, hoping to ease the pain.

"And they can't do anything about it?"

"No," Ed murmured in a pained voice.

"And I thought I had it bad," Morgan said with tearful eyes.

"You did, and please don't let this pull you down. I wouldn't have told you, but I might need your help since I don't want Kristen to be distracted from what she has to do in the next few weeks."

Morgan wiped the tears and looked kindly at Ed. "It won't be easy, but I'll do my best to keep it from Kristen, and in the meantime, if there's anything—and I mean anything—I can do, just ask."

"You're a sweet girl," Ed said and squeezed Morgan's damp hand.

"Been a long time since anybody's called me that," Morgan said emotionally.

"You're deserving of it."

"Thank you for coming into my life, although 'thank you' is just not enough; I love you, Ed."

"How lucky can I get? Two beautiful girls who love this old, broken-down man," Ed teased.

"This one loves you no matter how old you are and would do anything you ask."

"I'm glad . . . because when the time comes, I may ask you to do something that you might not agree with."

"For you, I will."

"Please remember that."

"Does Alice know of your condition?"

"I told her when I was in New York not to waste her time with me, but she foolishly didn't listen."

"I don't blame her; I wouldn't, either. Knowing you even for a day is worth more than knowing most men for a lifetime," Morgan said lovingly.

"You give me too much credit. Helping you and Kristen doesn't make me a great man or a benefactor," Ed said with a shrug. "What you girls give me in return is worth more than all the gold in the world."

CHAPTER 21

With eleven straight days of nonstop rehearsals under her belt, Kristen finally gave in to Sid's pleas and agreed to take Sunday off. The twelve-hour days had pushed the band to the limit, and two of the musicians threatened to quit. Kristen ignored the threats and told Sid she didn't want wimps in her band and didn't care if they walked. She expected them all to work just as hard as she did. Even though she'd never been on tour, Kristen knew it was going to be a grind, so they all might as well get used to it now. Sid was amazed by Kristen's drive and tenacity and told Ed he expected her to be ready in no more than a week; he'd already started to book the tour. The news lifted Ed's spirits until he realized he'd be alone when Kristen and Morgan were gone. Then suddenly, it occurred to him that this would be a perfect time for Alice to come for a visit. Health permitting, they could catch up with Kristen at one of the tour cities to see her perform, which Alice badly wanted to do. With that thought, he refilled his mug with strong black coffee, returned to the table, and called Alice.

"Good morning, Ed," Alice said sweetly, just as she had every time he called.

"Good morning to you as well. I hope I'm not interrupting your lunch."

"You're not. I'm waiting for my overworked daughter to come home."

"She worked today?"

"They had some kind of serious issue with a cyber-attack or something, and she had to rush to the office about five o'clock this morning."

"That's tough, especially on a Sunday morning," Ed said sympathetically.

"As I've mentioned before, she's on call twenty-four-seven."

"After a full week, has she had a chance to acclimate to being home?"

"I think she misses being in DC. As you know, it's another world there."

"Yeah, out of touch and full of double-talk," Ed said satirically.

"You sound very sharp this morning," Alice said happily.

"I got about four hours of straight sleep for a change, and the pain isn't all that bad."

"I'm so happy to hear that, especially since a couple of days ago, you were on the verge of taking pain pills."

"I toughed it out. Just not sure how long I can keep it up since it's getting much worse."

"You, without a doubt, are the toughest man I have ever known. Some of Frank's buddies were tough, but you're heads and heels over them."

"I appreciate you saying that. Now let me tell you the thought I had just minutes ago."

"Please do—you sound very enthused about it," Alice said eagerly.

"Sid told me yesterday that Kristen only needs about another week or so of rehearsals, so he's booking her tour.

Both she and Morgan will be gone twelve days, so I thought if you're willing, it'd be a great time to come to Vegas. We'll catch up with Kristen on the tour after you have a chance to see Las Vegas and do a little gambling," Ed kidded.

"That sounds wonderful," Alice said happily. "Not sure about the gambling, though."

"You just made my day, as that great American philosopher Clint Eastwood once said," Ed kidded.

Alice chuckled and said eagerly, "Did Kristen finally take today off?"

"Yes, had she not, Morgan and I were going to tie her to the bed while she slept," Ed joshed.

"I can't believe how hard she's working."

"Even Sid is amazed. He told me that of the five singers he managed, not even all of them put together could match her in that department—said she's like a tigress in a cage, and no one dares to get in her way."

"And how is Morgan doing?"

"She loves working for Sid and the showbiz atmosphere, and she's also become quite adept at running the house since she gets home a couple of hours before Kristen."

"Sounds like you've really hit the jackpot with the two girls."

"Make it three."

"What? You're taking on another?" Alice said in disbelief.

"I'm referring to you."

"Thanks for the thought, but I'm slightly past the girl stage."

"I believe no matter what age, there always remains a part of a little girl in every woman."

"I sometimes wonder," Alice said thoughtfully.

"By the way, will Mickey have a problem with you coming out to visit me?"

"No, she's pretty liberal in her thinking, and even if she wasn't, I still would," Alice said firmly.

"I truly appreciate that. Just don't want to cause you additional grief. You've already got more than you bargained for."

"Are you going there again?"

"Sorry."

"So since both girls will be home, you have any special plans?"

"As a matter of fact, I was thinking of taking them on a picnic."

"In January?" Alice said disbelievingly.

"We're supposed to have a springlike day, and I found this great place in the mountains less than an hour from here."

"Sounds wonderful; wish I was there."

"We'll do it when you're here. I think you'll love it; the views are absolutely breathtaking."

"Oh, oh, I hear the front door opening—must be Mickey."

"I'll call you tonight."

"You don't mind if I hang up?"

"Not at all, and say hello to Mickey for me."

Ed had no sooner hung up than Morgan and Kristen came bounding in, wearing oversize T-shirts and happy faces.

"Good morning," they yelped.

"Well, good morning to my sleepyheads. Aren't we full of energy and good cheer?"

"And how are you on this gorgeous morning?" Kristen chirped.

269

"Not that bad for a change."

"That's so great," Kristen said happily.

"How are you on coffee?" Morgan said as she started for the coffeepot near the stove.

"I'm still good, thanks."

"Did you talk to Alice and tell her the good news?" Kristen said as she sat down at the table.

"Yes, I just hung up. She's thrilled and wants to see you perform at a concert."

"She's coming?" Kristen said excitedly.

"Yes."

"Oh, that's great," Morgan said as she returned with two mugs of coffee. "Now we won't have to worry about you being alone."

"That's very sweet of you two," Ed said tenderly. "And now let me tell you what I have in mind for this beautiful springlike day if you're game."

"A dip in the pool?" Morgan kidded as she sat the mugs on the table.

"Not quite, but how about a picnic in the mountains?"

"Sounds like fun," Morgan blurted enthusiastically. "I've always wanted to, but for one reason or another, I've never been on one."

"What mountain?" Kristen said with a puzzled look.

"Mount Charleston. It's about an hour's drive from here."

"You've been there?"

"Yes, while you girls are working your little butts off, I've been checking out the area, and you'd be surprised how many great places there are to see."

"So that's what you've been doing when we can't reach you, and here we thought you were occupied with loose women," Morgan teased.

"I do that between my explorations," Ed said with a straight face.

"Aha, so we're partly right," Kristen said humorously.

Ed smiled and shook his head. "Well, you've got me. What can I say?"

"So you're cheating on us," Morgan said reprovingly.

"Every chance I get," Ed fired back with a grin.

"We're just gonna have to lock you in or take you with us to Sid's every day."

"OK by me," Ed said mirthfully. "So, Kristen, what about the picnic?"

"Yes, let's do it."

"You girls won't regret it," Ed said happily.

CHAPTER 22

It took all the willpower Ed could summon to get through the week without resorting to the pain pills. He did not want to distract Kristen from her final week of intense rehearsals and the all-out preparations for the tour. With the departure time in less than three hours, Ed felt quite dispirited, unlike the previous Sunday. As much as he wished the girls were up already so that they could spend more time together, he knew they needed to get all the rest they could after the frenzied week and what lay ahead. Even Morgan had been putting in long hours as well, and when they got home around seven or eight, they both crashed from exhaustion. Ed, not up to cooking, had their dinners catered once Morgan called with the time they'd be home and what they were in the mood to have.

With the rehearsals and the tour all set, Ed was even more impressed with Sid's show-business savvy and certain of Kristen's stardom. He just wished he'd still be around to see her reach the very top. He found it ironic that of all the significant moments in his life, this was the one he picked to be the most important one. And even more bizarre, he didn't feel guilty choosing it, but then again, a lot of what he did now no longer represented his lifelong thinking. Like most people, he had always considered the accumulation of material things the ultimate goal, but now, nearing the end, it no longer was of consequence. His deep reflection was suddenly halted by loud footsteps racing to the kitchen and Morgan and Kristen bounding in like two teenagers full of mischief.

"Good morning, Ed," they both sang out when they reached him.

"Morning, ladies, and it's about time you got up," Ed said affably.

"So what's for breakfast?" Kristen teased.

"Well, being that it's almost ten and a dreary Sunday, how about hot oatmeal and some toast since you'll be having lunch in a couple of hours."

"It'll be subs, which I ordered yesterday afternoon," Morgan said with a disapproving face. "Sid said no stopping, except for gas, until dinner."

"The man runs a tight bus, as the saying goes," Ed cracked and lifted the coffee mug to his lips.

"Speaking of the bus, have you seen it?" Kristen asked.

"No, it wasn't ready when I stopped by Friday; Sid said they were still working on it, including attaching the posters of you."

"Wait till you see the inside of the bus," Kristen said excitedly. "Our accommodations are, like, awesome. A king-size bed; an ample closet; a huge, brightly lit makeup mirror; a big-screen TV; a stereo and recording system; and topping it all off, a shower and separate bathroom."

"Sounds first class. What about the posters?"

"They're fantastic," Kristen crowed.

"Hot and sexy," Morgan boasted as she approached with the coffee. Mincing no words, she added, "Some men will probably have perverted dreams."

"The man certainly knows how to promote," Ed said mirthfully.

"Will you miss us?" Kristen said solicitously.

"More than you can imagine."

"You're including me?" Morgan said curiously as she took her chair.

"Yes, of course."

"You hardly know me, and all I've done so far is bring you a lot of grief that you don't need."

"What grief?" Ed said dismissively.

Morgan smiled and shook her head. "You are truly an extraordinary man."

"Nice of you to say that, but I'm far from it."

"I wish you were going with us," Kristen murmured wistfully.

"Maybe next time," Ed said offhandedly to appease Kristen.

"You promise?"

"Promises are broken when falsely spoken, and I won't do that."

Sensing Ed was quite discouraged and in pain, Morgan said cheerily, "OK, so who's turn is it to fix breakfast—Kristen?"

With it being Sunday, the street near Sid's office building, a couple of blocks off the main drag, was free of traffic, making it possible for the mammoth bus and a hitch to be easily parked. Ed pulled the SUV right up to the bumper and flipped the rear gate release, prompting Kristen and Morgan to hop out excitedly and retrieve their stuffed suitcases. As they struggled toward the bus door where Sid and the musicians were engaged in light-hearted conversation, one of the musicians noticed their plight and wisecracked, "You ladies need help?"

"No thanks—we'll just herniate ourselves," Morgan quipped.

Sensing the girls were in no mood to joke, Sid motioned to the musicians. "Couple of you guys give them a hand."

Being wise guys, they all clapped and passed remarks, which Morgan and Kristen countered by dropping the suitcases and taking a bow with their middle finger held over their heads.

"Smart-asses," Morgan snapped.

"Put them in their suite," Sid said somberly as the guys grabbed the suitcases and headed for the bus door, followed by Kristen and Morgan.

"It's enormous," Ed said to Sid once he reached him, then glanced at Kristen's huge poster on the side of the bus.

"Let's cross the street so that you can get the full view," Sid suggested.

"Really sexy and conveys her energy," Ed said keenly.

"Glad you like it."

"So you had a photographer at Drai's?" Ed said, mildly surprised.

"Not only a photographer but a video guy as well to record her performance. The snippets have been running on local TV stations in the six concert cities since yesterday, and her voice is on the country music radio stations."

"That's what I call an all-out blitz," Ed said approvingly.

"I hope you won't have a problem with it, but I spent an additional fifty grand over what we originally discussed."

"No sweat—I'll get the check to Donna tomorrow morning on my way to the airport to pick up Alice."

"Speaking of Donna, if you need help before Alice gets here, don't hesitate to call her; I'll give you her home number," Sid assured Ed, jotting the number on back of his business card.

"I appreciate that," Ed said and stuck the card in his pocket.

"Oh, in case you're wondering, by the time we finish Houston, which is the last stop, we should recover the entire investment, plus more," Sid said confidently.

"I had no idea," Ed said, surprised.

"Yeah, that's why most concert tickets cost an arm and a leg."

"You're charging top bucks, even though she's unknown?"

"By the time we get to El Paso, our first stop, she'll be known in all of Texas."

"You would have been one hell of a Madison Avenue man," Ed said with an approving grin.

"Maybe not—it's too damn demanding, from what I've heard," Sid joked.

"So what comes after Texas?"

"Grand Ole Opry. And an album."

"Will she have any songs of her own?"

"Willie, the bass guitarist who's been teaching Kristen how to read sheet music, has one ready called 'I Want a Country Man,' which will definitely get Kristen moving. He's also been working with her on the one she was writing about you, which should be ready in time for the album. From what Willie told me, it should be a monster hit, including the one he wrote."

"That's awesome," Ed said happily. "So you got a name for the album?"

"I'm thinking *Kristen Cole Sings Country Classic Golden Hits*."

"Great title," Ed said most agreeably.

"Think you'll be able to make one of the concerts?"

"Absolutely! I promised Kristen, and Alice also wants to see one."

"So she's definitely coming?"

"Yes."

"How long she staying?"

"Till you guys get back."

"Which concert you planning to see?"

"Think the Dallas one—either Friday or Saturday."

"Dallas is a good choice, and I would suggest the one on Saturday; by all indications, it will be huge. Give me a call before you come and I'll let you know for sure—and get you a honeymoon suite," Sid kidded.

"Yeah, right," Ed said with a grin.

Sid glanced at his watch and motioned toward the bus. "Gonna have to shove off, so come and see the inside of this five-star beauty."

"Yeah, and I need to say goodbye to the girls as well."

CHAPTER 23

At half past ten Monday morning, Ed checked his watch for the umpteenth time as he paced along the baggage carousel at the Las Vegas International Airport. He knew Alice's flight had landed and had been at the gate for at least thirty minutes; she would be coming down the escalator any moment now. The anticipation of seeing her again made him feel like a kid about to go on first date. The sudden appearance of passengers brought relief, and he searched for Alice in the crowd. He thought of heading to the escalator to be there when she came down but decided he might miss her with so many people. He decided to stay where he was since her suitcase was probably already on the carousal. Minutes later, Ed spotted Alice making her way toward him with an ear-splitting smile and waving her hand.

"Thanks so much for coming; you look fantastic," Ed said joyously as he hugged Alice. He immediately noticed something different and asked, "Cut your hair?"

"You like it?"

"Very much, gives you a youthful look."

"I don't know about that, but I'm glad you like it," Alice said with an appreciative smile.

"No, seriously, it's very becoming."

"Mickey suggested it. I've had shoulder-length hair just about all my life."

"So how was the flight?" Ed said as he guided Alice toward the carousel.

"A little bumpy as we neared Las Vegas, but otherwise very smooth, and of course, the service in first class was superb, for which I thank you," Alice said and squeezed Ed's hand.

"It's the only way to fly, and there is no need to thank me; I'm the one who's benefiting."

"Let's make that mutual," Alice said affably. "And how's the pain?"

"Much improved now that you're here," Ed fibbed for Alice's sake.

"I'm so glad—hope it lasts," Alice said optimistically.

"Have you heard from the girls yet?"

"Yes, just as I was leaving the house."

"Are they already in the first concert city?"

"They arrived in El Paso at dawn this morning."

"How many cities is Kristen doing?"

"Six, the last being Houston."

"And how are her nerves holding up?"

"She's a little wound up, needless to say, but with Sid's and Morgan's help, she'll get through it."

Alice shook her head. "I can't imagine what it's like to get on the stage and face thousands of screaming fans."

"The hardest part is the wait beforehand, but once the music starts, the nerves fade; that's what she tells me."

"Oh, that's my suitcase coming this way," Alice blurted as she glanced at the carousel.

"I'll get it," Ed said and promptly snatched it.

By nine o'clock after a sedulous day, Alice could barely keep her eyes open and was too tired to even carry a conversation. The three-hour time difference had caught up with her in a big way, as well as the munificent consumption of wine along with the sumptuous dinner at the Top of the World Restaurant, which had definitely been worth it, as Alice could not believe for the food or the view. This was followed by a glass of brandy when they got home and unwound in front of the glowing fireplace.

As hard as she tried, Alice could not stop yawning and finally reluctantly admitted she was totally spent.

"I'm so sorry for wimping out on you, but I'm falling asleep as I sit," Alice said wearily.

"I understand, and by all means retire for the night; it's been hell of a full day," Ed said sympathetically. "You have a choice of either Kristen's or Morgan's room. They changed the linens and tidied up."

"I'll take the one closest to the stairs," Alice kidded wearily.

"That would be my room."

"You don't mind if I don't stay in your room?" Alice said uneasily.

"Like I told you in New York, please don't feel like you have to avail yourself," Ed said forthrightly.

"I so appreciate your understanding."

"Quite honestly, I'm not even sure if I'm up to lascivious activity," Ed uneasily confessed and rose to his feet, then helped Alice do the same.

"Let's not talk about it now; we've got many days before I leave, and you never know how things will change," Alice said heartily, "and I'm very sorry for putting you in a position to have to say that."

"You don't have to apologize," Ed said kindly as he guided Alice to the stairs.

"I guess we're both old-fashioned and not in tune with the current times," Alice said as she struggled up the stairs with Ed behind her ,making sure she didn't stumble back.

"Your room?" Alice guessed when she reached top of the stairs and the first bedroom.

"Yes."

Alice stopped in the doorway when she reached Kristen's room and faced Ed. "Are you going to bed as well?"

"Not for a while. I'm going to wait for Kristen's call."

"Wish I wasn't so tired. I would love to hear how her debut concert went."

"I'll tell you all about it in the morning; have a restful sleep."

"You as well, and I'll say a prayer that you'll have a painless day tomorrow."

"I'm thinking of taking a pain pill tonight to see how well it works, and if it's OK, I'll take one tomorrow so that we can really cut loose and live it up. No constraints or inhibitions, just the pure joy of life. I want the next few days to be ineffable."

"I'm glad you've finally made up your mind to end the suffering," Alice said gladly, "and yes, I'll do my absolute best to help you make these days to remember."

Ed grinned and kidded, "I don't believe it—old-fashioned, conservative girl cutting lose."

"It's my last chance, too," Alice confessed with a sweet smile and kissed Ed good night.

CHAPTER 24

"Good morning," Alice said cheerfully as she made a beeline to Ed at the kitchen counter as he poured his second mug of coffee. She rose on her tiptoes and affectionately kissed him on the cheek.

"What nice way to start the morning, and same to you," Ed said happily. "Did you sleep well?"

"Heavenly, and you?"

"Believe it or not, I got up not long ago," Ed said contently. "I took a pain pill right after I spoke to Kristen and barely made it up to bed."

"You have any pain?" Alice said curiously.

"Negligible," Ed said happily and handed Alice a mug of coffee.

"Oh, that's wonderful," Alice said jubilantly and added a sweetener and cream to the coffee.

"So tell me about Kristen."

Once they got back to the table and settled in their chairs, Ed unpretentiously began, "She said the place was jammed, helped, perhaps, by a very popular local opening band, which Sid had smartly booked. She had a very bad case of the nerves and almost threw up, but she overcame it thanks to her band guys, who clowned and joked till she regained her composure. Once on the stage, at Sid's suggestion, she started off with 'Me and Bobby McGee,' which put her in the zone, and after that, she was on autopilot, doing the songs without the slightest stumble, pausing only for the thunderous applause. When she finished with 'Son of a Preacher Man,' the place went wild, and some audience members tried to get up on the stage. Fortunately, they were stopped by the security guys. Afterward, they had to wait nearly twenty minutes for the cops to clear the crowd away from the bus. She said it was incredibly thrilling with so many fans trying to get at her—but also a little scary. Sid told her on the way to the hotel that of the five girls he's managed, none had ever come close to having that kind of fan reaction."

Alice beamed. "Congratulations—you've got yourself a country megastar."

"Thanks, but it's all about Kristen, not me."

"You're too modest; it was you who believed in her, encouraged her, and gave her the opportunity."

"And now I'm fully paid," Ed said contentedly and took a swallow of coffee.

"Ed Goff, you are a truly a selfless man," Alice said glowingly.

"You're not bad yourself," Ed countered affably.

"So what merriment do you have in mind for us over the next few days and nights?" Alice said eagerly.

"We'll do surrounding sights by day, starting this morning with Hoover Dam, then back to Vegas for dinner at Ferraro's—an Italian restaurant—then do some gambling."

Alice shook her head and was about to comment when the cell phone in her bathrobe pocket chimed.

"Yes, it is a good morning, and no, you didn't wake

me up. Ed and I are having our coffee on this beautiful, sunny morning."

Ed rose from the table, mug in hand, and sauntered over to the coffeepot, allowing Alice to talk freely.

"Kristen told Ed she had an incredible debut concert. They loved her and attempted to rush the stage, but the security men stopped them. We just can't wait to see her in Dallas next Saturday," Alice bragged.

"Wish I could see her as well," Mickey said earnestly.

"Why don't you fly out to Dallas and join us? I'm sure Ed can arrange to have you backstage with us," Alice said.

"I would, but unfortunately, I'll be working the entire weekend."

"Your work hours are getting as bad as your dad's," Alice said, shaking her head.

"That's how it is when you work for the Bureau."

"You sound just like your dad."

"Speaking of Dad, I have a thought. Since you're going to be in Dallas, why don't you get together with the Richardsons; you haven't seen them since Dad's funeral."

"Funny you should say that. When I woke up this morning, that's what crossed my mind. I was going to mention it to Ed."

"You have their number?"

"No."

"Give me a sec to switch screens and I'll get it."

"You can do that?"

"You want Brad's and Janet's?"

"Just Janet's," Alice said and grabbed a pen from the table, jotting the number down on a paper napkin. "Thanks, sweetie."

"Got to go—my office phone is ringing. Bye. I love you. Oh, and please say hello to Ed for me."

"I most certainly will. Talk to you tomorrow."

"I gather Mickey won't be coming," Ed said as he made his way back to the table.

"She wanted to, but she'll be working," Alice said dejectedly. "I had no idea she was working those kind of hours till she moved back home. At this rate, she'll never get married."

"Can't she transfer to a different department where she'll have normal hours?"

"She loves what she's doing and is really good at it. She has received many commendations, and that's why they let her transfer to New York," Alice said with a mother's pride.

Ed shook his head. "For all those years, it was strictly men working long, crazy hours; now the women get to do it, too."

"I think it's pathetic," Alice said sourly.

CHAPTER 25

Alice rushed to Ed, who was stretched out on a pool-side lounge chair, taking advantage of the warm sun on this most delightful Saturday morning.

"I couldn't find you," Alice said plaintively when she reached him.

"Did you think I skipped out on you?" Ed kidded.

"Yes, I thought you left for Dallas without me," Alice countered lightheartedly and relaxed.

"Not a chance. I've grown accustomed to your beautiful face," Ed said with great feeling.

Alice sat down on the adjoining lounge chair with a look of satisfaction and connected with Ed's eyes. "And I no less with you; it's been quite a week of joy and bonding. In my wildest dreams, I couldn't imagine anything like it."

"So happy to hear that, and don't close the book quite yet. We still have another week, which I intend to make even more eventful," Ed said boldly.

Alice smiled affectionately and shook her head. "I can't imagine how you could top the one we just had."

"This past week was exciting; the next will be more sensuous."

Alice was taken aback. "Oh, really? Can you give me a little hint?"

"Nope," Ed said and glanced at his watch. "Think we need to start getting ready."

"What time's the flight?"

"Ten thirty."

"That's too bad," Alice said coquettishly and rose to her feet.

"You look fabulous," Ed said once on his feet.

"Thank you. This is the dress you bought me at Barney's our second night out."

"You give it class," Ed acclaimed.

"Ed Goff, are you flirting with me?"

"Just an honest appraisal," Ed said with an easy smile and guided Alice into the house.

Much to their delight, the flight was smooth as silk, and the service in the first class was par excellence. Ed had ordered his usual Wild Turkey, and Alice had a glass of pink champagne.

"You are spoiling me outrageously," Alice said euphorically.

"You deserve no less for putting up with a broken-down old horse like me."

"Please don't say that," Alice said emotionally. "You're the finest and most generous man I have ever known."

Ed nodded with an appreciative smile. "Oh, and by the way, I got us separate rooms, in case you're wondering."

Alice was surprised. "You didn't have to do that."

"I thought you'd be more at ease and not worry about what the others thought."

"They'll think I'm prissy and a goody-goody; please change it," Alice said sweetly and squeezed Ed's hand affectionately.

"Tell you what, I'll get a suite."

"Where are we staying?"

"Ritz-Carlton."

"Oh my God, that'll cost you a small fortune."

"Hey, we're on a first-class budget all the way."

Alice shook her head. "You're going to be broke before I leave."

"Can't take it with me," Ed said dismissively.

"I guess you took a fentanyl this morning?" Alice asked.

"First thing," Ed said with a grin.

"Will we see Kristen before the concert?"

"Definitely. By the time we get to the Ritz, she should be finished rehearsing. We'll get together with her and Morgan for rest of the afternoon."

"That sounds wonderful!"

"We'll meet with the band at the American Airlines Conference Center just before the concert, and guess what?"

Alice shrugged. "Tell me."

"We're going to take the tour bus from the Ritz to the concert venue with the girls and Sid."

"Sounds like fun," Alice said mirthfully.

Ed grinned. "We'll get to see firsthand what it's like to be a concert star."

"You think there will be a crowd waiting for Kristen?"

"For sure."

"Think they'll mob her?" Alice said with true concern.

"They'll be cops and security guys to escort her."

Alice shook her head. "And to think, less than three months ago, no one had heard of her."

"Only in America," Ed said humorously.

"Oh, I meant to tell you before we left—I spoke to the

Richardsons, and they want to get together tomorrow afternoon for a cookout at their house, if you're game."

"Yeah, why not?" Ed said enthusiastically. "We'll have breakfast with the girls and see them off, then head out to the Richardsons'. When we're done, we can either catch a flight back to Vegas or stay over another night—up to you."

"Yes, let's do," Alice said eagerly.

"I want you to be happy beyond your dreams," Ed said tenderly.

Alice smiled and shook her head. "I can't believe it's already Saturday—the week just flew."

"You know that old saying about time flying," Ed joshed.

"Yes, it's the most fun I've ever had in my life."

"I enjoyed it just as much, thanks to you and the little 'tangos,'" Ed said lightheartedly.

"Tangos?" Alice said with a puzzled look.

"That's what they call fentanyl on the street; Morgan told me."

"She's not into drugs?" Alice said with concern.

"No, but she's pretty streetwise. Was on her own in New York since fourteen."

"Oh, how awful," Alice said.

"She's had one hell of a lousy start in life—breaks my heart."

"And now she gets raped," Alice said, shaking her head. "Thank God you came along and took her in."

"Just wish I had more time to make sure she doesn't revert."

"I think she'll be OK," Alice said optimistically.

"Why do you think that?"

"Because you'll be too deeply imbued in her psyche, with you, and I'm speaking from that place," Alice confessed.

Ed was surprised by the admission but withheld comment. "She's very vulnerable."

"You've still got time to firm up her core."

"Hopefully," Ed said without conviction.

Alice was eager to change the conversation. "About next week—will we cut back on the sightseeing?"

"Most definitely. Unless you want to explore more?"

"Then we won't visit Tahoe?"

"Only if you want to; it's a day's drive or about an hour flight to Reno and then another hour by car if the roads aren't snowed in."

"I think I've seen enough of snow for this year and the next; let's just stay in Las Vegas and do the things you have in mind," Alice said amiably.

"You won't be disappointed."

"That being the case, can you give me just one little hint of what you've planned?"

Ed smiled and shook his head. "I might have known a woman's curiosity has no limits."

"Always," Alice cracked.

"OK, only if you're game: Sahra Spa, Salon & Hamman."

"Sounds sybaritic," Alice said with a probing look.

"It's a romantic spa that offers a centuries-old practice of purification. You get to lie down on a heated slab of stone for body detox, then a cooling bath, together with or without body cover, and after that, relax in a whirlpool and finish up in a stone lounge."

"You've done it?" Alice said curiously.

"No, Sid told me about it."

"OK, let's do it," Alice said gamely, much to Ed's surprise.

"After, we'll dine at the Picasso, which features

original artwork on the walls by Pablo, along with the cuisine of Spain and France."

"It all sounds fabulous, but that's going to cost you a million bucks," Alice said, shaking her head.

"I've already given you my view on that."

"You are absolutely overwhelming me."

"I want to leave you with a memory you'll never forget."

Alice looked at Ed tenderly. "You've already done that."

Ed shrugged. "So why stop?"

CHAPTER 26

I t was nearly one when Ed and Alice made their way through the crowded Dallas International Airport main terminal, looking around for Kristen and Morgan, who were to meet them at the baggage claim.

"Maybe they got stuck in traffic," Alice said thoughtfully as they started toward the exit with the intent of meeting them outside by the entrance doors.

"I'm sure they would have called if, in fact, they are," Ed said calmly and just then spotted Kristen and Morgan, both wearing barn-dance dresses and Mecate hats, making a dash at them.

"So happy to see you guys," Kristen blurted breathlessly and hugged Ed and Alice affectionately, then stepped aside for Morgan to do the same.

"Alice, this is Morgan, which you've probably guessed," Ed interjected as Morgan was about to hug her.

"Glad to meet you Morgan," Alice said most pleasantly.

"Same here. Can I take your wheelie bag?" Morgan said politely with an outstretched hand.

"Yes, thank you. I love you girls' outfits."

"It was Sid's idea; he wants us to convey a country image."

Ed smiled and shook his head. "The man doesn't miss a trick."

"You guys have a good flight?" Kristen said once they started for the exit doors.

"Smooth as a baby's butt," Ed joshed.

"Looks like somebody had a nip and a 'tango,'" Morgan quipped.

"Little miss smarty-pants," Ed teased back with a grin.

"Did you guys have lunch?" Kristen said once everyone was outside.

"Drinks and snacks. Have you?"

"It was really too early, and Sid thought we could all eat at the hotel when we got back."

"That'll be great," Ed said as they headed for the extra-stretch white limousine.

"First class all the way, plane to a limousine," Alice razzed, looking at Ed.

"It was Sid's idea, part of the image thing," Morgan interjected.

Once all were settled in the limo, Alice eagerly peered at Kristen, who was sitting directly across from her. "Ed said you had an incredible concert last night?"

"It was surreal. I remember walking, weak-kneed, out on the stage, but once the music started, I felt totally possessed by it, and I didn't come out of it till I uttered the last word of the final song. Then I heard the thunderous applause and cheers," Kristen said dreamily. "Maybe Morgan can give you a better account."

"It's was exactly as she said; Sid and I couldn't believe it as we watched Kristen, who, just minutes before, was about to collapse from a stage fright. It was a complete turnaround. She asserted herself like Tina Turner used to, and with each performance, she's becoming even more dominant. When she finished, they wanted more and whooped it up, and some even tried to get on the stage.

I've been to some wild concerts, but I've never seen that kind of fan reaction."

"C'mon—you're exaggerating," Kristen mildly protested.

Alice smiled. "And to think I get to see an evolving country megastar up close because of a chance meeting in an art gallery where we stopped to warm up."

"I thought you two lovely ladies stopped in because you loved art," Ed chided playfully.

"That's how you guys met?" Morgan said with a curious look.

"It was fate," Ed said congenially, "just like everything else that's happened so far."

"Including me?" Morgan asked eagerly.

"Yes, including you," Ed said definitively.

"How many more cities after tonight?" Alice said to Kristen.

"Three. The last one is next weekend in Houston, the heart and soul of country music."

"I thought Nashville was," Alice countered with a surprised look.

"Maybe once but not anymore; Texas is where it's a way of life," Kristen said knowingly.

"You're becoming a true Sid devotee," Ed teased.

"The man is a walking encyclopedia of country music," Morgan lauded.

"And a top-notch promotion man," Ed added thoughtfully.

"Kristen really lucked out," Alice proclaimed.

"And so have I," Morgan bragged.

Since it was past the normal time for lunch, the restaurant had only a handful of customers, and the service was extra prompt. While they ate, the conversation was lighthearted, spiced up by Sid's array of very funny jokes, much to the delight of everyone at the table. Even the service people lingered longer at the table so that they could hear the punch lines. When they'd all finished the splendid lunch, Sid, always the consummate host, lifted his glass of wine and offered a thoughtful toast.

"Here's to the lovely ladies who grace this table and made the lunch much more enjoyable."

"Now that's what I call a classy toast," Ed said with a nod.

The three women acknowledged the compliment with appreciative smiles and their glasses high.

With sips taken, the bill paid, and all ready to go, Sid made an announcement: "We'll meet here for dinner at six, and afterward, we'll proceed directly to the concert, so bring whatever you'll need with you so that you don't have to make a trip back to your rooms. Ed, let's you and I go over to Nolan's Pub next door and I'll bring you up to date on the finances."

Nolan's Pub, like the opulent dining room, was first class, with dimmed lighting, fireplace glowing, and mellow piped-in music—all conducive to unwinding after a harried day, and also like the dining room, the service was superb. No sooner were they seated at a small cocktail table than a very attractive waitress wearing a short black dress stopped by to take their orders. Sid ordered Jack Daniels, and Ed got a double Wild Turkey.

"You didn't eat much and looked somewhat out of sorts, so that's why I made up the excuse; I wanted to find out how you're really doing," Sid said with solicitude.

"The goddamn pain now never eases, so I'm finally using the fentanyl."

"You're getting relief?"

"I am, but I'm concerned my brain will turn to mush from using this shit for any length of time."

"Goddamn it, just when it's all coming together for Kristen," Sid said, shaking his head.

"Well, at least I get to see her on the bus to the stage, with fans waiting, so I really can't complain," Ed said passively.

"Guess you know she truly loves you and has worked her butt off to achieve the incredible dream in record time."

"Just don't let her flame out, and also keep an eye on Morgan for me."

"You have my word on both counts," Sid said solemnly.

"I'm deeply indebted and most grateful for all you've done for Kristen," Ed said emotionally.

"She's made it easy, and the credit is all hers," Sid said definitively. "Are you up to hearing our financial status so far?"

"Yes."

"I'm happy to say it's even better than I expected. With sellouts certain for the next three cities, we'll more than cover our investments and have enough left over for upcoming expenses."

"You've done one hell of a job in promoting Kristen; it's nothing less than incredible."

"Coming from a Madison Avenue man, I take that as the highest compliment," Sid said as the waitress returned with the drinks. "Danielle, your timing is exquisite—and your looks as well."

"I'll second that," Ed said gladly, and as soon as Danielle left, he raised his glass. "To the best damn manager in the music business."

"I appreciate that, and so you know, Kristen is making my job an absolute joy. She's got that something special that sets her apart from all the others I've managed," Sid said boldly. "Her physicality and magnetism are ineffable."

"I'll tell you honestly, she's accomplished more than I ever imagined."

"Wait till you see her; she's like a tigress when she hits the stage," Sid said grandly. "The genie's out of the bottle, and there's no stopping her."

"Now I can leave this world knowing that I did contribute something worthwhile," Ed said emotionally.

"That, my friend, is an understatement. There's no telling what she'll achieve," Sid said grandly.

"Kristen said you guys will be heading out to Nashville soon after you get back to Vegas."

"Yeah, I've got her doing a couple of appearances on Grand Ole Opry and then the record album.

"How long will the album take?" Ed said, thinking of his deteriorating condition.

"I'm aiming for ten days, but if you're concerned about being alone, Morgan really doesn't have to go."

"Well, if that's the case, I'll tell Alice not to come again since she's already put in her time."

"I gotta tell you, she's not only attractive but also one hell of a classy lady," Sid praised. "How long have you known her?"

"Not long. Met her in Omaha on the way to Vegas; she was visiting her sister for the holidays. We met in an art gallery."

"Where's she from?"

"New York."

"She's a gem."

"Yeah, definitely a keeper," Ed said positively. "If I didn't have this goddamn cancer, I'd snatch her up in a blink."

CHAPTER 27

When the tour bus pulled up at the rear of the American Airlines Conference Center, the vocal crowd was waiting for Kristen's arrival and had to be cleared by the cops for the bus to pull up near the back-door stage entrance.

"You believe this?" Sid exclaimed, shaking his head with a grin. "The crowd's getting bigger with each concert."

"I guess they love her," Ed said proudly as he cast his eyes from the crowd to Kristen. "You gonna be OK?"

"It's going to be a mad dash."

"Let's get at it," Sid said, rising to his feet. "Ed, you and Alice can either come with us or wait till we get inside the building and the crowd disperses. I'll have one of the security guards escort you to where we'll be."

"What do you say?" Ed said, glancing to Alice. "You want to experience the thrill of it?"

"Let's do it," Alice said gamely.

"So be it," Ed said sprightly and guided Alice behind the others to the bus door.

Alice paused just before stepping out and turned to Ed. "She'll never again have a normal life."

"There's no such thing as a normal life," Ed quipped.

With their arms stretched out and hands locked, the

cops and security guys strained with all their might to keep the eager fans from getting to Kristen as she rushed to the door, with the rest of the group a couple of steps behind. Once inside, they all relaxed, their faces flushed.

"So this is what it's like to be a country star," Alice said breathlessly to Kristen with a smile. "Don't know how you can do it."

"For the big bucks and adulation," Morgan cracked.

"And the joy of performing," Kristen added heartily.

"A very good summation, ladies; now let's all head to the green room and catch our breath," Sid suggested cheerily.

When they got to spacious room with plush sofas and matching armchairs, the band guys were already, tuning their instruments as they joked with each other.

"Listen up, guys! Please say hello to Ms. Alice and Ed."

They all responded with warm hellos and resumed their mirthfulness, much to Sid's delight, since he had asked them to be lighthearted and confident before every show to help relax Kristen and get her revved up. Ed and Alice, sitting across the room, watched with amusement and surprise as Morgan interacted with the musicians very easily and actually outdid them in terms of wisecracks.

"I hope you're enjoying the frivolousness," Sid said as he approached.

"They're hilarious—is that what they do before the concerts?" Alice asked.

"That's pretty much their style, but I asked them to include the girls since it helps Kristen enormously with the nerves."

"Sid, you are one amazing guy," Ed said approvingly as Sid sat down in an adjoining chair.

Sid acknowledged Ed's comment with a nod. "The group that performs before Kristen is a local favorite, which helps with the draw and also jacks up the crowd, so when Kristen takes the stage, they're more than ready for her."

"You don't miss a trick," Ed said with admiration.

"I had no idea how much effort goes into these concerts," Alice said in awe.

"That's why the tickets cost an arm and a leg," Sid said with a devilish grin and adjusted his Diamante hat.

"I meant to tell you on the bus, that is one handsome hat," Alice with an admiring look.

"Glad you like it, and I must say, you exude an aura of real class," Sid complimented.

"Thank you so much," Alice said amiably. "What is your long-term plan for Kristen, if you don't mind me asking?"

"International stardom—she's one of those rare entertainers who comes along once in a great while who has that special something that will make her a global star, and that's what I'm planning for her."

"Oh my, and here I am disbelieving of what she's already achieved."

"In the not-too-distant future, her singing will be overshadowed by her persona, like some of the great international entertainers," Sid said with certainty.

Alice smiled and turned to Ed. "What do you think of that?"

"That's way beyond what I envisioned."

"I have question," Alice said playfully to Ed and Sid when Kristen returned from the dressing room and joined the musicians and Morgan. "Which of you gentlemen picked that sexy outfit Kristen's wearing, or was that her idea?"

"It was me," Sid said, owning up, with a wink at Ed. "You don't approve?"

"Well, she certainly won't get sweaty, but she'll definitely be hot," Alice said lightheartedly.

"Couple of weeks ago, I watched a country concert on TV just to get ready to see Kristen's, and the girl was barefooted and wore a long, transparent nightgown—although, to her credit, she did have a bra and underpants on."

"I heard about that, and Kristen will definitely never do that, but she does have fabulous legs, just like Tina Turner, so why not show them?" Sid confided.

"It makes sense," Alice said agreeably.

"So what time are you guys leaving?" Sid said.

"We're staying overnight. Alice's very dear friends from New York who now live in Dallas and have invited us for a cookout tomorrow."

"Sounds like fun; let's get together for breakfast but let the girls sleep late."

"By all means," Ed said gladly.

Sid glanced at his watch and rose to his feet. "All right, guys, let's wrap it up; it's getting close to showtime."

Ed and Alice hugged Kristen as the stage grew dark and Sid, at the stand-up mic, introduced Kristen to an outburst of cheers and applause, prompting Kristen to bound on the stage like a bolt of lightning as the spotlight burst on her. When she reached Sid, she bowed several times and took the mic from his hand, then waited for him to leave the stage. She looked out to the sold-out crowd as the band softly played warm-up music.

"Ladies and gentlemen, before I start, I want to dedicate this show to someone very special in my life who

I love with all my heart and soul. His name's Ed, and he's just off the stage. So please welcome him warmly." Kristen then turned to her right and motioned for Ed to step out, which he did reluctantly. He waved to Kristen and the crowd, then retreated from the stage.

"Now, with your approval, I will dedicate this first song to Ed, which is most appropriate. It's called 'Till I Can Make It on My Own.'"

Ed was bowled over and looked to Sid, who was standing nearby with a wide grin. "Did you know she was going to do this?"

"Only after I heard, by chance, her and the band rehearsing it. I thought it was absolutely great—listen to the words, Ed."

Throughout the song, Kristen glanced back in Ed's direction, and when finished, she tenderly said, "I love you Ed."

The audience appreciated the gesture and gave Kristen a loud ovation, which she tearfully acknowledged, then regained her composure as the band exploded with "Son of a Preacher Man," which sent Kristen into frenzy and the audience into a fit.

"What beautiful thing that was to do," Alice enthusiastically affirmed to Ed. "She is really something special."

Throughout the concert, there was a steady din from the audience in appreciation of Kristen's performance, and she concluded each song to thunderous applause. To allow Kristen to catch her breath, the band would play a snippet of the next tune before the actual song. Finally, when Kristen got to the last song, which was requested vociferously throughout the concert whenever Kristen paused, she looked out with a grin and teased, "I think you've been trying to tell me something about a song made famous by a Texas girl named Janis Joplin, so in reverence to her, here it goes." And with that said, she tore into the song like an exploding grenade, traversing the stage from side to side, to and fro, pausing momentarily by the lead guitarist as he hammered on the strings.

Finally, with the last word sung and Kristen near collapse, the audience exploded with ear-splitting applause, whistles, and yahoos that were easily heard outside the huge venue. It was a night they would forever remember. After numerous bows and thrown kisses, Kristen slowly retreated from the stage under the spotlight, which clearly showed the sweat dripping down her face. When she reached the backstage area, Sid immediately wrapped her in a bath towel.

"You have surpassed last night, which I didn't think was possible," Sid boasted.

Kristen then turned to Ed's waiting arms. "Are you OK?" Ed said with great concern.

"I am now," Kristen said wearily.

"Thank you for what you did tonight," Ed said with utmost tenderness. "I'll remember it till my last breath."

Alice was next to hug Kristen and thanked her for a most memorable night and a very special friendship.

"The lively songs really take their toll," Alice said directly to Sid.

"It's part of Kristen's persona and what makes her such a great entertainer."

"I can't believe it's the same girl I saw at the karaoke place in Omaha just weeks ago," Alice said, shaking her head.

"This is what she was born to do," Sid said firmly.

"And you're the one who made it happen," Ed affirmed.

"Were the audiences this captivated with your other singers?" Alice said to Sid.

"Not even close with all five combined. There is no one like Kristen doing country or, for that matter, any other music—she is in a class by herself."

"Looks like you've given the world quite a gift," Alice said buoyantly to Ed, knowing how much it meant to him.

"She's justifying my life in a way I couldn't imagine in my wildest dreams."

"You've more than exceeded expectations in your contribution," Sid extoled.

"Is Morgan going to join us?" Ed said curiously as they started for the green room.

"Yes, and so is Ray Teal, the promoter; there's probably some kind of discrepancy in the attendance numbers and the bucks," Sid guessed.

Ed was surprised. "You've got her doing the finances?"

"She's a very bright girl and happily took that miserable chore from me, and I thank you for recommending her," Sid said with an appreciative grin.

As they approached the green room, Morgan and Ray Teal finally showed, both looking somewhat agitated.

"Problem?" Sid said congenially.

"The damn computer froze up in the middle of a printout, and we had to get a tech guy to come over and get the damn thing running," Ray said with disdain. "So we missed the whole show, which I badly wanted to see, especially when we heard the noise coming from the hall all the way in my office—it was definitely louder than last night."

"And here I thought you ran off with Morgan," Sid cracked as they entered the green room.

"I tried, but she refused," Ray said with a devilish

grin, then turned to Ed and Alice. "I'm Ray Teal, and I profusely apologize for my outburst."

Ed and Alice assured Ted no apology was needed and introduced themselves as well.

"In twenty years, I've never seen or heard such a vociferous reaction, and we've had some of the biggest entertainers around," Ray declared. He then turned to Sid. "How about staying over another day?"

"We've got a concert Monday night in Austin, and besides, what kind of turnout could we get on Sunday night and without a sufficient promo?"

"I'll handle that and financially guarantee you," Ray said confidently.

"Wish I could do it, but there's just no way. Kristen needs a break; you saw what she puts out at these concerts," Sid said regretfully to his longtime friend. "We'll do it next time."

"Ed, she's your girl—what do you say?" Ray said slyly.

"When it comes to showbiz issues, Kristen is strictly within Sid's domain," Ed said firmly.

"Well, you can't blame me for trying," Ray conceded. He then said to Sid, "When do you think you'll be down this way again?"

Sid shrugged. "I honestly don't know, but when we are, I promise you more than two nights."

Ray nodded appreciatively. "I have a feeling she'll be in demand by more promoters than you can count. You've got yourself a superstar, the likes of which we haven't seen in quite some time—you lucky bastard."

"Luck had nothing to do with it," Sid said in jest with a wink at Ed.

"I'd like to suggest something if you don't mind," Ray said directly to Sid.

"Go ahead."

"You should consider getting Kristen a female backup trio so that she can catch her breath after those physical numbers."

"You have read my mind; that's exactly what I'm going to do when we get back to Vegas."

"If you're interested, I know several backup singers who can also dance and are looking to hook up with a country star."

"They in Dallas?"

"Yes, and they've performed here several times."

"Can you set up a meeting for tomorrow morning, about ten?"

"They're roommates; I'll call them tonight and arrange the meeting."

"Thanks," Sid said appreciatively. "I guess we're done here, so let's head for the bus and take our lumps," Sid joshed.

CHAPTER 28

After returning to Vegas from the concert, Ed was determined to make the coming week even greater than the previous one, starting with the Sahra Spa, Salon & Hammam. He gathered whatever energy he had left in his tired body for what he knew would be his last hurrah. With the pain mostly sedated by the medication and his spirits chemically elevated, Ed focused on making Alice happy in ways she had never been before. Every wild and crazy notion that popped into his drugged brain he pursued with abandon. Alice at first was reluctant, but she sportingly went along with it, and much to Ed's delight, she began to enjoy it and even made some suggestions. In true Las Vegas style, they made no distinction between days and nights and did whatever caught their fancy. For the first time in their lives, they let themselves be truly free, unconcerned about what others thought or the proper decorum. Alice, even more than Ed, appreciated the newfound freedom and made up her mind not to revert to her old ways. Her greatest regret was that Ed would not be around to share the coming good times with her.

When Saturday evening rolled around, they were more than ready for the wild week to end. Both were exhausted beyond their limits, and spending a normal night at home was more than welcome, especially for Ed, who surprised Alice with his physical stamina, which she knew was a supreme effort. In fact, she wondered if he would ever recover. He looked gaunt and pale, and her heart broke for him. She wished she could help him, but in reality, there was very little she could do other than stay positive and provide encouragement. This being their last night together in Vegas—and quite possibly their last night ever—she wanted so much to give herself, sensing Ed must have thought about making love for the last time in his life. With that thought in mind, Alice made herself extra sensually appealing, starting with an extended bath in fragrant oils, which left her hair lightly scented. Thinking they would probably make love during her two-week stay, she'd brought her sheerest black lace nightgown, which would accentuate her smooth, milky skin.

Ed had been in bed for nearly an hour when Alice emerged from the bathroom looking stunningly beautiful and much younger than her age. She slowly made her way to the bed with the sexiest saunter she had ever done in her life. She was determined to arouse Ed even before she got in bed. Her effort was not wasted; Ed noticed and was moved by her grace and allure. At this moment, he imagined her to be the epitome of desirability and lustfulness. Her fragrance as she neared was intoxicating and added to her sexuality. When she finally reached the bed, Ed was in a lustful trance. Alice smiled lusciously and purred.

"You like?"

"That's an understatement of all time," Ed gushed.

"You've got room for me?" Alice teased.

Ed was stunned by Alice's imitation of the sexiest of the movie stars in their most provocative similar scenes.

"Not that much, so we may have to squeeze," Ed teased back.

"We'll just have to make do," Alice said and mounted the bed, "and I do apologize for your long wait."

"It was worth every minute and then some," Ed said affably, with the look of a man about to realize his most desirous fantasy.

"I will do anything you ask," Alice whispered enticingly.

Ed, as always, was first to wake, but too exhausted, he decided to remain in bed. He turned from his side onto his back and glanced at Alice in the dawn light. She was soundly asleep and looking very peaceful, with a happy expression on her still, beautiful face. All sorts of pleasant thoughts came to him, of the life that could have been with Alice, but the pain in his gut reminded him it would never be. Apoplectic with his lot in life, he reached for the fentanyl pills on the nightstand, popped two into his mouth, and swallowed hard. It took very little time for the medication to numb the pain and disengage his brain from its constraints, which would enable him to do things that he wouldn't be able to otherwise. His thoughts slowly turned to the reality of the coming day and Alice's departure just hours away, and he wished permanent sleep would overtake him so that he wouldn't have to face the downcast day.

"Good morning—how long have you been up?" Alice said sprightly as she opened her eyes.

"A while," Ed said wearily.

"Been thinking?" Alice guessed.

"Yes."

"Care to share?" Alice said and propped herself on an elbow near Ed's face.

"About what might have been," Ed said reflectively,

"but it's too hurtful to talk about, so let's just appreciate the days we had and our remaining hours."

"I understand. And just so you know, it was the two greatest weeks of my life, bar none, which I'll cherish as long as I live," Alice said and kissed Ed passionately.

"You know what I would say right now if it wasn't for the goddamn cancer?"

"What?"

"I love you."

Alice burst into tears. "I love you, too—hold me tight."

"Gladly," Ed murmured and firmly wrapped his arms around her.

"Can we stay like this for a while?" Alice whimpered as she sobbed.

"We've got time."

"You want me to stay till after the girls get home or even longer?"

"It'll only be a couple of hours after you leave, and you've already stayed longer than you probably intended," Ed said kindly.

"How can you say that after what I've told you?" Alice said, hurt by his words.

"I'm sorry; the pills are messing with my brain."

"You've taken one already?"

"Took two," Ed confessed.

"The pain's that bad?"

"The second is to help me mentally get through this wretched day," Ed said dejectedly.

"Maybe I should take one as well," Alice said half seriously.

"I wouldn't recommend it; you've already taken on too many of my dubious ways."

"You know, if it wasn't for Mickey's award and promotion ceremony Monday morning, I wouldn't leave yet."

"You're the sweetest, kindest, most caring woman I have ever known—no exceptions."

"And you're the most generous man in every way, and you have treated me like I always imagined I would be but never was."

"The man was a fool," Ed said straight out.

"I feel so guilty since I've done very little to reciprocate."

"You're totally wrong there. What woman in the world would stick by a dying man she just met and brighten his last days?"

Alice brushed the tears from her reddening face. "And you, my love, deserve that; I'm just not sure if I've done a very good job of it."

"But you have, especially last night, for which I must apologize."

"Apologize for what?" Alice said with a puzzled face.

"Taking so long to climax."

"You have nothing to apologize for; you made love to me in a way I've never known," Alice said intently and kissed Ed with great feeling.

"There is one great regret I'll take to my grave," Ed said woefully.

"What?" Alice murmured.

"That I didn't have more time with you."

"You still have time," Alice insisted.

"Perhaps," Ed said without conviction.

"I'll come back right after Mickey's ceremony."

"As much as I would love you to, this has to be our final goodbye," Ed said firmly.

"I don't understand. Why don't you want me to come back?" Alice said dejectedly.

"I don't think I can stand to do this again," Ed said with tears in his eyes. "Once in a lifetime is too much."

"Ed, I love you so," Alice murmured and kissed Ed repeatedly as a torrent of tears cascaded down her cheeks and washed Ed's sallow face.

They remained embraced in silence, unable to find words of comfort, and drifted off to an uneasy slumber, which ended all too soon when Alice awoke with a scream from a hellish nightmare.

"What's wrong?" Ed gushed, his eyes still shut.

"A very bad dream," Alice gasped.

"It's over," Ed said reassuringly and held her tightly. "You want to tell me?"

"I'd rather not; it was too grotesque."

"Was it about me?" Ed rightly guessed.

Alice shook her head dismissively, even though it was. "It's almost nine; I need to start getting ready."

"While you're doing that, I'll start the coffee and make you breakfast."

"Aren't you having any?"

"Don't think I can, and it's got nothing to do with the usual reason," Ed said with a sour face.

"You need to eat something to regain your strength before the girls get home; otherwise, they'll think I didn't take very good care of you," Alice said seriously.

"They know better," Ed said assuredly.

"I really hope so," Alice said and reluctantly got out of bed. "I won't be long."

"I'll have your breakfast ready," Ed said and got out of bed as well.

After breakfast—of which Ed had none—Alice cleared the table hurriedly and returned with a pot of coffee in hand. She refilled Ed's mug, then took her seat.

She intended to convince Ed to let her come back. "It's just not fair," Alice said plaintively.

"What?"

"You not wanting me to come back."

"Why would you want to?" Ed murmured. "Look at me—I'm wasting away as we speak, and it's not going to stop."

"How you look doesn't change how I feel about you."

Ed grasped her hand and looked deeply into her teary eyes. "I appreciate that so very much, but please understand, you've got to leave me with some pride," Ed said pleadingly.

"Is that the real reason?"

"Yes."

"I'll accept it, but grudgingly," Alice said.

"The time we had together was truly extraordinary, so let's leave it at that and not ruin it with something hideous."

Alice glanced at her watch. "It's getting to be that time. Will you please call me a cab?"

"I'll drive you."

"I can't let you do that after you've taken two pain pills and some slugs of the booze; you're in no condition to drive," Alice insisted. "Let's just say our goodbyes here; it'll be much more meaningful than at the busy airport anyway."

"I just don't feel right about sending you off in a cab; it seems so cold and unappreciative."

"That's nonsense after all you've done," Alice said.

"You deserved it," Ed murmured gladly, then called for a cab.

The finality of what was pending overwhelmed them both, and they could no longer hold their emotions in check. Alice rose from the table and asked Ed to hold her as a torrent of tears cascaded down her cheeks. Ed grabbed a napkin from the table and dabbed her face, then suddenly burst into tears as well.

"Look who's acting like a little girl," Ed gasped.

"How can you say that?" Alice uttered between her sobs. You're more of a man than any I have ever known."

"You are by far the most incredible woman I've had the luck of knowing, and thank you for coming into my life, even if only for a short time."

"Will you call me often?"

"Every day."

"Promise?"

"Yes."

CHAPTER 29

Kristen and Morgan returned from the triumphant tour flying high—until they walked into the house and were met by Ed at the door. They couldn't believe how terrible he looked in just a week since they'd last seen him. He had lost more weight and looked totally spent, even though he gamely tried to be lively as he hugged them.

"You look worn," Kristen said, generously camouflaging her great concern as they proceeded to the kitchen, where the aroma of brewing coffee filled the air.

"Like I told you on the phone, we really painted the town, and I definitely overdid it, but I'll recoup in a couple of days," Ed said to placate the girls.

"Alice should have stopped you, knowing how seriously ill you are," Morgan said critically.

"Please don't blame her; it was all my doing," Ed pleaded as they sat down at the table.

Kristen looked directly at Ed with a puzzled face. "Is there something I don't know?"

"Yes, I was going to tell you in the next day or two," Ed said reluctantly and drew a deep breath, "I have stage four pancreatic cancer."

"God, no!" Kristen screamed and jumped to her feet. "That can't be. You said it was the wound."

315

"I didn't want you to be distracted and lose focus on what you had to do," Ed said as he rose from the chair and hugged Kristen.

"So what does that mean?" Kristen murmured uneasily through her sobs.

"Less time than I hoped for," Ed said in a choked voice.

Kristen pulled back and raised her head. "Monday morning, I'm taking you to the best cancer doctor in Las Vegas, and I don't care how much it costs, and if he can't help, I'll find one somewhere who will."

"I appreciate that very much, but there's nothing that can be done at this stage; I've seen one of the best oncologists in New York, but unfortunately, it was already too late."

"Didn't you have any telltale symptoms?" Kristen said with a puzzled look.

"They misdiagnosed it and attributed the problems to my war wound."

"Goddamn them," Kristen screamed, "bunch of fucking worthless assholes!"

"It happens," Ed said in a subdued voice and pulled Kristen back into the hug.

"You should have sued the fucking bastards," Morgan said angrily.

"It wouldn't have saved my life, and I had no one who would have benefitted."

"But at least you could have made their lives miserable—the useless fucks."

"It wouldn't have mattered," Ed said indifferently and released Kristen.

"I won't leave you now, even for a minute," Kristen said as she wiped her eyes, "and my singing will have to wait."

"No, please don't do that," Ed said pleadingly. "I want you to go on with what you're doing; that will make me very happy."

"But you need me."

"I'll stay with Ed," Morgan said immediately, "and he's right—you need to go to Nashville and do the Grand Ole Opry and, most of all, record the album for Ed."

"I just don't feel right about it. I should be here," Kristen insisted.

Ed reached down and gently held Kristen's tear-stained face in his hands. "Hey, I'm not going to croak before I hear the album and my song that you've written."

"You promise?" Kristen whimpered.

"With all my heart and will."

"Will Alice be coming back?"

"She wants to badly, but I don't want her to, especially now that Morgan will stay."

"Tell Alice I'm quite capable of taking care of you to ease her mind," Morgan said firmly.

"Let's sit; I was going to go over some important things with you girls in a day or two, but since we're on this unpleasant subject, I might as well do it now and get this morbid crap over with."

"Would you like me to get you some coffee?" Morgan asked.

"Yes, please."

"Kristen?"

"No, my stomach wouldn't be able to handle it right now."

Minutes later, Morgan returned with two mugs, handed one to Ed, and warned, "It's really hot."

"I need to let you girls know what to expect. I have appointed Ted Stevens, my attorney on Staten Island, as the trustee of my estate. He will see to it that you girls receive timely amounts of money as you need it for as long as the estate lasts. Upon my demise, he will meet you here in Vegas and go over the details of the will and answer any questions you may have. I've known him for over twenty years and trust him explicitly, so I know he will do right by you, and he'll be there if you need advice or have an issue."

"You've included me in your will?" Morgan said disbelievingly.

"Yes, of course. I updated it," Ed said heartily.

"But I'm nothing to you, and you hardly know me," Morgan said with a quizzical look.

"I know that deep down, you're a caring person with a good heart who deserves a break. I judge people by what's in their heart and not by their mistakes."

Morgan couldn't contain her emotion and burst into tears, letting all the hurt and pain that she had known come gushing forth like a broken damn. Ed rose and took her in his arms, and he held her tightly till, minutes later, she finally stopped.

"I'm so sorry—I got your shirt all wet and stained," Morgan murmured, her face a total mess from the ruined makeup.

"It's OK."

"I'll go up and get you a dry one," Morgan insisted and took off.

Ed noticed Kristen's downhearted look. "What's wrong, my little thrush?"

"I don't feel like you love me that much anymore," Kristen murmured.

Ed was totally taken aback. "Why do you think that?"

Kristen hesitated before she finally answered, "You seem to favor Morgan now."

"I love you more than ever, and I'm sorry for giving you that impression. Please understand, I'm running out of time, and I want Morgan to know that I love her as well. You have a most special place in my heart, and no one can ever take it. As a matter of fact, I need you to do me a huge favor; when I'm gone, please stay close to Morgan so that she doesn't revert to her old ways.

Very soon, you'll be sitting on top of the world, with fame and wealth beyond your wildest dreams, and she'll be looking up to you, so please make sure you take care of her like a sister and make her feel like she's important, too. Will you do that for me?" Ed said, looking into Kristen's teary eyes.

"I promise with all my heart, and I'm very sorry for doubting your love," Kristen said just as Morgan returned with Ed's fresh shirt.

"Hope this one's OK," Morgan said as she handed the shirt to Ed.

"It's fine, thanks," Ed said and promptly changed shirts. "As long as we're on this unpleasant topic, I might as well get to the final item, and that's pertaining to the disposition of my remains. I have made all the necessary arrangements to have my body cremated immediately after my demise, and I ask that you two dispose of my ashes soon as you get them, without any fanfare."

"You don't want a Catholic service with a priest and all?" Kristen said with a puzzled look.

"I'm not going to be a hypocrite."

"Hope you change your mind," Kristen said.

"OK, enough of this doleful conversation. What do you say we celebrate the incredible concert tour and Kristen's stardom with some Dom Pérignon?"

"Are you kidding?" Morgan said, mouth aghast.

"When you become a megastar, you celebrate with nothing less," Ed said with a grin. "Now if one of you ladies would saunter to the fridge, the bubbly should be sufficiently chilled."

CHAPTER 30

Two days into Kristen's intensive rehearsals with the female backup threesome, Sid decided to call on Ed after Morgan told him she didn't think Ed was going to last much longer. She only shared the concern with Sid and not Kristen, knowing she would not be able to handle the dismal truth and would most likely stop rehearsing and opt out of the Nashville trip. With this doleful news, Sid decided to visit Ed on the spot. When he got to the house and Ed opened the door, Sid was taken aback by how badly Ed had deteriorated. He now understood why Kristen was so driven and insisted they leave for Nashville the coming Friday rather than a week later, as Sid had proposed.

"So how you doing?" Sid said uneasily and hugged Ed.

"Seeing me as I am should give you a fairly good idea," Ed said dejectedly, then guided Sid to the living room, where they both sat down on the sofa in front of the low-grade flames in the fireplace.

"Is the medication controlling the pain?"

"It is, but I'm taking more and more each day, and I'm about to run out."

"I'll go get it," Sid said eagerly.

"I need a new prescription, and I don't have a doctor

here. I don't know what the hell I was thinking," Ed said, shaking his head in disgust.

"Not a problem—I'll get my doc to write you one, and as a matter of fact, I'll have him stop by after his office hours and check you out. His name's Dr. Berg, and I've known him for about fifteen years."

"A doctor who makes house calls?" Ed said in disbelief.

"He owes me big time for getting him prime seats and tables at top shows over many years."

"And now I'll owe you as well," Ed weakly kidded.

"You can repay me right now with that Wild Turkey," Sid said with a nod to the bottle on the coffee table.

"Don't blame you for not waiting to collect," Ed quipped as he generously filled two glasses.

"Maybe you shouldn't mix the booze with the pain meds," Sid said with concern.

"You think it's pernicious to my health?" Ed said dryly.

"You're right; I guess 'here's to your health' is inept, so let's toast to Kristen's huge success."

"And you for making it happen."

Sid acknowledged the compliment with a nod, and they both took substantial swigs.

"Kristen tell you she wants to head for Nashville Friday?"

"Yes. Are they ready?"

"I would have liked to have them rehearse for a few more days since the backup girls are still not in sync with Kristen's moves, but I'll go along with her decision," Sid said amiably.

"Not surprised they're having a hard time keeping up with her gyrations. What about their vocals?"

"Their singing is great."

"One out of two ain't half-bad," Ed said with an anemic grin and took another swig.

"So, will Alice be coming?"

"She wants to, but I'd rather she didn't."

"Why?" Sid said with a puzzled look.

"I don't want her to watch me wither away and croak," Ed said bluntly.

Sid nodded. "I understand."

"I need one more favor," Ed said hesitantly.

"Name it."

"Keep an eye on Kristen and Morgan when I'm gone, and don't let them stray too far off the path," Ed said with a heavy sigh. "You know better than I do; they'll have temptations every day for all kinds of things."

"You have my word," Sid said firmly.

"Thanks."

"Listen, I can postpone the trip to Nashville."

"I really appreciate that, but I want her to go and record the album, and if I'm lucky, I'll still be here to hear it."

"Speaking of the album, I almost forgot; Reed finally finished the barn-burner song he wrote for Kristen, which is the best thing I've heard in years, and he is about finished with the one Kristen started—she'll have two big-time hits, no doubt."

"Funny, she hasn't mentioned it."

"She probably wants to surprise you, so please don't say anything."

"You know something?" Ed said thoughtfully. "I still can't believe how quickly it all happened for her."

"You know something? Neither can I." Sid confessed. .

"It wouldn't have without you."

"And Madge," Sid said and rose to his feet. "I really need to go—see you when we get back."

"I'll be here," Ed said sportingly and walked Sid to the door.

323

"Be expecting Dr. Berg later today," Sid said, pausing at the door.

"I will. Thanks is just not enough for all you've done for Kristen," Ed said emotionally and hugged Sid at the front door.

CHAPTER 31

Kristen's trip to Nashville started Ed's downward spiral. With the pain increasing in severity, he'd been taking even more fentanyl, washing them down with liberal mouthfuls of booze. His life force was now artificially sustained by the man-made nostrum, which Ed now consumed without regard for the consequences. Dr. Berg urged Ed to check into a hospital, where he would receive more relief with around-the-clock intravenous morphine, but Ed stubbornly refused to even consider it, insisting he would tough it out to his last breath at home, with Morgan's help. She had given Ed her word: no matter how bad he got, there would be no hospital or hospice for him. She also agreed to help him maintain the charade that he was doing better than he really was for Kristen's and Alice's sake whenever either called. He desperately wanted Kristen to finish the album—the crowning achievement to the worthiness of his life and her undisputable, huge success.

"It's me again," Kristen said anxiously as Morgan stepped into the living room with phone in hand.

"I'm just about to check on him," Morgan said as she neared Ed. "You're in luck—looks like he's waking up."

"I want to talk to him," Kristen said impatiently.

"I'll put him on; just give him a sec to get his bearings,"

Morgan said and helped Ed sit up, then handed him her cell phone and headed for the kitchen.

"Sorry for the delay," Ed said groggily. "Those little devils really zonk me out."

"Not a problem. Did you have a good nap?" Kristen asked sweetly.

"That's all I'm doing lately."

"You're catching up on all the sleep you've missed in your life," Kristen kindly kidded.

"No doubt. And how's the recording going?"

"Have one more song to do, which I intend for us to get done tonight, no matter what, and then I'm catching the first flight home."

"Seems like you've been gone forever," Ed mused, totally unsure of the time frame.

"Actually, eleven days, and I promise not to leave you for a second once I'm home."

"Morgan could really use a break," Ed said thoughtfully. "She's been with me every minute since you left and even sleeps on the other end of the sofa."

"I'm jealous," Kristen teased.

"She's really been incredible, so please be good to her, and love her as I do you."

"Oh, they're signaling me—they must be ready—so let me get this thing over with, and then I'm home," Kristen said eagerly just as Morgan returned with a mug of coffee.

"Go finish the album, and always know how very much I love you and how proud I am," Ed said with tears in his eyes.

"I love you, too, and don't you dare go anywhere before I return," Kristen said apprehensively. "Is Morgan there?"

"Yes, she just brought me coffee. Bye, my precious thrush," Ed said as tears rolled down his cheeks. He handed Morgan the phone in exchange for the mug.

"Kristen?"

"Walk away so that you can talk," Kristen said anxiously. "Tell me the truth; how is he really doing?"

Morgan felt trapped. She had given her word to Ed not to divulge his true condition, but she knew Kristen would never forgive her for not telling the truth if Ed suddenly passed. She decided to leave herself some wiggle room.

"He's hanging tough, but he's getting very weak—just unable to eat anything."

"Try to force him to have something, even if you have to shove it in his mouth," Kristen insisted.

"Believe me, I'm trying," Morgan grumbled.

"They're ready for me, so I've got to go, but call me immediately if Ed starts to get worse. I'll have Sid hire a private jet to get me home."

"Hopefully it won't come to that," Morgan said uneasily and crossed her fingers.

"Then I'll see you sometime tomorrow morning," Kristen said and clicked off the phone.

"She give you a hard time?" Ed said kindly when Morgan got back.

"About you not eating," Morgan said reluctantly.

"Sorry about that."

"I wish there was something you could eat," Morgan said, utterly frustrated.

Ed was deeply touched by Morgan's genuine concern and attentiveness in his final battle, as well as her desperate tries to lift his spirits. Having mulled over what was in the best interest of Kristen and Morgan and the impact on them of watching him slowly die, Ed decided to spare them from that saturnine experience.

"There is some nutrition in the Wild Turkey," Ed joshed.

Morgan reached for the bottle on the coffee table and peered at it before pouring some. "It's nearly empty; I'll run out and get some more."

"Do you mind? It's almost dinnertime."

"It'll take less than twenty minutes," Morgan said.

"I know, but you're wearing yourself to a frazzle, and I feel so badly for putting you through this hell."

Morgan shook her head and teared up. "You're the first man who ever truly cared and showed me love and did not take advantage of me."

"I wish I wasn't checking out so that I could have tried to make up for all the bad you've known in your life," Ed said honestly and squeezed Morgan's hand.

"You've already done so much, and you gave me the chance to change."

"I'm so very proud of you; always know that," Ed said with a loving smile. "I've got one more favor to ask. You already know I've made all the arrangements regarding my remains. As to the last act regarding the disposition of what's left of me, I would like you and Kristen to take my ashes to the overlook near where we had the picnic and set me free."

"We'll do it," Morgan said woefully and peered at Ed skeptically.

"Now please go so that you can have your dinner before you start looking wretched like me," Ed teased.

As soon as Morgan left for the liquor store, Ed got a notepad and a pen and sorted his thoughts for what to put in the note to Kristen.

My dearest Kristen,

I write this note with my mind unclear, so please forgive me if perhaps it doesn't make sense. The pain has reached an unbearable level, leaving me with just one choice, which you and Morgan likely will not agree with, but I do this with you both in mind to spare you the gruesome death watch. I'm certain that when you read this, the album will be done, and that completes the incredible journey that you and I joyfully shared. You will go on to a phenomenal life and achieve things beyond your dreams.

I wish, of course, I could have seen it, but just knowing that you will is almost as good as being there. I ask just one more thing of you; please be good to Morgan and love her always as I you. She's got a great caring heart and will always be there for you as she's been there for me. I hope you will forgive me for skipping out on you, but it's the only way for me to end this hellish pain.

With all my love eternally,
—Ed

Ed tore off the note and, bleary-eyed, read it deliberately, then folded it twice and set it on the coffee table. He then reached for the pill vial, emptied the contents directly into his mouth, and washed it down with what was left of the Wild Turkey.

Morgan hollered twice when she walked through the front door, but Ed did not respond. Sensing something amiss, she set the bag on the floor and rushed to the living room. Ed was slouched on the sofa with glazed eyes, staring at the pill vial on its side on the coffee table. Morgan dropped to her knees next to Ed and reached with one hand to touch his ashen face.

"Ed, Ed," Morgan cried out.

"You're back," Ed barely murmured.

"Did you take all those pills?" Morgan said with a glance at the empty vial.

"No more pain."

Morgan immediately retrieved the cell phone from the back pocket of her jeans and said with panic, "I'm calling for an ambulance."

"Please don't," Ed begged and grasped Morgan's hand with the cell phone.

"I just can't let you die," Morgan said frantically.

"It's best this way."

"I need to call Kristen, then."

"Not till after," Ed pleaded and nodded at the coffee table. "I wrote her a note so that she doesn't get angry at you."

"I love you so much," Morgan murmured, then rested her head gently on Ed's chest and wrapped her arms tightly around him.

Ed pulled Morgan's head closer to his face and looked directly into her tear-filled eyes. "I love you as well, and please don't ever forget."

"I promise," Morgan said and once again gently rested her head on Ed's chest. Listening to his fading heart and his labored breath, she knew the ethereal moment was close at hand.

Mere minutes later, it was over.

"God, please take his soul," Morgan cried out, tears bursting from her sodden eyes.

EPILOGUE

It was a beautiful springlike day with a few billowy white clouds resembling cotton balls scattered about against the dark-blue sky. The warmish sun was tempered with a refreshing light breeze; in every way, it was a perfect day to be outdoors doing almost anything—except for what Kristen and Morgan faced. They were on the way to Mount Charleston to perform Ed's last request and let the mountain winds consume what was left of him. Emotionally spent, they drove in silence and dry-eyed, having spilled innumerable tears eulogizing Ed at the lugubrious service attended by Sid and the members of the band. Morgan pulled the SUV a few feet from the waist-high rock wall overlook, with Las Vegas shimmering in the distance like a mirage in the setting sun, which spilled its rays on the nearby clouds, tinting them pinkish gold.

"I'm glad no one is here and it's almost sunset," Kristen said as she pushed open the car door.

"Maybe Ed's up there in the clouds, looking down on us," Morgan mused and got out as well.

"I hope he is, so that he can share in this last farewell since there won't be a grave to visit."

"So how we gonna do this?" Morgan blurted when they reached the barrier.

331

"Tip the urn and pour the ashes slowly over the side as I sing, and the wind will do the rest."

"You going to sing the song you wrote for him?"

"I just can't," Kristen said tearfully. "I'll do the one he loved so much—'You Needed Me.'"

"That's perfect," Morgan whimpered, "a beautiful tribute that exactly describes your relationship and your love."

"It'll be from both of us; he loved you as well," Kristen said and punched the song on her cell, then began tearfully.

When it was done, Kristen took Morgan's hand and looked directly into her eyes. "It's you and me from now on and no one else."

CPSIA information can be obtained
at www.ICGtesting.com
Printed in the USA
LVHW051127120723
751664LV00005B/257